In The Shadows
By Craig William Emms

Cold Fish Books

This novel is entirely a work of fiction. The names, characters and incidents portrayed in it are the work of the author's imagination or are used fictitiously.

First published in Great Britain by Cold Fish Books 2015
www.coldfishbooks.com

Copyright Craig William Emms and Linda Barnett 2015

Craig William Emms asserts the moral right to be identified as the author of this work

A catalogue record for this book is available from the British Library
ISBN 978-1-910310-09-0

This book is dedicated to Linda...at least our own diving trip to Egypt many years ago didn't end up in a shooting match, unlike some of our other adventures! Seriously though, this book, as with all of the other books in the John Smith Series, has been a joint venture with Linda. I do the writing but Linda does everything else that has helped make the series as successful as it's turned out to be. She takes the cover photographs and produces the covers, reads through the first and many subsequent drafts of the manuscripts, letting me know where I've gone wrong, or have missed something out, or even occasionally where I've gone too far. Then she copy-edits, proof reads (along with our good friend Jonny Jones) and spends hours formatting the raw manuscript into a form that is acceptable to Kindle, and finally uploads the finished article on to the Amazon website. In short, without Linda, there would be no John Smith. On top of all of this she works hard at her own things, including beginning to write her own series of books, puts up with my frequent bouts of PTSD and depression, and makes me feel human again. I love her to bits.

Also by Craig William Emms and featuring John Smith

ONE HEARTBEAT A MINUTE
PUBLIC ENEMY
HEART OF STONE
THE SMILING COAST
THE BROTHERHOOD
PEGASUS

If you read *In The Shadows* and enjoy it please leave a review on Amazon or contact the author via the Cold Fish Book website at www.coldfishbooks.com

You can become a friend of John Smith, 22 SAS on Facebook, or 'Like' the 'John Smith Series' page on Facebook (there are occasional competitions and freebies on this page).

THE STORY SO FAR...

The Brotherhood is the fifth story in the John Smith series, following on from *One Heartbeat a Minute, Public Enemy, Heart of Stone* and *The Smiling Coast.*

In *One Heartbeat a Minute* we are introduced to John Smith as a young paratrooper who is recruited by MI6 to become a spy against the Rhodesians. We follow John's exploits as a young soldier throughout the Rhodesian Bush War and later when he serves as a trooper in the Special Air Service Regiment of the British Army.

After fighting for his country with distinction in a dozen wars and conflicts around the world Smith is falsely accused of being a paedophile and murderer. He sets out on a rampage of revenge, death and destruction that leaves the police force and the security services bloodied and reeling.

In *Public Enemy*, the second story in the series, John Smith is tracked down to his hideaway in West Africa. Forced to flee, he faces Muslim terrorists, an IRA hit man (employed by the British government to kill him) and vicious Somali gangsters in a British prison.

Only by befriending other ex-servicemen and facing his enemies head-on does Smith find a way to stay alive and earn his freedom.

In the third book of the John Smith series, a short story called *Heart of Stone,* Smith has retired to a peaceful life with the woman he loves, in Norway. But can there ever be peace for a man like John Smith? When the Iranians find out where he is they are intent on carrying out the death sentence that their leader has proclaimed on him. But will the hunters become the hunted?

In *The Smiling Coast*, the fourth story in the series, Smith finds himself back in West Africa. This time he is on the trail of Nigerians involved in the illegal trading of wild animals, a growing threat to the security of many countries in the developing world. He teams up with a Dutch wildlife expert and the two men discover that it's not only wild animals that the gangsters are concerned with, but the international trafficking of children as sex slaves as well. Smith finds himself drawn into an adventure that can only end in bloodshed and tears.

Meanwhile back in the UK, Smith also becomes involved with 'The Brotherhood', a group of ex-forces vigilantes who have decided to take on organised criminals including the Albanian Mafia. His participation draws the unwanted attention of the British security services. Will they find out that Smith is still alive?

In *The Brotherhood*, the fifth story in the series, Smith and the other original members of The Brotherhood return to the UK after their successful, if somewhat tragic mission in West Africa. While they gather intelligence in preparation for their final attack on the Albanian Mafia they also deliver their own form of justice to a group of travellers who beat up and kill an old man and to the British Pakistani gangs who are abusing and raping young vulnerable girls in the north of England. But all the time they are under constant pressure from the security services and the National Crime Agency, organisations which are desperately trying to infiltrate The Brotherhood and bring it down. Will John Smith and The Brotherhood overcome all of their problems and take out the Albanians once and for all? Or will the joint task force set up by MI5 and MI6 to destroy the vigilantes get their own way?

In the sixth instalment of the series, a special short story; *Pegasus*, John Smith is recuperating from the wounds he sustained in his one man attack on the Albanian Mafia. He is struggling with his physical and mental health and finds himself still trying to come to terms with his best friend's suicide.

Then there's a chance meeting with an old man in the village pub. This turns into a night of story-telling about one of the most famous airborne assaults in history - the taking of the bridges over the River Orne and the Caen Canal (Pegasus Bridge) in German-occupied France on D-Day. The old soldier talks about landing right next to the bridges at sixteen minutes past midnight on the 6th June 1944, and how they overcame the German garrison and captured the bridges intact. Smith is totally gripped by the old man's tale and learns how they held the bridges against overwhelming odds until they were relieved in the afternoon by Lord Lovat's Commandos.

The two old warriors discover that they have much in common, and over numerous pints of beer their conversation makes it easier for Smith to begin to put his own ghosts to rest.

Read on now to find out what becomes of John Smith in the seventh book in the series: *In the Shadows*...

PROLOGUE

Foreign and Commonwealth Office: Update to travel advice.
Press release
March 31, 09.54 BST

The Foreign Office is updating its travel advice pages to reflect a heightened global threat to United Kingdom nationals travelling overseas.

The government regularly reviews and updates its travel advice to make sure it provides the most up to date information and advice for British nationals travelling overseas. Given coalition action in Syria and Iraq and the growing global threat to UK nationals through terrorism and kidnapping, we have decided today to update our travel advice to reflect this.

The government is adding the following information and advice to all of its travel advice pages:

"There is considered to be a heightened threat of terrorist attack globally against UK interests and British nationals from groups or individuals motivated by the conflict in Iraq and Syria.

In addition there is a growing threat of kidnap against British nationals in North Africa and the eastern horn of Africa.

You should be vigilant at this time."

This change is being made to travel advice globally in response to the generalised threat. The government will continue to reflect any specific credible threats in travel advice in the usual way.

ENGLAND

ONE

6th September 2010
Checkpoint Kingshill, Babaji District, Helmand Province, Afghanistan

The sixteen-man patrol of 5 Platoon, B (Malta) Company of the 1st (Cheshire) Battalion, The Mercian Regiment moves forward slowly through the open ground between two compounds. It's still early morning and the temperature hasn't risen high enough to generate the sweat and bring out the swarms of flies that dominate their life in this desolate hellhole of a country. Normally there would be the sound of crowing cockerels and playing children but this morning the compounds are quiet. Perhaps too quiet. All of the men deployed on this 'ground domination and assurance patrol' around Checkpoint Kingshill can feel the tense uncertainty in the air, Lance Corporal Billy Machin amongst them.

Suddenly the peace and quiet is shattered by the staccato blast of a machine gun. Billy can hear the supersonic 'crack' and 'thump' as high velocity rounds whip past his head, followed almost immediately by the ear-splitting bangs of rocket-propelled grenades exploding all around the patrol.

"Take cover!" yells the patrol's commander, Sergeant 'Pony' Moore as the men throw themselves on to the dusty ground. Billy hits the dirt heavily, his body armour and load-carrying equipment landing awkwardly and digging into his ribs. A few rounds throw up little spurts of sand as they land a metre in front of him.

"Red Fire Team! Two hundred metres! Slightly left of axis, just where the mud brick wall ends, there's a ditch. Enemy MG in ditch! Rapid fire!" The clatter of weapon's fire strengthens as the left half of the British Army patrol returns fire on the Taliban

13

ambushers in the ditch, the right half keeping their heads down for a few vital seconds while Sergeant Moore takes stock of the patrol's predicament.

"Stop!" Red Fire Team hold their fire and of course the insurgents start up again with their own. "Is anybody hit?" Billy looks around at the men either side of him, as he's been trained to do, examining to see if they're okay. It's only then that he realises that Ricky, his best mate, is lying in a circle of bloodied earth just three metres away. *Shit!* He scuttles across to him sideways like a crab, trying to stay as low as he can while the enemy bullets continue to whip over his head. He reaches his mate and pulls him over, almost retching as he sees that a round has entered his throat and punched its way out of the back of his neck through his spine. Ricky's dead. He must have died instantly in the first burst of Taliban fire.

Billy feels the bile rise up in his throat and for a few seconds he freezes, unable to move or to shout. His heart is hammering away in his chest like a trip-hammer on speed and the sweat begins to flow down his face and into his eyes.

"Is anybody hit?" Only Sergeant Moore's voice repeating the question rouses Billy from the horror of the moment. He pushes his mate's body back over so he doesn't have to continue to look at his face and his open staring eyes.

"Eldridge is dead, sarge!" His voice cracks as he shouts back over the clatter of the insurgent's machine-gun. He ducks down as yet another rocket-propelled grenade explodes in a shower of dirt and a cloud of dust off to his right.

"Are you sure?"

"Yeah! He took one in the throat, sarge!"

"Okay, Billy! You and Boyd grab his webbing and drag him back to that wall behind us. The rest of you, rapid fire!"

Ten SA80 assault rifles and two Light Support Weapons send around three hundred 5.56mm rounds per minute at the ditch where the Taliban are hiding. Just like any normal human being, Billy feels a great reluctance to stand up in that hail of fire, even though most of it is directed away from him, but his training and his innate courage kick in. He pushes himself up and grabs one of

14

Ricky's webbing straps in his left hand, while holding on to his rifle with the other. Jack Boyd hurries across from the other side of Ricky's body, gives Billy a look that needs no words and grabs hold of another webbing strap. Together they stumble and grunt as they drag back the lifeless body of their mate, only pausing for a few seconds as Jack stops to throw Ricky's rifle over his shoulder, using its sling. There's no way that they're leaving a weapon behind that the bastard Afghans might use against them in the future. The distance to relative safety is only thirty metres but it feels as though they're running half a marathon as they heave and sweat, until finally they can tumble into the ditch in front of the wall. There's always the chance that their ambushers have set booby traps; Improvised Explosive Devices in the ditch, but neither Billy nor Jack give a shit at this precise moment. They drag Ricky's body into cover and let go of him, desperately trying to suck air into their labouring lungs. All they can feel is the blood pounding in their ears after the exertion of the past few minutes.

"Stop! Fire and manoeuvre! Red Fire Team prepare to move back. Move!"

Pony's voice is loud as he shouts out his orders but it conveys a great calmness and confidence that helps to steady the younger members of the patrol. The right hand fire team minus Billy, Jack and Ricky continue to send rounds in the direction of the Taliban while their pals in the left hand fire team scuttle a short distance sideways to put off the enemies aim before leaping to their feet and scarpering backwards ten metres. They then slide to a halt, sink to the kneeling position and send more rounds back at the Taliban as their mates in Blue Fire Team get up and sprint backwards, passing their line by roughly another ten metres before they sink to the knees, turn and give the Taliban some more shit. Meanwhile, the Afghans have repositioned themselves about fifteen metres to one side using the cover of their own ditch and suddenly a long sustained burst of fire comes from their 7.62mm Russian-made belt-fed RPK machine-gun in its new position, spraying rounds into the British patrol and knocking one of them from his feet. Then another rocket-propelled grenade comes in from the opposite side of the open area and explodes just behind Sergeant Moore, sending him sprawling on to the ground as he's riddled with shrapnel from the blast. Amazingly Pony pulls himself to his feet, hurt but still alive and fighting, and still shouting out:

"Red Fire Team! Prepare to move! Move!"

Finally all of the patrol get back to the relative safety of the ditch alongside Billy and Jack. All of them except for Corporal Johnny Phelps who had been knocked from his feet by the Taliban machine-gun fire, which almost severed his left leg.

"Shit, sarge! Corps is still out there!"

The initial shock of nearly losing his leg wears off during the brief firefight that follows and Corporal Phelps begins to scream as the pain kicks in with a vengeance. Billy knows that there is no way that he can leave another of his mates exposed in the middle of that open ground and without thinking he jumps up from the tenuous cover of the dry ditch he is lying in and races across the twenty metres out to where his mate is lying. As he runs he fires off so many rounds so quickly in the direction of the ambushers that his rifle barrel begins to glow red hot. As soon as he arrives at his mate's side he picks him up in a fireman's lift over his shoulder and starts to stagger back while the rest of the patrol lays down a withering curtain of covering fire. All of the time Billy tries to make sure that his mate's leg, which is only hanging on by a splintered bone, a few ligaments and half-severed muscles doesn't become separated from the rest of his body and fall into the dirt. Taliban bullets kick up dirt around his feet and more RPGs explode in the open area behind him but the sustained rapid fire of his mates helps to put the insurgents off their aim and encourages them to keep their heads down as much as possible. Billy finally stumbles down into the ditch and willing hands reach for Johnny Phelps and help him down into cover.

In 2005 the British Army had introduced a fundamental change to the way that casualties were dealt with by fellow soldiers during their initial treatment for gunshot or blast wounds on the battlefield. The army had stopped teaching soldiers about 'ABC' (Airway, Breathing, and Circulation) and switched instead to 'CABC' (*Catastrophic haemorrhage*, Airway, Breathing and Circulation). At the same time they also, for the first time ever, issued everyone with tourniquets. The logic behind this act was the fact that the one *avoidable* way of dying on the battlefield is from the loss of blood, especially from a limb or limbs, and a quickly and appropriately applied tourniquet can stem the flow of blood and stop this from happening. The first thing that Billy's mates do after his heroic rescue is to apply a tourniquet around the top of Johnny's leg. Then Billy joins the rest of his patrol as they pour even more fire at their Taliban ambushers and one of the patrol's Combat Team Medics rushes over from an adjacent ditch under the covering fire to carry on with Johnny's treatment. The medic stuffs special dressings impregnated with substances that stick to damaged blood vessels deep into Johnny's wounds, and once the bleeding is under control he loosens the tourniquet that has stopped him from bleeding to death in the first place.

Meanwhile Sergeant Moore and the patrol's signaller have called for air support. A few minutes later two Apache attack helicopters arrive on the scene and blast the Taliban insurgents that ambushed Billy's patrol with a devastating lethal mixture of Hellfire Missiles, Hydra air-to-ground rockets and 30mm shells from their M230 chain guns mounted underneath their fuselages. Following behind the Apaches is a Chinook helicopter carrying a Medical Emergency Response Team made up of a consultant, an emergency nurse and two paramedics, along with an armed protection team. Barely fifteen minutes after the initial contact with the Taliban insurgents has begun, and only ten minutes after being hit, Corporal Johnny Phelps is on his way back to a hospital and being treated on the flight with plasma, which helps his wounds to clot and halts any further bleeding. Within twenty minutes he is lying unconscious on an operating table in the Role 3 Hospital at Camp Bastion undergoing an emergency operation to save his leg.

It's only about an hour later - when the rest of the Mercian patrol are all relatively safe back in their FOB (Forward Operating Base) that the true terror of the situation hits Billy; he begins to shake so badly with delayed shock and fear that he can't even hold a bottle of water to his parched lips to take a sip.

10th June
Armed Forces Day, Guildford, Surrey

Billy shudders as the vivid flashback of that fucking awful day fades away in his mind's eye.

"What's up, mate? You look like a dog's nicked your biscuit." Billy is sitting in the front driver's seat of an old BMW. Darren looks across to him from the passenger seat.

"Nothing..." He shudders again as the memory continues to fade. "Nothing Daz, it's just...." Billy looks back at him, and Darren sees the expression of pain in his eyes. "...you know how it is, mate. It's Armed Forces Day again. Every time it comes around I remember my mates that I lost over in Afghanistan."
Darren nods his head.

"Yeah, I know what you mean, Billy. I do too."

"Most of the time I don't think about it. You know what I mean?"

"Yeah."
Both of them fall silent for a minute or two, their thoughts turned inward as they remember. Then Billy sighs.

"I miss having John around."

"Yeah."

"Have you heard anything from him?"

"I got an email from him about two weeks ago."

"How's he doing?"

"Okay, mate. He said he was running a few miles every day and felt a lot fitter. His wounds are not hurting so much. How about you? Have you heard anything from him?"

"Yeah. He gave me a bell a few weeks ago. Asked me if I still felt bad about Nigel."

"What'd you say?"

"I told him the truth. Said that I still felt stunned and angry over what he did...you know...the suicide. We had a long chat about it."

"Did it do any good?"

"Yeah, I think so."

"Did he say what he's up to these days?"

"Not really. You know what he's like. Keeps everything close to his chest. He did sound a lot happier though. You know, more at peace with himself."

"That's good."

"Yeah. I still miss him though."

18

The men drop into silence brooding over their own thoughts. After a few minutes Billy speaks again, looking out of the windscreen at the blue, cloudless sky.

"It's a nice day for the parade."

He's in his late twenties, slim and slightly feminine in appearance. His girlish face is accentuated by his long sandy-coloured hair, which is drawn back tightly and tied into a long ponytail hanging down between his shoulder blades. His womanly looks would only fool someone who doesn't know him however as they conceal a body that is as tough and wiry as a terriers under his loose sweatshirt and jeans.

Billy joined the British Army when he was seventeen and had served for just over five years initially in the Cheshire Regiment, then later in the 1st battalion of the Mercian Regiment when it was formed during the restructuring of the infantry in 2007. During that time he served operationally in both Iraq and Afghanistan, and it was during a tour in the latter theatre that his cool temperament under fire had earned him a Military Cross. The commendation for his gallantry award simply says that he carried a wounded comrade to safety while under enemy fire, risking his own life in the process, and that the decoration was awarded for 'an act of exemplary gallantry during an active operation against the enemy'.

His mate, Corporal Johnny Phelps didn't just survive that ambush; his leg was saved as well, and today he runs around and plays football with his two young sons. And he owes it all to Billy, who ran out into that hailstorm of bullets and rocket-propelled grenades to carry him back into cover. Needless to say, they're still best mates.

However, neither Billy's exemplary service in the army nor his Military Cross had cut any slack with the British justice system when Billy got himself into trouble after leaving the army. His younger brother had been in a fight after a night's clubbing in their local town, and ended up stabbing someone. When he was being interviewed by the police about the incident Billy had acted impulsively and stupidly to try and save his brother from a prison sentence. He lied and told them that his brother had been at home when the fight occurred. Of course, DNA evidence found on the handle of the knife and bloodstains on his clothing had proved beyond doubt that his brother had carried out the stabbing, so Billy had been charged, tried and found guilty of 'perverting the course of justice'. He had been sentenced to four years in prison. On the other hand, in a perverse twist of fate his brother had escaped a prison sentence and been put on probation.

Billy served two years in Winson Green nick in Birmingham before being released but during that time he met the guys who were to change his life forever, namely Nigel, Darren, Matt, Brummie, Daljit and of course, most of all – John Smith. They had all become best friends and since his release Billy had been through a lot with them, including coming out of the closet and admitting to them that he is gay. When he'd told them he was very unsure about what they might say. He had felt like his heart had been in his mouth but none of them had batted an eyelid. There had been some good-natured banter taking the mickey somewhat but it seemed his declaration and honesty had merely served to make their friendship stronger and he loved them even more for that. In Billy's mind the only negative aspect to their alliance had been Nigel's suicide at the end of the previous year, and Billy still choked up when he remembered finding his body hanging from an apple tree in that orchard. It had cut him to the bone and he still has nightmares about the moment that he realised that big Nigel who was so strong and on the surface filled with fun, was dead and would be gone from his life forever.

Billy shudders at the memory and hardly hears Darren say:

"Have you ever been on one of these marches?"

It takes Billy a second to come back to the present, put two and two together and realise what his mate's referring to:

"An Armed Forces Day parade? No. I was on the parade when the Mercians marched through Worcester when we came back from our Afghan tour, but that's the only big parade I've ever been a part of. How about you?"

"Nah. Us signallers don't get to go on many parades. We leave that to you grunts!"

"Mmmm. You were probably too busy making a brew in the back of your Land Rover!"

Darren is not like Billy in appearance at all. He's in his late thirties, short and stocky with crew-cut hair and a thick moustache. He served for seven years in the Royal Corps of Signals as an electronics and communications expert and had completed a tour of Bosnia, two tours of Iraq and three tours of Afghanistan. Despite his cushy-sounding job he'd still been involved in a few fire-fights with the insurgents in Afghanistan while helping different units to set up their comms at their Forward Operating Bases. Even signallers were expected to fire back when attacked by the Taliban.

After he had left the army Darren had used his considerable technical skills to become a very successful private investigator, spending most of his time compiling photographic and video evidence of married men and women having extra-marital affairs. Then one day, completely out-of-the-blue, he had gone home early from his job only to find his naked wife in bed with another man, grunting and groaning as they fucked each other. It had been a total shock to him and he had lost control and beaten the crap out of his wife's lover, putting him into hospital for a month. As a consequence he had received a three year sentence for 'grievous bodily harm'. Of course his own exemplary service to his Queen and Country had been ignored by the pitiless judge sitting high and mighty on his bench. He had never served his country in the armed forces and had never been shot at or risked his life in any way whatsoever, so it meant nothing to him. Needless to say, Darren is now divorced from his wife, though still paying maintenance through the Child Support Agency for his four teenage kids. It was while he was inside Winson Green Prison that Darren had met Billy and the others.

He grins at Billy and shrugs his wide powerful shoulders:

"Yep. More than likely! Any idea which units are taking part in the parade?"

"I had a look at the Order of March this morning in the newspaper. There's loads of different units here today, including some of your lot." He starts to count them off on his fingers: "Plus there's the Royal Artillery, Royal Dragoon Guards, Light Dragoons, Coldstream Guards, Royal Regiment of Fusiliers, Royal Anglian Regiment, my old mob; the Mercians, the Paras and the Rifles, plus the Royal Navy, Royal Marines and the Air Force Regiment."

"Jesus. Gonna be a big one!"

"Yep, and that's not counting all of the veterans and the British Legion branches. They reckon about four to five thousand in total."

"Crikey. Let's hope we can keep it peaceful then."

"Yep."

Their musings are interrupted by Billy's mobile phone ringing. He answers it:

"Billy. Yep. How many of the wankers? Great stuff, cheers!" He hangs up and turns to Darren, who has a questioning look on his face. "They're close. They've been trying to get through to the route of the parade but the coppers are doing their bit. They're putting on a show of force; all helmets, batons and riot shields, blocking them off whenever they try to turn towards the main road. This is the only route that's been left clear for them."

"How many?"

"Our dickers reckon about eighty. They're still shadowing the twats and they should be appearing around that corner..." He indicates the end of their street about a hundred metres away with a nod of his head. "....in about ten minutes."

"Perfect! I'll go and warn Daljit and the rest of the lads." Darren climbs out of the car and jogs across the road towards a side street.

TWO

10th June
Armed Forces Day, Guildford, Surrey

Billy feels his nerves tingling as the first of the eighty radical
Muslim protesters appear at the end of the street walking purposely
from around the corner. Most of them seem to be aged between
twenty and forty and they are dressed in a variety of clothes,
ranging from western-style jeans and jackets through to long robes
that fall around their ankles. All of them have thick luxuriant
beards and are wearing the short, rounded skullcaps known as
Taqiyah. Many of them are carrying placards attached to long bits
of wood, but the placards are held low to stop them being obvious.
Billy can't read what's written on them as they are covered with
cloth, probably to stop the group being harangued before they can
even get close to the parade. The protesters lengthen their stride
when they see that the road ahead of them is clear of policemen.
    Billy dials a number on his mobile from memory:
    "They're just starting to enter the street, Daz," he mutters.
Then he listens for a few seconds. "Okay, willdo. Standby…" He
watches as the last of the Muslim protestors turns into the street.
"Let them get a bit closer…."
    "…standby…."
    "…standby…."
    "Go, go, go!"
Suddenly he hears the pounding of feet echoing in the street behind
him as a group of men charge into the road from where they were
hidden from view along a side street. The first of the group of
Muslim protesters come to an abrupt stop as they stare wide-eyed
in surprise at the new arrivals, and the men behind almost walk
into them. Voices are raised in anger.

The newly arrived group of approximately thirty men surges past Billy's car and with obvious discipline they form themselves into two silent, menacing ranks stretching across the street facing and blocking off the protesters. Like the Muslims they are dressed in a variety of clothes and are from approximately the same age group. All of them carry transparent riot shields on their left arms which are tucked against their upper bodies. They are also wearing thick belts around their waists supporting a large webbing pouch. In addition a handful of the grim-faced men are also wearing the traditional Muslim Taqiyah on their heads and sporting thick beards, just like the protesters. Billy quickly joins them, slipping into the rear rank next to Darren.

For a minute or so the street is quiet and still. The men formed into two ranks face forward, their faces calm as they silently size up the Muslim protesters in front of them. For their part, the protesters appear to be shocked at the arrival of these newcomers. They mill around, not knowing whether to carry on and try and force their way through their lines or retreat and find another way through. They had known that they were going to face trouble and counter-protesters today, but they had been expecting a disorganised rabble of white people, perhaps from the racist English Defence League, mouthing off, insulting them and their religion and their God. No way did any of them ever expect to face any opposition as obviously disciplined and organised as this and it has completely thrown them off their stride. A few of them even look around for a sign of a policeman, perhaps perversely expecting them to help. Needless to say there isn't a copper anywhere in sight. Typical. You can never find a policeman when you want one.

The group of radical Muslims begin to argue amongst themselves in low angry voices, being calmly watched by the still and silent ranks of men in front of them. Eventually one of them, probably one of their leaders and organisers, steps forward. He totally ignores the white men in the line in front of him and deliberately faces one of the few bearded men in a Muslim skullcap that are amongst them:

"As-salāmu `Alayka. Peace be upon you".

"As-salāmu `Alaikum wa Rahmatullahi wa Barakatuh. Peace be unto you and so may the mercy of Allah and His blessings."

24

Once the polite formalities are over the leader of the protesters breaks into a southern London accent:

"Who the fuck are you lot?"

"It doesn't matter who we are."

"Well, step aside, brother. We are on a peaceful protest. We have every right to be here."

The man's voice is loud but there is an undercurrent of confusion and fear in it. The other man that he chose to address replies, and although he speaks loudly so that the other protesters can hear him plainly, there is no hint of confusion or fear in his voice:

"Fuck you. You're no brother of mine."

"We're here on a peaceful protest! We have every right!"

The man stares with hard eyes into the protester's face.

"If you're here on a peaceful protest, why are you carrying those placards? I can guess what they say. Something like: Soldiers go to hell? Or is it Murderers, Rapists, or Baby Killers?"

The protesters leader returns his stare with hate-filled eyes.

"The army of the kuffir is murdering our Muslim brothers! Are you with us, your brothers, or are you with *them*?"

The other man sneers back at him.

"I'm not with you, you twat. You're just a bunch of fucking extremist fanatics. This is *my* Brotherhood. Have a good look at them." He waves his arm to take in the ranks on either side of him. "All of us have served our country in places like Bosnia, Iraq, or Afghanistan. We were all soldiers once and we've been through hell and back. These are my real friends, my *real* brothers!"

"But you're a Muslim! Why are you siding with these kuffirs?" He almost spits the last word. Then he asks suspiciously: "Are you a Shia?"

The man laughs back at him.

"No, I am not a Shia. If only it was all that easy, eh? No, I'm a good Sunni."

"Then why?"

"Because I'm a Muslim. I believe in Allah, the All-Merciful and the All-Seeing, and I believe that the Islamic faith is a religion of peace, love and understanding and I'm proud to be a Muslim! But I'm also proud to be British! What's wrong with that? What's wrong with being a *British Muslim*?"

"Because the British oppress us! That's why!"

25

The Muslim ex-soldier nearly chokes on his laughter:

"*Oppress* us? How?" He looks around angrily at the faces in the front of him. "It's obvious that you lot believe what you want to believe, or what you've been told to believe by your Imams and your leaders. But we're not oppressed in this country. We Muslims have exactly the same rights as everyone else, no matter what their religion is. We're allowed to worship in our own Mosques! We even have our own bloody schools! How are we oppressed eh? Go on, tell me!"

"Yeah, mate. You're talking out of your arse!" A big white ex-soldier next to him chips in. "You don't see us protesting outside your mosques do you? You don't see us waving bloody placards with things like: Baby Killers written on them when some bloody Muslim fanatic murders a load of women and kids with a suicide bomb, do you? Eh?"

There's a loud murmur of agreement from the lines of ex-soldiers at their words.

The protester's leader shouts back:

"We are oppressed by the British government!" There are loud shouts of agreement from the men behind him.

The Muslim ex-soldier stands for a moment staring down at the protesters. Then all of a sudden his manner seems to change as he realises that he will never be able to get through to these men, fellow believers or not, no matter what he says or does.

"You know, you're so different from me that I don't even know what you believe in."

The protesters murmur angrily amongst themselves at his words, obviously insulted, and begin to push closer to the ranks of men facing them, some of them raising their placards threateningly as clubs. The leader of the radicals answers, his voice dripping with loathing for the man in front of him:

"I believe that Islam is the one true faith!" There are loud shouts of approval from the men with him. "If you side with the kuffirs then you are nothing but a dog!"

"You're the dog! You're not a true Muslim, or you wouldn't be here! You wouldn't be here to break the law and cause trouble!"

"What law?" The extremist is almost frothing at the mouth now in anger. "Muslims are not obliged to obey the man-made laws of the kuffirs. We believe only in Sharia! God's law is the only law! Allāhu Akbar! God is Great!" The whole group of eighty radicals begin to chant along with him, the sound of their unified voices echoing along the street like a wall of noise: "Allāhu Akbar! Allāhu Akbar!" Some of them rip the cloths from their placards and brandish them above their heads, pumping them up and down in time to the chanting. Sure enough, as the ex-soldier had guessed, they bear slogans such as: 'Baby Killers!' 'Cowards!' 'Muslim's Against the Crusades!' and 'Soldiers go to Hell!'

When finally they begin to run out of steam and it starts to quieten down a bit in the street, another man speaks up from the front rank of the ex-soldiers facing them. This one is tall, dusky-skinned and wearing a turban; he's obviously a Sikh:

"Turn around and fuck off." His voice is low and menacing but it still carries to all of the protesters. "Go now, and in peace, and you'll be able to walk home. Fuck with us and you'll be eating hospital food for a month!"

The Sikh's pronouncement elicits a few grins and nods of heads from his comrades. Daljit Singh Bohgal served for fifteen years in the Army Air Corps as a weapons technician. But despite his loyal service to the crown he had still been found guilty of a fraud that he had not committed, and spent a total of four long years in Winson Green Prison, where he had met John Smith, Billy, Darren and the others. He is every inch a true Sikh warrior and even though he has been badly treated by the country that he was born in, it is very clear from the look on his face that he still loves Britain. It's also clear that he hates these radical Muslims with all of his heart. However even his attitude and presence doesn't look like it's going to stop the protesters, as they just get angrier at his words.

"We have a right to protest!" one of them shouts.

"That's right, mate," another of the ex-soldiers jeers. "And do you know why? Because blokes like us have fought and given their lives to make sure that you have that right!"

"Then let us pass!"

"Yeah! Move over!"

"Get out of our way!"

"Allāhu Akbar!"

"Allāhu Akbar!"

Bashir Mahmood, the Islamic ex-soldier that the radical's leader had addressed first of all raises his hand for quiet, but he is ignored by the angry protesters, who begin to move forward again. Bashir is a thirty-five year old Pakistani-born English man. For twelve of those years he served as a soldier in the 2nd Battalion of the Yorkshire Regiment, formerly known as the Green Howards before its amalgamation with other regiments in 2004. He had made staff-sergeant in the army, and although he had not been posted to Afghanistan he had served in both Northern Ireland and Bosnia, and had seen a handful of enemy 'contacts' in these trouble spots where he had handled himself very well. He loves the army and would still be in it now if his father had not been taken seriously ill a few years before. His dad had owned and run a newsagents in Keighley near Bradford, and when his illness eventually led to his death in 2006, Bashir had thought that the time was right for him to leave the army and to take over the running of his father's shop. He has done well since then and now owns two shops after opening another in a nearby village. He is also in the running to be a councillor in the local council elections in Keighley. Standing next to Bashir is his best mate, Dave Bowers, a huge blonde-haired northerner who served with him in the same regiment.

Bashir raises his own voice to be heard above the angry voices of the protesters. In his army days his staff-sergeant's voice could be heard from one side of a windy parade ground to the other and as he raises it now he causes the protesters to pause in their tracks:

"Stand fucking still!" He face is locked in a grimace. "We're not fucking stupid, you twats. We know why you're here today and what you're planning to do! We know that some of you are carrying tear gas canisters!" His words cause more than one of the Muslims to look at each other in shocked surprise, wondering how these men know their dark secret. "There's no fucking way that we're going to let you disrupt the parade today. So just fuck off back to the rocks you fucking live under, you slimy bastards!" Perhaps unsurprisingly his words don't have the desired effect. The protesters blood is up now and they suddenly surge forward, hoping to scare the smaller group of men facing them with a show of aggression and to force a way through their lines by using their sheer superiority in numbers.

28

"Batons!" Daljit the big Sikh shouts the order, and the thirty ex-soldiers all reach into their pockets and pull out matt-black telescopic truncheons. There is a loud rasp as wrists are flicked and the batons are extended to their full sixteen inches of toughened stainless steel tubes. "Shields!" Thirty round transparent riot shields are raised and tilted upwards and forwards to protect their faces and upper bodies. The bright sunshine glints off the 53cm diameter, 3.5 mm thick polycarbonate shields that weigh just 1.5 kilogrammes but are as tough as steel.

The Muslim radicals pause in their advance momentarily at the menacing sight, but only for a few seconds before they heave forward again, placards raised and faces snarling as they throw themselves forward.

"Fuck the crusaders! Allāhu Akbar! Allāhu Akbar!" Daljit's roaring voice can be heard again over the sound of the eighty angry men moving towards them:

"Remember your training, lads! Go for their knees, elbows and collar bones! I don't want anybody killed! Just hurt the bastards!"

Then the two groups meet, the eighty Muslims wading into the two thin lines of ex-soldiers, smashing their placards down on shields, faces and heads.

THREE

10th June
Maidenhair Drive, Rugby, England

"Bloody hell."

"What's up with you, Barry?"

"I'm bored, mate. Bored to shit." The two men are staring out of the window at a house on the other side of the street. Barry is looking over the body of a digital camera fitted with a large telephoto lens which is set on a tripod. His mate has a pair of binoculars hanging around his neck. "How long are we going to be stuck here? That's what I want to know."

"Until something happens, Barry." This announcement comes from a frumpy looking woman in her mid-thirties seated at a table behind the two men. She has a pair of headphones over her head but only one ear is covered by an earpiece. "You heard what Miss Robbins said; we're stuck here until that bastard shows up."

"Bloody hell!"

"It could be worse." This is from another man who has entered the room. "We could be stuck in a bloody hedgerow somewhere in all sorts of weather. You guys don't know when you're lucky!"

"Yeah. Righto, boss. Sure." Barry's voice is full of sarcasm. His field supervisor has a quick look out of the window then moves back to sit at the same table as the woman.

"You could always ask for a transfer over to the team that's watching this twat's brother."

"Balls to that! They're stuck in a bloody van!"

"Exactly, Barry. You just don't know when you've got it easy, mate. Didn't they warn you when you joined that working for the

Firm was one percent action and ninety-nine percent being bored out of your bloody skull?"

"Mmmm. More like ninety-nine point nine nine percent! How long have we been stuck in this bloody place so far?"

"Nine weeks, mate. But the team before us was here for about eight months."

"Bloody hell!"

"There's movement." The woman is concentrating on the sounds coming through her headphones. "He's just saying goodbye to his missus." The supervisor looks at his watch, then jots down a note in the logbook lying on the table.

"Like bloody clockwork. His lift will be here in a second or so." As expected a few seconds later there's the sound of an old battered Series 1 Land Rover pulling up in the street outside and the loud honking of a horn. "What'd I tell yer? Okay, Jim, my lad. Off you go. You take point on the bike this morning and I'll follow in the Audi. When he gets to work I'll meet you in the office across from his factory."

"Righto, boss." The man with the binoculars around his neck checks that his pistol is secure in his concealed shoulder holster, drops the binos on the table next to the woman and grabs his motorbike helmet. He winks at the woman and laughs:

"Don't forget that it's Barry's turn to mow the front lawn today!"

He laughs on his way out.

"And up yours as well!" Barry's rejoinder follows him out of the door.

Across the street a tall, stocky man in his early thirties exits the front door of his house dressed in dark jeans and a dark blue T-shirt. He has bright ginger hair cut fairly short, a moustache and a short goatee beard. Before turning and planting a quick goodbye kiss on his wife's cheek, the man waves at his mate in the Land Rover. His wife is roughly the same age as him, very attractive and clutching a young toddler to her chest. The man ruffles his son's hair then jogs out and jumps in the vehicle. With a spurt of dust and diesel fumes the Land Rover pulls away from the curb and heads off towards the junction at the end of the street.

Two minutes later a brand new Honda CBR900RR Fireblade motorcycle moves off after the Land Rover from the side entryway of the house opposite, its 999.8cc inline four-cylinder engine purring with pent-up power, easily able to catch up with the old four-by-four. After another couple of minutes the door to the garage of the same house opens and a top-of-the-range Audi Q7 SUV pulls out on to the road and follows in the same direction.

FOUR

10th June
Armed Forces Day, Guildford, Surrey

The street suddenly erupts with sound as the mob of eighty enraged radical Muslims surges forward into the double rank of the thirty ex-soldiers. As they rush headlong to the line swinging their fists and smashing down their heavy placards like clubs, they suddenly find themselves missing their intended targets and losing their balance as the ex-soldiers unexpectedly and smartly step backwards two paces. Then with a quick change of direction their adversaries forge forward and their sixteen-inch telescopic batons dart into view around the edges of their riot shields to deliver short sharp sideways blows to the protester's knees, thwacks on to elbows and strikes downwards on to exposed collar bones.

Despite their superior numbers the first of the radicals to encounter the front line of ex-soldiers stumble to a standstill as a dozen grunting men drop their placards in agony and grab at bruised bones, howling in pain. But there's too many of them crowding in the narrow street and those behind continue to surge forward, pushing the ones in front of them into a melee of jabbing and swinging batons. The first rank of ex-soldiers bows slightly towards the middle of the street due to the sheer weight of the attack but the second rank stands firm, legs braced, helping to keep their comrades upright amongst the jostling, swearing and shouting humanity in the thick of the fight. Some of the men there reach ahead to jab at the faces of the protesters over the shoulders and shield rims of their comrades. Then, as suddenly as the attack started the radicals begin to retreat, shocked by a level of disciplined violence that none of them have ever experienced before. They aren't battle-hardened troops; they are civilians, and they have never participated in a stand-up fight with grim-faced professional soldiers before. The ex-soldiers, on the other hand are all veterans of this kind of action. All of them have already proved their courage to themselves and to their mates; they have been in combat and faced people who have been trying to kill them. In response to the radicals giving ground the ex-soldiers begin to step forward in unison, continuing to swing and jab at exposed bits of body with their batons, inflicting more and more injuries and pain on the radicals.

Then the Muslims at the front turn, push backwards and manage to break away from the fight, retreating a few metres and leaving a small gap between them and the line of ex-soldiers. Those with any breath left continue to scream defiance and insults at the men who have beaten them back, but they make sure that they stay a good distance away from the threat of those nasty swinging batons and the agony that they can inflict.

For a few minutes there's a stalemate as the large group of radicals mill about and try to figure out what they are going to do next. A handful of them still want to risk getting stuck in with the grinning men in front of them, but they can't convince the others to attack again. Loud, vicious arguments break out amongst them as the worst of the injured, clutching themselves in pain, push their way through to the back of the group, wanting to escape from this sudden hell and just go home. They hadn't signed up for this. They'd thought it would be an easy day, shouting and jeering at the infidel's troops as they marched past, protected from the worst of the violence of angry everyday people by the kuffir police. None of them had expected this sort of opposition nor this level of violence against them. In ones and twos they begin to slip away into the empty street behind them, hoping not to be spotted by the others.

Then the first of the teargas grenades come looping over the heads of the protesters, to land amongst the ex-soldiers.

Daljit is the first to see the danger and he shouts out the standard British Army warning to a gas attack:
    "Gas! Gas! Gas!"
On hearing the warning the rest of the ex-soldiers automatically close their eyes and hold their breath, reaching around to the large webbing pouches on their belts. Buckles are torn upwards and a

variety of respirators are pulled from the pouches. Most of them are of the older S6 and S10 NBC (Nuclear, Biological and Chemical warfare) types, but a half dozen of them are the new General Service Respirators, which have been used in the army since 2011.

The men slide the elastic fastenings over the back of their heads and then pull the respirators tight down on to their faces, releasing their breath in explosives shouts of: Gas! Gas! Gas! to expel any air and chemical smoke that may have been scooped up in the face pieces. British soldiers are trained to don their respirators in less than nine seconds, and the training pays off today, as it has many times before: 'On in nine, saved in time!'

Four M7A2 CS gas grenades land on the road amongst the lines of ex-soldiers. The canisters are simple in design, being basically a grey cylinder of sheet steel with holes in the top and bottom and a bold red stripe running around the cylinder. They contain a detonator, a pyrotechnic device and about one hundred and twenty grams of CS inside the steel tube. CS, or Chemical Smoke is predominately made up of a compound called o-chlorobenzylidene malononitrile, which occurs in solid form at room temperature. To operate a CS grenade it is held in the hand holding the handle in place. The grenade's pin is then pulled out to arm it. Next the grenade is thrown releasing the handle which in turn fires off the detonator igniting the pyrotechnic inside the casing. The pyrotechnic creates hot gases which convert the solid CS compound into an aerosol which is released from the holes in the cylinder, producing the tear gas which looks like a dense white cloud of normal wood smoke.

However, unlike normal smoke CS gas reacts with moisture on the skin and in the eyes, causing a horrible burning sensation which makes anyone exposed to it immediately shut their eyes. There are also numerous other effects caused by the gas which include tears streaming copiously from the eyes, fits of coughing, excessive snot running from the nose and more burning sensations of the eyelids, nose and throat areas. On top of these symptoms, which are bad enough, CS also causes disorientation, dizziness and restricted breathing. If the skin is already sweaty or sun-burned the CS will cause it to feel like it is burning on contact. In highly concentrated doses CS can also induce severe vomiting. All of these effects combine to partially disable anyone caught in CS smoke without protection, reducing their ability to fight or cause trouble, which is why it is commonly used to disperse rioters.

The worst effects usually wear off after an hour or so, although the feeling of burning and highly irritated skin may persist for hours, especially if you inadvertently forget and later rub your eyes with contaminated hands. The gas persists for a long time on clothing, at least until the items are washed, so a journey home in a car or a train after being caught in a CS attack can be particularly uncomfortable.

The gas grenades produce a thick white cloud of smoke along the two lines of ex-soldiers. However they are all safe from its harmful effects as they have responded quickly to Daljit's gas warning and donned their respirators before getting caught in it. The radical Muslim protesters on the other hand have never been trained in how to protect themselves from the effects of CS, nor have they been trained in how to use it correctly - not even in the simple concepts such as seeing which way the breeze is blowing before throwing your grenades. As the four grenades spew out their gas cloud the CS rises into the air for about three or four feet and accumulates before it is slowly whisked back through the ranks of the ex-soldiers by a slight breeze into the massed body of the protesters themselves.

The protesters who have not already run away from the fight find themselves coughing and spluttering as the CS drifts through them. Their eyes and noses run profusely and some of them are bent double as they spew up their guts, while others stagger away back up the street, watery eyes stinging like hell and throats burning.

If the radicals had managed to get close enough to the marching soldiers and the thousands of men, women and children that are lining the street to watch the Armed Forces Day Parade through the narrow streets of Guildford, waving their flags and cheering the troops, the tear gas grenades would have caused mass panic. Some of the older people might have been overcome and gone into respiratory failure, perhaps even dying, while young children could easily have been trampled and injured as a result. Of course none of this would have mattered to these radical extremists. They would have laughed at the panicking kuffirs who are, after all, only unbelievers, and therefore just the same as animals in their eyes.

As it stands, there is a lot of laughter on the street where the protesters have met the disciplined ranks of The Brotherhood, but it's a strange sort of strangulated sound. The sort of sound that can only be made by seriously amused men who are wearing respirators and have just witnessed a load of useless wankers gas themselves. There's a few tears flowing inside those respirators but it's not from the effects of the CS.

FIVE

10th June
Armed Forces Day, Guildford, Surrey

Billy, Daljit and Darren are sitting around a wooden table in the garden of the Britannia Pub along the Millmead, a road in Guildford. It's late in the afternoon and they are nursing the last remnants of their drinks; non-alcoholic lagers for Billy and Darren and a Coke for Daljit, as they're all facing long drives to get home.

"Well, the parade went okay. It's been a good day, lads," says Darren, raising his glass and taking a sip.

"Aye, it sure has," agrees Daljit, suddenly grinning. "Especially when them silly twats gassed themselves!"
They all laugh quietly at this comment, in a similar manner as to how as they've been laughing on and off ever since it had happened that morning.

"Their faces, man! When they realised that the CS was drifting back at them. I'll never forget the looks on their faces!" Billy's own face is almost split into two by the size of the grin on it.
Daljit's eyes start to water and he reaches up a hand to wipe them.

"Oh fuck!" he splutters loudly, and the other two suddenly stop laughing and look at him with concerned expressions.

"What's up, Dalj?" asks Billy, obviously concerned at the sudden change in his mate's demeanour.

"Are you alright, mate?" enquires Darren anxiously.
Daljit's head has dropped, so that he's looking down, but now he raises it again and his eyes are brightly red-rimmed and streaming with tears.

"Shit!" he says. "I forgot I'd got gas on me hands. Now I've rubbed it into me bloody eyes!"

38

The other two men stare at each other for a moment, then suddenly they're howling with laughter. After a second or two the big Sikh joins in with them.

It's a lovely warm and sunny afternoon and the guys are in a relaxed mood now that Daljit's eyes are almost back to normal and have stopped streaming tears. That's the trouble with CS gas. Once it's on your hands or clothes it's a real bugger to get off in the short term. When any residue makes contact with something like moist eyes, the effects just flare up again. It can only be removed with a good scrub of hot water and lots and lots of soap, and neither Daljit nor the others have had a chance to do that all day, as they've been running around on the periphery of the parade making sure that the radical Muslim protesters didn't get a chance to regroup and have another go at causing trouble.

The small garden of the Britannia Pub contains about a dozen tables. It's not that busy and only four of them are occupied by couples and groups of friends. The garden is surrounded by a low brick wall with a white-painted picket fence on top of it. From where they are sitting the three men have a good view out over the small car park to the River Wey slowly flowing past them about thirty metres away, and as they chat they are also idly watching the people who are walking along the riverbank.

The three men have known each other for a long time and have shared a lot together, including their time in prison and some of the more dangerous missions that they've undertaken in The Brotherhood since their release. They are three of the 'originals' of the close band of ex-soldiers who started up the organisation from scratch. They were all there on that New Year's Day in Tobago when Nigel had first come up with the idea, only eighteen months ago.

The Brotherhood is a group of like-minded ex-forces men and women who have joined together to act as vigilantes and fight against serious and organised crime on the streets of the United Kingdom. They started out with just the initial eight members, or the 'Magnificent Eight' as Billy likes to call them, two of whom, Sam the Man and Nigel, are now dead. Sam was killed when The Brotherhood took on Nigerian gangsters in West Africa and was pivotal in successfully saving the lives of some child sex-slaves.

39

Nigel is no longer with them because he killed himself at the end of the previous year, most probably due to a severe bout of depression combined with Post Traumatic Stress Disorder.

The organisation has now grown from these humble beginnings to comprise over two thousand five hundred active members, and tens of thousands of 'non-active' supporters. All of them are ex-serving or currently serving members of the British Army, the Royal Air Force, the Royal Navy and the Royal Marines, and they occur everywhere in British society. Some are politicians or local councillors, others are police officers, probation officers, prison officers, social workers, dentists, doctors, lorry drivers, road sweepers, business owners, waiters and waitresses, nurses and traffic wardens. You name the profession or the job and there's probably a person somewhere in the UK who does it and is also a member of The Brotherhood, or at least affiliated to it.

Up to now The Brotherhood's activities, which sometimes involve very violent tactics, have led to a huge decrease in the amount of serious crime, especially that committed by organised crime cartels. Their biggest success so far has been the virtual annihilation of the Albanian Mafia in the UK. Coversely, they are paying a price for this success and the methods they use. Every police force in the country is after them, as well as a dedicated joint 'desk' of MI5 and MI6 personnel.

However, in the secret world of the Security Services, nothing is ever as it seems to be. Unbeknownst to anyone else the two Director Generals of the Security Services had secretly worked hand-in-hand with The Brotherhood to take down the Albanians. Even now, as one part of their services continue to hunt down The Brotherhood and find a way to infiltrate them, the two bosses are happily using information given to them by The Brotherhood to weed out other criminal organisations and to take the credit for it themselves. This is not just a case of the right hand not knowing what the left hand is doing, but rather the right hand not even knowing that the left hand exists! And mixed up with all of this is one rather special man; a man known to everyone simply as John Smith. A man whose real name is unknown to anyone but himself.

A former soldier in the Parachute Regiment of the British Army, Smith had been recruited by the Secret Intelligence Service (MI6) in the 1970s to act as an agent in the Rhodesian Army after it had declared unilateral independence from Britain. Serving for several years during the Rhodesian Bush War and constantly fighting the insurgents there, Smith, had worked his way up through their Special Forces, eventually becoming a sergeant in the Rhodesian Special Air Service Regiment. The information he had passed back to his spy masters had on several occasions saved the lives of the leaders of the so-called African freedom fighters, including the man who would eventually become the President of the country; Robert Mugabe.

After the Rhodesian war ended, Smith had returned to the UK and had found himself serving in the British Special Forces. He had been one of the troopers who had famously assaulted the Iranian Embassy in May 1980, freeing the hostages and killing the terrorists who had kidnapped them. Then he had served in numerous other wars and hot-spots around the globe including the terrorist conflict in Northern Ireland, the Falklands War, the war between Chad and Libya and the invasion of Afghanistan by the Soviets. At this time his luck had finally run out and in the snowfields of Afghanistan Smith had been captured and tortured by the Soviets for three long months before eventually breaking.

When he finally returned home, Smith was a changed and damaged man. However he had once again been recruited by the Secret Intelligence Service as an operative in a very, very secret part of their service known as the Increment. Here he had been used as a cold-blooded assassin for three years before almost completely breaking down. Even then he had still gone on to serve again as a Special Forces soldier in the First Gulf War and as an agent in Slovenia during the beginning of the crisis there.

Finally he was abandoned by both the army and the Secret Intelligence Service and had fallen apart. But the spooks couldn't leave him alone; they had to cover their tracks as Smith knew just too many of their dark little secrets. So they framed him with the abduction, rape and murder of a young teenage girl and Smith was sentenced to spend the rest of his life in prison, discredited and disgraced.

That had been a big mistake - on the part of the spooks.

Smith escaped from the courtroom where he was being tried and had gone on the rampage. He destroyed the police department that had charged him and murdered the prosecutor, the judge and the Secret Intelligence Service handler who had set him up. Then, just for good measure, he had blown up the Police National Computer and the National DNA Databank as well. After this he disappeared.

Eventually, of course, Smith had been found. He was hunted down in The Gambia, a small country in West Africa where he had been hiding under a different name. But before he could be assassinated he had fled the country and had ended up on a plane flying across the Atlantic which had been hi-jacked by North African terrorists. Their aim was to crash the airliner into Buckingham Palace and wipe out the entire British Royal Family as they had gathered to celebrate the Queen's birthday. Smith had taken on and killed the eight terrorists single-handedly just in time to save the Royal Family, but he was very badly injured, almost fatally.

Back in the UK Smith survived his wounds and was finally carted off to Winson Green Prison to serve out his life sentence. He may have saved the Royals and a plane full of civilians, but he had still murdered people while on his rampage. It was in prison that Smith had met Nigel, Billy, Darren, Daljit, Brummie and Matt. They had helped him to escape during a daring kidnap of the Royal Couple; Prince William and his wife Kate. At the same time he had managed to convince the authorities that he had been killed in a massive underground explosion.

At that point in time he had been free from retribution by the British government, but a man like Smith can't live the quiet life for long, and since then he had enjoyed several adventures with his mates from prison. Now he is back in the good books of the security services' bosses, after handing them the Albanian Mafia on a plate.

"Are you lads up to anything interesting?"
Billy takes a swig of his non-alcoholic lager and grimaces slightly at the taste.

"I'm looking into the gangmasters operating in East Anglia," says Daljit, his eyes calmer but still bloodshot from the CS gas.

"Yeah? What's all that about then?"

"There's a bunch of thugs over there who are running huge gangs of foreign labourers and hiring them out to farmers to pick

42

their crops." He pauses and looks at his mate's faces. "I know that doesn't sound like the stuff we normally get into, but these poor mugs are treated almost like slaves. They live in atrocious conditions, work very long hours and earn just a pittance, plus the gang masters are extremely violent and abusive towards them. It's early days yet, but our initial findings indicate that organised crime is involved in a big way."

"Hmm. Who are these gangmasters? A bunch of foreigners?" Billy looks interested, especially at the mention of organised crime.

"Surprisingly not all of them. There are a few Polish and Lithuanians involved, but a lot of them are British too, and there's also quite a few Irish gang masters. It's a right old mix."

"Sounds like a nightmare."

"It is, but I'm working on something now to put a stop to at least one of them."

"Great stuff. How about you, Darren? Anything interesting coming up?"

Darren dejectedly shakes his head as he answers:

"Nah! Not a dickie-bird. It seems to be going really quiet. I think we've been doing too good a job!"

"Yep. It does seem to have quietened down a lot since we took out the Albanians. Most of the organised criminals are keeping their heads down, I reckon." Daljit smiles. "Which reminds me, have you heard about Smiler and Ginger?"

"Not for a while. What are they up to then?"

"Well, they were at a bit of a loss when they got out of nick. Nigel kept them busy for a while by getting them involved in some operations, but since his…suicide, well, they've been getting bored. John talked it over with Linda. I think he was worried that they might turn back to crime again, but Linda came up with the idea that they might enjoy running one of our half-way hostels for homeless servicemen. They weren't that impressed by the idea to start with, but now they've been running the hostel down in Devon for a couple of weeks and they really seem to be enjoying it."

Both Billy and Darren smile at this news.

"I reckon they'll be great at that. They're both good at getting on with other blokes."

"Yeah, just so long as they don't start teaching them how to nick motors!"

They all laugh.

"Funny enough," adds Daljit, "one of the courses they're running is for 'operations'; they're teaching a few of the guys how to bypass car alarms!"

"Jesus!" splutters Darren. "That's like putting the fox in charge of the hen coop!" They look around guiltily at a couple sitting a few tables away as they all burst into laughter again. The couple just smile back, not at all offended by the group of visibly happy men.

"What are you up to then, Billy?" asks Darren. "Anything I can help with?"

"Yeah sure, Daz. Always glad of some help. I'm heading up a new team that's putting pressure on a few business owners around the country."

"Why's that then?"

"Oh. It started with my brother. He got a job at a fast-food place in Worcester, but he was only earning about four quid an hour. Well below the national minimum wage."

"I thought that it's illegal to pay people less than the minimum wage?"

"Exactly, mate. I had a word with Daljit and Brummie, and we're going to bring it up as a possible operation at the next council meeting. They've given me a team of blokes to start investigating how common it is in the UK."

"Any luck with that, Billy?" asks Daljit.

"You'd be surprised, Dalj. Official figures reckon that about sixty thousand workers in Britain are being paid under the minimum wage, but from what we're turning up it's probably going to be a hell of a lot more than that. Maybe as many as a hundred to a hundred and fifty thousand workers!"

"Jesus! That's terrible!"

"I know, mate. The worst thing though is that the majority of their employers are turning out to be rich bastards. They're not doing it because they can't afford it. They're just greedy wankers. I've found one place where they're paying their security staff one pound fifty an hour! Can you believe that?"

"Bloody hell."

"Too true. Anyway, we've been given the go ahead to try putting some pressure on a few of the employers to see if it'll work."

"What sort of pressure, Billy?"

Billy grins evilly at this.

"You know, mate. The sort of pressure that we're really good at: a bit of violence and intimidation!"

"Sounds great! Definitely give me a call, Billy!"

"Roger that, Darren. I've got one real bastard coming up in the next couple of months that you can help me with. He's an Indian geezer who owns thirteen restaurants and fast food joints and employs over a hundred staff, most of them illegal immigrants. They also rent houses and rooms from him at extortionate rents, and he pays them all less than four quid an hour. One of our members works in a local bank where this bloke has an account, and she's slipped us a record of how much money he's saved with them. It turns out that he's a bloody millionaire, and this is only one of several accounts that he has spread over many different banks. The bloke's an out and out wanker."

"What're you planning to do with him?"

"Well, I thought we'd have a quiet word with him first and let him know that we're on to him. If that doesn't work then we should start destroying some of the property that he owns, such as his brand new Merc. Eventually he'll get the message, I hope. Fancy a go at that, Daz?"

"Sure, Billy. You can count me in."

"Well, as John would say..."

They all join in at this point, laughing.

"....Super!"

EGYPT

SIX

10th June
Hurghada International Airport, Egypt

"Christ, I'm dying for a fag!" Mike's hands are shaking badly
as he fumbles to pull a cigarette from the packet and from the
corner of his eye he can see a frown forming on Dwayne's face.
"What?" he says. Then it dawns on him: "Oh shit! Sorry, Dwayne!
I forgot that 'fag' means something else entirely to you Yanks. It's
not my fault you took a perfectly good language and butchered it!"
Dwayne can tell that his friend is just a bit wound up from the lack
of cigarettes. Mike finally manages to get a cigarette free from the
pack, shoves it into his mouth and lights it with a cheap throwaway
lighter that he'd just bought with the fags from a local vendor
outside the airport terminal building. His whole body shudders as
he draws the smoke deep into his lungs, holds it there for a count
of five seconds and then exhales it slowly back out. It's only a
moment before the rush of nicotine hits his brain and he can finally
feel himself relax.

"Why the fuck they've stopped people from smoking on
bloody flights I'll never know. Tosspots!"
Mike's companion and good friend Dwayne is massively built with
wide shoulders and a deep chest, bulging biceps and thighs, and a
square-jawed, handsome face. He towers over Mike's respectable
six feet two inches by another four inches. Looking down at his
friend Dwayne sees Mike grinning:

"You Brits, man. You've always got to moan about something
or other." Mike grins back up at him, happy now that he's
poisoning his lungs with God knows how many toxic chemicals.

"Too right, mate. It wouldn't be any fun if you couldn't have a moan about it." His attention is grabbed by a grey minibus weaving towards them through the airport car park. "Hey Sheila!" he shouts at his wife. She's standing with Dwayne's wife Margot amongst a small group of other tourists about twenty yards away, next to a small mountain of their luggage and diving kit piled high close to the exit from the terminal. "It looks like our vehicle's here." He gestures towards the minibus, which pulls up in front of the group. There's a hand-written sign on a piece of cardboard propped up on the dashboard. It reads: 'Ibrahim's Camping and Diving Safari'.

"Finish your fag first, Mike. The driver will help us get the kit on, I guess." Mike cannot fail to note the subtle sarcasm in Sheila's voice, but he's very happy sucking on his cancer stick and so decides to make light of it. He whispers to his friend:

"She's the worst kind of anti-smoker, Dwayne. Ever since she gave up herself about eighteen months ago!"
Dwayne just shakes his head in disgust as Mike inadvertently blows a whiff of smoke into his face.

"Jesus, Mike! What's in that thing?" Dwayne drawls in his distinctive Midwestern twang, his nose twitching.

"Dunno, mate. Probably camel shit. It's a local brand."

"Sure smells like it."
After another few drags on the fag he's finally satisfied, at least for a while, so he tosses the butt into a nearby ashtray and wipes at the sweat forming on his brow.

"It's bloody hot, mate."

"Well, we are in Egypt, Mike." The big man smiles, looking just for a second like a young excited boy. Then he claps his huge hands together. "Come on, let's help the womenfolk load our gear away or we'll never hear the last of it."

"Too true, blue." Even Mike's beginning to feel the excitement of the moment. "We're here at last ,mate. Let's get some bloody diving in! Yehey!"

"Yo!"
They high five like a couple of school kids.

Mike Oldport and Dwayne Huntsbringer are an odd pair of friends. They had met about six years before when Mike and his then girlfriend Sheila were travelling through the States on holiday. They are both passionate about sub-aqua diving and they were on a diving holiday in Florida, working their way along the Keys, and stopping whenever the fancy took them to have a dive from a beach or cove. The weather was hot, the diving fantastic and Sheila had even managed to get plenty of close encounters with cuttlefish, which were her favourite form of sea life. The couple were driving east along the Overseas Highway between Boca Chica Key and Key West at the southern tip of Florida when their hire car suddenly overheated and they'd had to pull over and stop. When Mike lifted up the bonnet he'd been enveloped in a cloud of steam from a split radiator hose. Dwayne and Margot just happened to be driving by, on a holiday of their own, as he emerged red-faced from his unexpected steam bath. Sensing that they were tourists (which wasn't hard to see), Dwayne had felt a moment of pity and pulled over to give them a hand.

Dwayne had a spare can of water in his car and a roll of gaffer tape that they used to temporarily repair the split hose. He's like that, not going anywhere without spares for everything and always ready for any emergency. It's probably down to the training he had when he served as a US Army Ranger. He was with Bravo Company, 1st Battalion of the 75th Ranger Regiment in the first Gulf War, so he knows his stuff. Not that he talks about it much.

Once the engine had cooled down and they'd tipped Dwayne's water into the radiator, Mike and Sheila invited their rescuers out to a seafood dinner at a restaurant called Bistro 245 overlooking Mallory Square in Key West as a thank you. Their friendship blossomed over shrimp and lobster fettuccine served with asparagus and chèvre and since then Dwayne and Margot have visited the Brits every two years at their home in Ely in Cambridgeshire. Dwayne had even been Mike's best man and Margot had been Sheila's Maid of Honour at their wedding, and in return the Brits had visited their American friends every other year in their hometown of Denver, in the State of Colorado.

Mike and Sheila have both been very keen sub-aqua divers for a number of years, having first met when they were taking a PADI (Professional Association of Diving Instructors) Open Water Diver's course in Swanage, Dorset. They became diving buddies during the course and did their first dives together under Swanage

Pier and off Chesil Beach. During that first meal together with Dwayne and Margot, Mike and Sheila did nothing but talk about diving and not surprisingly their enthusiasm for their pastime rubbed off on the Americans, so they all agreed to meet up again the following day and go diving together. Mike and Sheila took Dwayne and Margot out one at a time into the Gulf of Mexico, and the American couple were bowled over by the experience, really enjoying themselves. One thing led to another after that, and Dwayne and Margot eventually took their own diving courses once they returned home to Colorado. Now they are all on their first diving holiday together. None of them has ever dived in Egypt before, but it is the Mecca for anyone with any interest in diving, so they're all really looking forward to a chance to dive on the legendary coral reefs of the Egyptian Red Sea.

SEVEN

10th June
Coastal Road, Egypt

'Ibrahim's Camping and Diving Safari' is a locally run company that had come highly recommended by some old friends of Mike's who'd used them when they had been on holiday a couple of years ago and really enjoyed their trip. Unlike most tourists who come to Egypt and dive in the very well-known and often crowded waters around Sharm-El-Sheikh, Mike and Sheila were drawn to Ibrahim's because the company's itinerary included diving in remote locations along the western seaboard of the Red Sea, from below Quseer, located about halfway down the Egyptian coast, right through to the Sudanese border in the south. The company had described some fantastic spots along the coast with great coral reefs that have not been dived before. Of course, the location is well off the beaten track and there are no tourist facilities so there would be no hotels or lodges for them and they would have to camp at each new location. For Mike and Sheila this just adds to the whole romance of the trip in their view. Who couldn't be excited about camping on the edge of the great Eastern Desert where it joins the Red Sea? Then diving on pristine coral reefs that no one has ever dived before? It sounded almost too good to be true and when they had got in touch with Dwayne and Margot, they hadn't needed much persuasion to come along on the holiday of a lifetime.

The driver of their minibus is Egyptian and as they head south along the coast road and the light of day gradually fades, they start to learn some of his night time driving habits. The main one is that he likes to drive in the pitch black darkness with the headlights switched off, just occasionally flicking them on every quarter of a

53

mile or so for a second or two to orientate himself. Mike is pretty annoyed by this, not only because it's unsafe but also as he is a nature buff and constantly stares out of the windscreen, hoping to catch a glimpse of the local wildlife crossing the road ahead in the glare of the headlights. That's why he had chosen the front seat of the minibus for himself and Sheila, so that they could see clearly out of the windscreen. It's pretty frustrating for him that the lights are off so much, although he does get a brief glimpse of two foxes just after they pass through Safaga. One is definitely a Red Fox, like the ones back home in England, with its white-tipped tail and reddish coat, but he is pretty sure that the second is a Ruppell's Sand Fox, because it is much smaller, has a pale, sandy-coloured coat and huge great ears. This is a new species for Mike and goes a long way to making the journey less frustrating for him.

In the end though, even Mike can't keep his eyes open anymore and he begins to drift off, lulled by the absolute silence and darkness of the desert night and the motion of the minibus.

Suddenly he is jerked awake by the ear-splitting blast of the minibus horn. It's still night-time, but he guesses that they've arrived at Quseer, the last major town they need to go through before they head even further south into the empty desert. The driver has his lights on all the time now, as the narrow dusty street in front of them is filled with bustling crowds of people. He begins to sound his horn almost non-stop as he slows right down to a crawl. There are people everywhere and most of them seem to be walking down the middle of the road. Some are even tugging donkeys along behind them with lengths of old rope. The minibus is a bit like a ship breaking through a thick layer of ice in the Antarctic as the crowds of people reluctantly part before it, and more than one person is clipped on their shoulders by its wing mirrors as it forces its way forwards, but they don't seem to mind.

Along the side of the road Mike catches glimpses of the open fronts of shops, lit up and doing a roaring trade even though it's quite late. He can see huge rolls of colourful cloth laid out on top of rickety tables, pots and pans, shoes, batteries, piles of sticky-looking dates, in fact just about everything you can think of is for sale along the roadside, including such incongruously modern things as DVDs and CDs. The place is absolutely heaving with people. He glances across at Sheila's face and sees her eyes are sparkling with excitement at the sights, which are very strange and new for both of them. He reaches across and grabs her hand and she gives him one of her most beautiful smiles. Mike's heart wells up inside of him. He reflects that Sheila is not only a wonderful person to share his life with, she's also gorgeous and very, very smart. She's about five foot ten inches in height, and even though they're both in their mid-thirties now, she still has the deliciously slim and willowy figure of a girl half her age, but with ample curves in all of the right places. God, he loves this woman of his!

As the minibus creeps slowly on even Sheila finds it hard to keep up her interest as they continue slowly making their way along the crowded road. It's been a long day (and night) for both of them so far with a long drive down the M11 Motorway in the UK to Gatwick Airport, followed by a boring three hour wait before boarding their flight. Not to mention the seven hour flight to Hurghada and the two or three hours on the road south since landing. Mike looks back at Dwayne and Margot and can see that they are both fast asleep, which isn't surprising as they had flown out to them in Cambridge from the States only the day before.

Mike looks around the minibus at the other sleeping occupants. Neither himself and Sheila, nor Dwayne and Margot had been on an organised tour of this kind before, and it had been interesting to find out about the people who have joined them. There's a young Scottish couple who look very fit and athletic. Mike had found out that she is a producer for the BBC and he's something to do with the City, probably a stockbroker – they look wealthy enough and have a load of brand new top-of-the-range diving kit with them. There's also a Dutch couple who are closer to their own age. The man is a veterinary surgeon. Dwayne laughed when he was talking to them earlier, saying that he too was a 'vet', but of a different kind altogether of course. After quitting the US Army, Dwayne became a professor of history at a Denver community college and Margot is an editor in an academic publishing house. The last two couples are English. One of them is a lorry driver and his wife who have left their three young kids at home with an aunt while they enjoy their break. The last couple appear to be a miss-matched pair. She is a very beautiful lecturer at Warwick University and he is an ex-soldier who writes war novels. He looks too much of a rough-diamond to be sharing his life with an academic, but they seem to be very much in love. Of course, the one thing that all of the tourists on the minibus have in common is that they are all qualified and enthusiastic sub-aqua divers.

Mike Oldport was born in a council flat on a housing estate in Coventry and went to a state-run comprehensive school where, if the truth is to be told, he didn't do very well. He was much too naively idealistic and independent to enjoy being told what to do by a bunch of school teachers and was always getting into trouble. But he's done okay since then, as it wasn't long after leaving school that he started up his own business. He began his working life by working hard in a car factory for a year and saving up his hard-earned cash to buy a small printing press. At first he used his bedroom in his parent's house as an office and production site, printing up small numbers of flyers for school fetes and the like. Now Mike owns eight large printing companies across the West Midlands and East Anglia and he's worth a couple of million pounds.

Sheila works with Mike and is a co-director of the business, handling all of the publicity and public relations. She is a very clever woman, and it's thanks to her that their business has tripled its income during the last few years, and that's in spite of the recession. She gets on well with all of their customers, so well that sometimes Mike thinks that they only come back to his company for repeat jobs because of her sparkling personality, even when they can probably get their printing done in Hong Kong or Singapore for a lot less. She really wins them over.

Finally the slow forward motion of the minibus through the main street of Quseer comes to an abrupt end. Almost instantaneously a harassed-looking Egyptian businessman in a cheap shiny suit knocks on the door of their minibus. It seems that he's been waiting for them to arrive for some time, for as soon as the driver lets him in he starts to have a right go at the poor man, haranguing him loudly in Egyptian and gesturing more than once at his wristwatch. Finally he seems satisfied that he has reprimanded the driver enough and turns to the passengers, putting a sickly smile on his face.

"Hello English peoples," he starts off confidently. "Many, many apologies for delay." Turning back to the driver he gives him another mouthful of angry Egyptian and then looks back to face the passengers again. "Need passports please."
Mike looks at Sheila. Sheila looks back at him with an expression that says: 'What the hell is he talking about?' Mike turns around to look over his shoulder at Dwayne and Margot who have both just woken up. They look completely knackered and totally confused as they have both been roused from a deep sleep bought on by the jet lag they're experiencing. Mike turns back to the Egyptian in the suit who seems to be getting more and more agitated.
"What do you mean? Passports?"
The Egyptian just looks at him uncomprehendingly and Mike suddenly realises that he doesn't understand any English at all - he must be saying it all parrot-fashion. He just holds out his hand and repeats:
"Need passports, please."
Mike is used to being asked for his passport to check into a hotel, but never in the middle of a busy market street by an absolute stranger when there are no official personnel in sight. Mike looks out of the window, hoping to see a passport control office or similar official looking building on the street but there's nothing except the same kind of buildings and shops that they've been passing and staring at for the last twenty minutes. Dwayne, more awake now, catches Mike's eye and shrugs. Well that's not a lot of help, he thinks to himself.
"Why do you want our passports?" Mike asks again, slowly and clearly, hoping against hope that the Egyptian will understand his doubts, even if he doesn't understand their language. The man in the suit repeats his gesture of proffering his hands and says:
"Need passports, please."

At this point there is a lot of anxiety and confusion in the minibus. None of the passengers know what's going on and nobody is eager to hand over the only identification documentation they have. They've just arrived in a foreign country, parts of which are in turmoil because of the political nonsense taking place in the big cities like Cairo and Alexandria after the 'Arab Spring', and here's a complete stranger asking them for their passports.

Mike looks around the minibus and he can see from the expectant looks on everyone's faces that somehow he has been appointed as their official spokesman. God, how did I end up in this position he thinks to himself. I don't want the job; I don't know how to make that man understand - I haven't got a clue what to do. He feels an enormous sense of relief when Dwayne, the ex-Ranger's voice breaks in, coming to his rescue:

"Police?" Dwayne asks the guy in the suit. "Are you a policeman?"

The guy just looks at him in exasperation and says:

"Need passports, please!"

They notice that his voice is getting higher in pitch and louder in volume. Dwayne taps Mike on the shoulder and whispers:

"I don't think we're going to get anywhere with this guy."

Mike nods in agreement. "But I don't want to give our passports away without knowing where they're going."

Mike nods again, thinking out loud:

"Why don't you and me go with him, Dwayne. Let's make sure that everything is kosher?"

"Yup. That sounds like a good plan, old buddy."

Dwayne and Mike talk briefly to the other passengers. It seems they are in agreement that their proposed plan of action is probably the best idea. None of them are very keen to let their passports be taken, but they seem to trust that Mike and Dwayne will look after them. Dwayne has the sort of strong, honest face and straight forward personality that most people feel at ease with and trust, so they dig into their bags and pockets and hand their documents over to him.

Mike smiles at the Egyptian, and again in a slow, loud and clear voice he says:

"Okay, pal. Here's the passports, but we're coming with you." He shows him the documents and hears Dwayne sigh at his 'Englishman abroad' type speech. The suit is a little confused at first, but when Mike and Dwayne stand up and move to the front of the minibus he seems to suddenly understand and gives them a very relieved smile.

"Good! Good!" he says. "Need passports, please!"

Mike turns and gives Sheila a little smile saying: "Hopefully we won't be long" and steps down from the minibuses door into the heat, dust and noise of the Egyptian town. He feels the presence of Dwayne behind him as they both follow the guy in the suit into a dark alleyway leading off from the street. Although Mike feels a little moment of anguish as they walk along behind the Egyptian, his feeling are tempered by having Dwayne with him. He feels buoyed up with the large confident man close by. After about thirty metres the alley opens up onto another, narrower street and with a feeling of intense relief they see the entrance to a police station right in front of them. The doorway to the station is open and light is billowing out on to the street from inside, illuminating a battered police car in the road, along with a couple of Egyptian police officers lolling around and smoking cigarettes. Mike turns around to give Dwayne a grin when suddenly all hell breaks loose behind them.

EIGHT

10th June
Quseer, Egypt

As Sheila watches Mike and Dwayne step out of the minibus, she can't help but look at Mike's bum. They've been together for some ten years now, but she's never seen a sexier one in her whole life; so pert and firm he could crush a walnut between his buttocks. It's not just his bum though; to Sheila Mike is without doubt the sexiest man alive - and kind, sweet and smart. She just loves him to bits.

She's very aware that Mike knows how to look after himself so she does not feel unduly worried as she watches him leave the minibus and walk off into the darkness of the Egyptian street. Besides, he's got Dwayne with him, she reassures herself. He just exudes strength and she knows how careful he is. Sheila is confident that the two men will be okay no matter what happens. Despite this she has to push aside a sharp pang of anxiety as they disappear into an alleyway following the little sweaty Egyptian in his ridiculously shiny suit. Sheila is happy to hear Margot's voice from behind her:

"Do you mind if I sit next to you, Sheila?"
She looks up to see her peering over the back of her seat. Her accent is not as pronounced as Dwayne's but Sheila always marvels at how husky her voice is. Sheila can see that she's also feeling a touch of concern by the look on her face, so she pats the fabric of the seat and encourages her friend to sit beside her.

"Of course not!"
Margot quickly slips around and perches next to her. She is a good ten years her senior, but you'd never guess it. There's hardly a line on her perfectly proportioned face and her skin is as smooth as the

proverbial baby's bottom, as Mike would say. Sheila feels a flush of welcome friendliness as Margot reaches over and grabs her hand, and she squeezes it back. Margot and Dwayne are the best friends that anyone could ever have and Sheila is suddenly glad that they're here together.

"I hope they're not too long," she says.

"Me too!"

The minibus jolts slightly as someone on the street outside bumps into it and Sheila looks out of the window. The illumination in the street is not great as it's only really the result of the diffused light given off from a number of windows and open doors in the surrounding buildings. However the harsh light from the minibus headlamps that the driver has left on help her see more. It's like an alien world out there, about as far from Ely in Cambridgeshire as you could ever get. There is a sea of faces moving slowly past their windows as the crowd outside surges and wanes like a tide as they flow past them. There are men wearing loose robes, with dark mahogany-coloured skin that's wrinkled and lined by the heat of the desert. Young boys and girls with jet black hair and huge dark eyes that peer excitedly at them through the windows. Sombre black-faced North Africans chewing some kind of plant in their mouths and lots and lots of the most beautiful women, some bare-faced and wearing head scarfs. There are also quite a few women dressed from head-to-toe in their black burqas with only their dark eyes showing through a narrow slit. Sheila is forcibly reminded that Egypt is a predominantly Muslim country and she feels a slight surge of panic as the word 'terrorist' also pops unbidden into her head.

Her thoughts wander on to the warning that their travel agent had given them about a handful of terrorist atrocities which had taken place recently in Egypt. But she also remembers his reassurances that the majority of these had been carried out against the Egyptian security forces because of the domestic political situation after the 'Arab Spring' and not against western tourists. She also knows that terrorist attacks are always carried out against targets where there are lots of people gathered together and fortunately they are going far away from the crowds and out into the desert, so they'll be in no danger at all. Now, however, her mind is working overtime and she has to admit, surrounded as they are by a crowd of staring, and seemingly hostile faces, his words do little to comfort her.

Then, out of the blue, but almost as if her thoughts are some sort of prophesy they are assailed by a burst of loud bangs in the street.

Sheila can see the faces outside the window all turn in the same direction, but she is unable to make out what they are looking at. Then there is another loud burst of ear-splitting noise and her heart drops to her stomach as she realises that it's gunfire. Suddenly the street is filled with screams and shouts and Sheila can see the panic and fear written across the features of the Egyptian's faces outside. They begin to run, shoving and pushing each other in their haste to get away from whatever is happening. She's terrified as she watches a few people fall on to the road only to be trampled in the stampede as everyone desperately tries to get away. It's absolute pandemonium out there. There are more gunshots and they are much closer now.

Margot pulls at her arm: "Get down, Sheila! On to the floor!" She instinctively follows the other woman, dropping down to her knees and feels the hot metal of the minibuses floor through the material of her trousers. They both duck down, keeping their heads low. One of the other passengers starts to scream and the sound is terrifying in the confined space.

Suddenly there is a loud banging on the door of the minibus. Sheila risks a look upwards and she can see a black man pounding his fists on the glass of the door's window just in front of her. He's shouting and brandishing something long and dark in his hands but she can't make out what it is and their driver is shouting back at him in terrified Egyptian. Out of the blue there is an almighty bang as the door window explodes inwards, showering Sheila and Margot with shards of broken glass. The women spontaneously use their arms to try and shield themselves. Sheila risks another quick look and she can now see that the black man is undoubtedly holding a gun. He pushes it in the broken window and fires point blank at the driver. His head explodes in front of her and the inside of the minibus is showered with hot blood. Sheila gags as vomit rises in her throat.

The black man leans inside and uses the manual lever to open the door and then jumps up on to the step. Sheila has never ever seen anyone like him before; he's small and skinny with very black ashy-coloured skin and he has huge yellow buck teeth that jut from his mouth. He grabs the dead body of the driver and heaves it out the door, then screams at the passengers in a language Sheila does not recognise and which sounds like the crazy jabbering of some kind of monkey. None of the passengers move; they're all glued to the floor by absolute terror hardly daring to make a sound. Sheila can just hear the passenger who was screaming now sobbing loudly together with the low voice of her husband who is doing his best to comfort her.

The black man can see that no one understands him and he seems to lose his temper. He raises his gun into the air and pulls the trigger and a stream of bullets smash their way out of the roof and through the luggage piled on the roof-rack. The sheer noise hammers at the passenger's senses and makes them cringe on the floor and soon the stink of the gunpowder makes Sheila wretch again as it fills the minibus with an acrid cloud. Then another black man appears at the vehicle doorway. This one is tall, though he's as skinny as the short one, and his skin is a lighter brown colour. Something about this one makes Sheila feel very afraid especially when he looks at her. His eyes radiate poor hatred. He jabbers away at the first man in the same strange language and the short one grins, laughs harshly and spits a big blob of disgusting phlegm on to the floor. He then hands his gun to the tall man who clambers on board and just stands there glaring at the passengers, hate and loathing emanating from insane-looking eyes while he covers them with the gun. Meanwhile the short one climbs into the driver's seat and starts the engine up. With a jerk the minibus starts moving forward in the abandoned, empty street.

As the tall gun man turns to jabber again at the short one the air is suddenly filled with the high-pitched screaming of an alarm that is so loud it pierces Sheila's ears painfully. He spins back around and darts towards the back of the minibus. She can't see what's happening but he's obviously furious at someone in the back because she can hear the thuds as he lays into one of the passengers there as he screams loudly. Then she hears glass breaking again and the sound is followed by a long burst of gunfire. Sheila thinks he's firing at someone or something behind them. He screams in anger again and stomps forward. Sheila risks

63

a quick look at his face and wishes she hadn't. He is obviously seething with anger and hatred and literally drooling from his open mouth and looking quite insane. He catches her looking at him from the corner of his eye and smashes down at her with his rifle. She doesn't remember it connecting. Suddenly everything is blackness.

NINE

10th June
Quseer, Egypt

Behind them Mike and Dwayne hear the loud hammering sound of gunfire. They look at each other for about half a second and then they're running back the way they came as fast as their legs will carry them. Mike can hear high-pitched screams and shouts from the street where they left the minibus and then there's another blast of gunfire. He was running fast before but now the terrifying sound puts an added spurt of energy and fear into his body and he rockets forward.

They hit a crowd of Egyptians fleeing from the gunfire and even the huge bulk of Dwayne is slowed down to almost a crawl as they run into a seething mass of panicked and terrified people trying to go in the opposite direction. The larger man uses his size and strength to elbow and push people aside as he powers forward and Mike slips into his wake, being jostled every agonisingly slow step of the way. They hear a couple of single shots ahead and keep on forcing their way through the crowd, but it's almost impossible to make any headway, as at least a hundred Egyptians are frantically trying to squeeze past them through the narrow dark alleyway. Then, as suddenly as it had appeared the crowd begins to thin and at last Mike and Dwayne can move quicker, just in time to hear a long blast of gunfire that sounds like it's in some sort of enclosed space. Mike can hear Dwayne grunting as he pushes aside the last few Egyptians in his way and then at last they're clear and sprinting the last few yards.

They emerge from the suffocating blackness of the alley into the dimly-lit street just in time to see their minibus jerk forward and then pick up speed as it starts to accelerate. What the hell is going on? The question blasts through Mike's mind. Where has all the shooting come from? Where the fuck is our minibus going? He searches desperately for a glimpse of Sheila in the windows as it shoots past him, but he can't see her anywhere. Where the hell is she?

Both men instinctively start to sprint after the receding minibus and Dwayne reaches out a long arm, almost managing to brush the back of it with his fingers, but the vehicle's going too fast now and they can't catch up. However they don't stop trying and both stretch out their legs and pump their arms to pick up more speed. Mike's heart is hammering inside his chest and he's sucking in a bucket-full of hot dusty air into his lungs, but it does no good and he can see the minibus fast disappearing in front of them along the street.

Then unexpectedly Mike watches amazed as the rear emergency door on the right-hand side of the minibus is flung open and a body comes flying out and bounces on to the road. On no, they haven't killed someone he pleads to himself. The body springs up from the tarmac and he can see that it is a woman and she starts to run back towards them. As she races nearer, the rear window of the minibus explodes and glass flies everywhere. Then Mike sees a crazy-looking black face above a long rifle as they both appear out of the now open gap. He can see the flashes as the black man fires the rifle before he hears the shots themselves. Then he feels Dwayne's big hands on him throwing them both into the dust by the side of the road. Mike looks up from the ground and can see spurts of dirt and tarmac as the bullets whip into the dusty tarmac, working into a long jagged line past where they lie. Then the firing stops as the minibus disappears into the dark and the near-deserted street is suddenly and eerily silent, except for the sound of their laboured breathing and the blood pounding in their ears.

They've gone. Sheila, Margot, the other passengers, the minibus. They've all gone.

Mike screams out loud in his fear and frustration, and the sound echoes off the buildings.

I've lost her. I've lost Sheila!

TEN

10th June
Quseer, Egypt

It takes a while for Mike to pull himself together. He's got so many
questions floating around inside his head but the main ones are:
What the fuck just happened? and Where's Sheila? Is she okay?
Unfortunately there are no answers. He feels helpless and hopeless.
He just sits there in the dirt of the street, unable to take it all in.
Why is this happening to us?

Dwayne slaps him around the face. Not hard enough to hurt
him, but enough to sting like hell and make him pull himself
together.

"Come on, Mike. We've got to do something….anything.
Let's get back to the police station. They must know what's going
on?" His tough handsome face has taken on a look that Mike has
never seen there before. He looks mad. Not crazy mad, but mean,
angry mad. For the first time since he's met him Mike feels a little
bit afraid of Dwayne.

"What about the woman?" Mike says, his voice hoarse after
all the running.

"What woman?"
Dwayne looks perplexed.

"The one that got out of the minibus, mate! I saw her running
towards us." Instead of answering Dwayne steps out into the street
and looks along the route that the minibus took. Mike jumps up to
join him, searching with his eyes amongst the dim lights from open
doorways and windows. "There she is!" He points at a dark bump
lying next to the road about seventy yards away. "I think."

"Come on, Mike!" Dwayne starts running again towards the slumped figure and Mike follows him on legs still shaky from all of the sudden activity.

As they get nearer Mike can see that the figure is moving. She's alive thank God! He feels an instants sharp hope that it might be Sheila. Then he senses that her whole body is shaking and he can hear loud sobs. Both men automatically slow down as they approach, shocked by the sheer distress contained in the sounds. Dwayne crouches down and gently lays a hand on the figure. They can't see who she is yet as she's lying in a pool of darkness.

"Margot?" Dwayne's voice is desperate and Mike feels a split second of irrational jealousy surging through him. No! It can't be Margot! It must be Sheila! Then both of their hearts are broken.

"Who?" It's a stranger's voice.

Despite their disappointment Mike and Dwayne recover quickly, and they don't think that the woman really notices. Dwayne quietly asks her if she's been hurt as he gently runs his hands over her body, feeling for injuries in the dark.

"I...I don't think so....I just twisted my ankle."
Mike is burning with questions about what's happening and whether Sheila is okay and who the black bastard with the gun is, but a stern look from Dwayne makes him keep his mouth shut. At least for now. They help the woman to her feet and move into the pool of light spilling from a deserted shop front. Then they recognise her. She's the university lecturer who was a part of their group, the one who was with the ex-soldier who writes war novels. She looks very different now. Before she had been perfectly composed and an absolute stunner, but now she's very, very distraught. Her eyes are red-rimmed and puffy, her face is pale and waxy and streaked with a mixture of dust, sweat and tears. Her hair is an absolute mess.

Once they've established that she's not injured Mike can't contain himself any longer and he starts to ply her with questions. Dwayne stops him again. Mike knows he's right to do this but he can't help feeling more than a little annoyed at him. Apart from the mad look that's still in his eyes Dwayne appears calm and collected and Mike can't understand it. My world has just blown apart, doesn't he feel the same? Inside his head he's screaming: WHAT THE FUCK IS GOING ON?

"Can you tell us what happened?" Dwayne asks her gently and suddenly Mike realises that Dwayne feels the same way as he does. With his training as a Ranger, he is much better at keeping his emotions under control but Mike can still hear an edge of fear to his voice. The woman has a faraway look in her eyes and they're unfocused. Dwayne peers at Mike over her shoulder and mouths: "She's in shock." Mike almost laughs out loud. Who the fuck isn't?

Dwayne is holding her by the shoulders and Mike gets the feeling that he wants to shake her to get her to talk, but, of course doesn't. He just pulls her to him as she begins to sob again and a huge shudder hits her body. The three are standing in the street when the cops finally arrive, and they've got guns.

Mike and Dwayne know that they've got guns because as soon as they screech to a halt beside them in their Nissan pickup, four police officers tumble from the vehicle and point hand guns at them, screaming in a jabber of Egyptian. Suddenly Mike is terrified that they'll be shot for something that they haven't done; something that has happened that they've had no control over.

The four policemen are dressed in dark blue pullovers, trousers and flat berets, and they look almost military-like. Their faces are angry, but Mike is sure that they're almost as scared as he is from their wide eyes. This doesn't make him feel any better. They scream at the two foreigners again and the dark holes at the end of their pistols barrels which are aiming at him look enormous to Mike.

Dwayne responds first. He talks to them in a calm and quiet voice, slowly raising his hands into the air to show that they are empty:

"Okay. Okay. Let's take it easy guys. I'm an American."
Mike follows his example, raising his own hands high.

"English! I'm English!" he jabbers back at them, his voice sounding high-pitched and thin compared to his mate's. Mike fights for control and amazingly his own voice begins to lower in pitch and sound calmer. "Tourists. We're tourists, lads. Just tourists."

Mike and Dwayne's efforts seem to have the desired effect and Mike can see that the coppers are relaxing a little, although they do not lower their guns at all. One of them steps forward. Mike doesn't know if he's in charge but his voice is calmer too, though of course Mike still can't understand what he's saying. When he gestures to the ground with the end of his pistol Mike gets the jist of what he wants though.

"I think he wants us to lie down, Dwayne."

"Yep, I guess so. We'd better do what he wants, but make sure you keep your hands where he can see them and do everything in slow motion. They're very nervous."

"Them and me both!" Mike blurts out, earning him a reproving shout from another of the policemen. "Okay! Okay! We're lying down. Look!"

He slowly sinks to his knees, and even more slowly he puts his hands on to the dirt of the street in front of him so that he can lower the top half of his body. He hears Dwayne murmuring calmly to the woman to do the same as he also gets down on to the ground.

Then the breath is forced from Mike's lungs as he feels a knee descend hard into the middle of his back. His hands are jerked painfully backwards and he feels the cold touch of handcuffs as they're snapped shut around his wrists.

"Tight!" he stammers. "They're too tight!" He feels the steel bracelets dig into his flesh and bring tears to his eyes. But whoever is on top of him either doesn't understand or doesn't care, or both. He just jerks Mike's handcuffed wrists backwards and Mike feels a stab of shear agony rip through his shoulders and upper arms. Then he is kicked hard in the ribs.

Suddenly he can't take it anymore and he snaps. He starts to struggle, wriggling his body and shouting at the top of his lungs: "You're a load of fuckers! What are you doing about my Sheila! What the fuck's happening!"

Then everything goes black for Mike.

ELEVEN

11th June
Quseer, Egypt

Mike wakes up and for a moment everything is okay with him. It's like he is just pulling up out of a deep sleep and Sheila is sitting next to him on the minibus. He is warm and can feel the vibration from the engine as they motor southwards towards their camp. He's got a feeling of intense contentment.

Then as he opens his eyes his serenity is shattered.

He finds himself lying on a hard bed in a strange room; the heat that he can feel is from a bright lamp shining quite close to his face and the vibrations that are going through his body appear to be coming from a large rickety air-conditioning unit mounted on the wall behind him. A dark-skinned face is staring down into his. It is very serious looking.

Mike jerks upwards but as he does so he is hit by a feeling of nausea and suddenly everything comes flooding back into his mind; the trip in the minibus, the gun-shots, the sight of the minibus rapidly driving away into the darkness.

"Sheila! Where's Sheila?"

Even to him his voice sounds gravelly and hoarse. He feels a hand on his shoulder, gently easing him back on to the bed.

"It's okay, Mr Oldport. Just try to relax." The voice comes from the dark-skinned Egyptian touching him.

"What's happening? Where's Sheila?" He feels hysteria threatening to engulf him.

"Sheila? Is she your wife?"

"Yes, yes! Where is she?"

71

"Try to remain calm, Mr Oldport. I'm sure that your wife is okay. The captain will speak to you soon."

"Captain? What captain?"

"The captain of the police detachment here in Quseer. He is with your friends at the moment. I will take you through to him if you wish?"

Mike struggles to clear his head, shaking himself physically only to be hit by a killer of a headache.

"What's wrong with me? I don't feel too good?"

The Egyptian smiles. Mike looks at him and realises that he's well into his sixties if he's a day.

"You've had a bang on your head and you're in the police station's infirmary. Apparently, one of the police officers who picked you up was a little….how do you say it? A little too excited. I'm afraid that he knocked you unconscious."

Mike remembers now.

"Who are you?"

"Oh, I'm sorry! I should have introduced myself. I'm Dr Youssef Osman. Captain Mounir called me to treat you. How do you feel?"

"Okay, I guess. I've got a pounding headache though."

The doctor reaches into a bag on the table next to the bed.

"Here. Take these. They will help with your headache." He hands Mike two small white tablets and a glass of water. "It's okay. They're just Paracetamol."

Mike swallows both of them quickly.

"Where's Dwayne?" he asks.

"Is he the big American?"

"Yes."

"Well, if you feel up to it, we can go and see him now? He's with the captain."

"Okay."

Shakily Mike sits up wary of the pain in his head. He slips his feet over the edge of the bed and gingerly puts them on to the floor.

"Let me help you, Mr Oldport. Here, lean your weight on me." Mike does as he suggests and the old Egyptian feels surprisingly strong as he helps him get to his feet.

It's only a short walk from the infirmary to the captain's office, along a dimly lit corridor. Mike is helped to the office by the doctor as he's still feeling wobbly and sees Dwayne sitting at a large wooden desk. He feels a rush of relief. Dwayne looks back over his shoulder at him and Mike is guessing that he feels the same too, as a huge grin momentarily lights up his face.

"Hey Mike, buddy! How're you feeling?"
Mike rubs a tender spot on his scalp.

"Okay, I guess."
He also sees that the woman who escaped from the minibus is sitting next to Dwayne. She looks a lot better than the last time he saw her. Her face is clean and not nearly as puffy and red-eyed. She manages to smile at him too. Then he sees that another person is sitting on the other side of the desk. He's a slim man in the blue uniform of an Egyptian policeman, about mid-thirties with jet black hair and a thin moustache. He looks embarrassed as he stands and leans forward over the desk, extending a hand towards Mike.

"Ah, Mr Oldport I presume. I am Captain Abdu El Mounir. I must apologise for my officer treating you so badly. I can assure you that he has been severely reprimanded!"
He doesn't know what it is about him, but Mike instantly takes a liking to this policeman. He has a very cultured voice and a charming, well-educated manner. His English is impeccable.

"Thank you. But I'm not worried about that. I just want to know what's happening. Where's Sheila and Margot? What's happened to them?"
He feels another wave of nausea threatening to make him throw up and he's grateful when the policeman lifts a chair forward for him and Dr Osman guides him into it. The captain gives the doctor a querying look.

"Mr Oldport has a touch of concussion, but thankfully it's not serious, Inshallah, God willing. He does have a bad headache and a touch of nausea though."

"Thank you, doctor. Shukrān, thank you. I appreciate you coming out so late to look at our guest."

"Not a problem, captain. I will go to my home now. Please do not hesitate to contact me again if Mr Oldport begins to feel worse."

"We will. Thank you again, doctor. Tisbah 'ala khayr, good night."

"Yeah. Thanks, doc."

"My pleasure. Wintu min ahla, good night to you all."
He smiles at them and withdraws from the room, bowing slightly in the direction of the captain. As the door to the office closes behind the old Egyptian, the captain retakes his seat on the other side of the desk. Dwayne gives Mike a comforting squeeze on his arm.

"Just try to relax, Mike. The captain here was just talking to us about what's happened."
Mike tries to do as Dwayne says but his heart is way down in the pit of his stomach and a feeling of absolute terror is threatening to overwhelm him.

Captain Mounir leans forward.

"I was just explaining to your friends here that it seems that your wives and the other members of your party...." He nods in acknowledgement to the university lecturer. "....appear to have been kidnapped. From eyewitness accounts it seems that three or four men, possibly Somalis, discharged their firearms into the air, panicking the civilians in the street and causing them to flee in fear of their lives."
Mike's heart lurches at the mention of Somalis and an image of the black face in the rear window of the minibus as it drove off appears in his mind's eye. He has to interrupt:

"Somalis? You mean terrorists?"

"It's impossible to say at this time, Mr Oldport. This may be a terrorist act, or it may be motivated purely by money. We're not sure yet."

"Money? You mean ransom? This could be a kidnapping for ransom?"

"Possibly. As I said, we don't know yet. Two of the Somalis forced their way on to your vehicle and shot the driver dead."

"Oh fuck!" Suddenly he feels sick again.

"Yes, I'm afraid so, Mr Oldport. The two Somalis then drove off in the minibus following behind the other man or men, who were in a Toyota pickup truck."

"Where are they now, captain? Did any of your men follow them?" Dwayne's voice sounds tight and strained.

74

The captain looks him straight in the eye as he replies, his own voice taking on a clipped edge:

"Two of my men were on patrol to the south of Quseer. They heard about the shooting over their radio and attempted to intercept the Somalis."

"Fantastic! Did they stop them?"

For the first time Mike feels a surge of optimism. However the look on Captain Mounir's face causes the hope he feels to deflate as soon as it blossoms.

"I'm afraid to report that we found the bodies of my officers by the side of the road about fifteen minutes ago. They had both been shot numerous times."

"Shit!" Mike only just manages to keep the contents of his stomach where it should be at this news.

"Quite." The Egyptian agrees.

TWELVE

11th June
Quseer, Egypt

"I'm really sorry to hear about your two men, captain."
Dwayne's voice is subdued and grave. "We can only thank them
for trying to save our loved ones."
The Egyptian inclines his head in acknowledgement of the
sentiment. Then his eyes become harder.

"We have numerous vehicles and men searching for the
minibus and the Somalis as we speak, and a military helicopter is
on its way from Hurghada to help with the search, but I'm afraid
that it will be several hours before dawn and the Eastern Desert is a
big place. You should prepare yourselves for the idea that we may
not find them any time soon."
For a few moments everyone in the room is silent as they
contemplate the captain's words, then Dwayne turns to the
university lecturer.

"Excuse me, Miss."
She looks up at him with tears in her eyes, and corrects him
automatically:

"Doctor...I'm a doctor." Then she shakes herself as if
wakening from a bad dream. "My names Belinda...Belinda Clarke,
with an 'e'."

"Okay, Belinda. I'm Dwayne Huntsbringer, and this is Mike
Oldport." His voice is gentle. "Could you tell Mike what you told
me earlier, what happened on the minibus and how you managed
to escape?"
She takes a deep breath, trying hard to control her emotions:

"It's like the captain says. A few minutes after you
and....Mike....left with our passports, we heard shooting in the

76

street. Then this awful man forced his way on to the minibus and he….he shot our driver in cold blood. It was appalling!"
She shudders at the memory and Dwayne calms her down by gently taking her hands in his.

"Just take your time, Belinda. It's okay."
She lets out a sob:

"Then another black man came into the minibus and the first one climbed into the driver's seat and we started to pull away. That was when Dave, he's my partner, he….he leant across me and opened the emergency door. The alarm went off and then he told me to run for my life and sort of pushed me out of the door! The last thing I saw of him was him standing up to fight with the black man, and then I was rolling on the ground!" Her whole body is shaking by now and tears are flowing down her cheeks. "I heard Dave shouting again for me to run, so I did. I was absolutely petrified! Then I heard the window smash at the back of the minibus and the black man was shooting his gun at me. I just ran as fast as I could!"
She breaks down completely now and both Mike and Dwayne put their arms around her. Her whole body is being wracked by huge sobs. Eventually she starts to calm down again.

"Did you see my….our wives?" Mike asks her in a whisper. "The blond and the redhead near the front. Did you see them? Were they okay?"

"Yes. They were sitting together and I saw them dive down on to the floor when we heard the shooting."
Mike felt an immense release of pressure. That sounded just like the sort of sensible thing that Sheila and Margot would do. He shares a look with Dwayne and can see the relief on his face too.

"Your partner was very brave, Belinda and so were you."

"I just hope that he's okay. Those men were frightening. I hope that Dave is okay."
She collapses in their arms again, sobbing her heart out.

77

THIRTEEN

11th June
Somewhere in southern Egypt

Sheila doesn't regain consciousness for a while, and when she does she can hardly see for the dreadful pain pounding behind her eyes which makes her squint. She's still sitting on the floor of the minibus at the foot of the front seat but now she is cradled in the arms of Margot. The American soothes her as she jerks awake and just for a moment or two she can't remember where they are or what's happened. Then it all comes rushing back and she lets out a sob of fear.

"Ssshhhh, dear." Margot gently wipes Sheila's hair out of her eyes and her calm smile helps the English woman pull herself together. Gradually her eyes open more and she looks around. The first thing that she sees are the dreadful hate-filled eyes of the tall black man leering down at them as he leans against the dashboard. He grins at Sheila and it scares her to death. She starts to shake uncontrollably. "It's okay, dear. Sssshhh." Margot's voice calms her again.

"Where are we?" Sheila whispers. "What's happening?"

"I don't know, dear. I think we've been kidnapped."

The black man suddenly lurches towards them and waves the barrel of his gun in their faces. He shouts and though they don't know what he's saying they can guess that he wants them to stop talking. He is so close that the two women can smell him, and he stinks of sweat and dirt. They're splashed by his spittle and almost gag. They both lower their heads in acquiescence.

Then he leans back against the dashboard and says something to the driver, the short ugly one with the buck teeth, and they both laugh harshly. Sheila risks another whisper to Margot:

78

"How long was I out of it?"

"About an hour. There was a gunfight just after we drove out of Quseer. There's another vehicle in front of us and I think that they shot at someone by the side of the road but I couldn't see anything. It was over pretty quickly and since then we've been driving in the dark." The two women keep their heads close together and their voices as low as they can.

"Any idea where we are?"

"No. I think we're driving south along the coast road, but I'm not sure." Sheila sees the tall black man look at them again and she closes her mouth. He looks slightly insane and she doesn't want to keep on upsetting him.

The two women remain sitting on the floor of the minibus. Neither have watches and their mobile phones are not to hand. They have lost track of time. Sheila's headache recedes, but is soon replaced by a pain in her lower back where the edge of the seat is sticking into her, and it's not long before the muscles in her buttocks and legs start to ache fiercely from the lack of movement. There's an awful draft coming through the smashed window on the door, and though the air is warm, almost hot, it doesn't help to ease the aching and the dust she can taste in her mouth. She feels as dry as a bone.

Sheila peers up out of the windscreen past the figure of the black man but it's just pitch black beyond. The only variation is the occasional glow of lights in the darkness, perhaps from distant buildings. Every now and again the driver flashes his headlights on but when he does all she gets is a brief glimpse of an empty road in front of them, though sometimes she catches sight of the rear of another vehicle on the road ahead. She can feel that they are belting along at a hell of a speed though and the minibus sways from side to side as it hits small bumps and hollows in the road's uneven surface. She just prays that they don't run into anything, or perhaps, she thinks, it would be better if they did. At least if they crash they might have a chance of escape if they survived it, and it would certainly wipe that bloody insane grin off that black bastard's face. She can feel hatred begin to grow inside her every time she looks at his bloody face.

She doesn't know how long they are sitting on the floor, but it is still dark when she feels their speed begin to diminish. The two North Africans, at least that's what she guesses they are, look at each other and the driver says something to the tall one which makes him turn around and stare out of the windscreen. The driver flicks on the headlights but again all that Sheila can see is a view of the road ahead with deep blackness beyond. She takes the opportunity to try and ease her aching muscles as he looks away by stretching as far as she can in the confined space in the foot well of their seat. Then suddenly he exclaims out loud and points excitedly at something and the minibus slithers to a ragged halt.

FOURTEEN

11th June
Somewhere in southern Egypt

The driver switches off the minibus engine and both of the black men jump out of the door. Then Sheila hears them jabbering away in their weird language with someone else in the dark. She risks raising herself on to her knees to have a peek to see whether the keys are still in the ignition. They are not there of course; the driver must have taken them with him. It's sheer bliss to be on her knees and stretching her aching back muscles. She feels like she's been run over with a truck and from the look on Margot's face, the older American is feeling the same.

For the first time Sheila looks around and can see some of the other passengers behind her. The English couple are just behind her and to the left. The husband is a big man with receding hair, probably in his late thirties. She remembers that he's a lorry driver back in the real world. His wife is pretty and a few years younger than him, she guesses. Both of them look strained and very frightened, but the husband manages a slight smile when he sees Sheila peeking around the front seat. He has kind eyes.

"Are you okay?" he mouths silently and Sheila whisper in reply:

"Yes."

Then her eyes are drawn to a figure lying in the aisle between the seats. It's a man, and he's lying on his back. His face is covered with blood and she supresses a loud exclamation of shock. At first she can't see who it is but then she realises that it's the man who was with the beautiful university lecturer, the ex-soldier who writes war novels. The upper part of his face and head looks smashed in and his hair is matted to his scalp with the dried blood.

Beneath it his skin looks very pale. The Dutch veterinary surgeon is on his knees beside him and Sheila can see that he's gently massaging the man's wounds. She guesses that he's trying to see how badly injured he is.

Then the shouting outside stops and Sheila quickly falls back into her place next to Margot. She's only just in time as the minibus lurches under the weight of the two black men climbing back in through the open door.

The tall one starts screaming at the passengers and gesturing with his rifle for them to stand up. Sheila grasps Margot's hand again and she can feel absolute terror threatening to overwhelm her. What's going to happen now? Are these men terrorists? Are they going to kill us? She feels ashamed suddenly as her bladder gives way and she feels the warm stickiness of her own urine soaking her panties and trickling down the inside of her trouser leg. She is so scared she can hardly stand up and Margot grips her tightly and helps her to her feet. Her legs are shaking like a bowl of jelly. As the acrid stench of her piss fills the inside of the minibus the Africans sniff and then burst out laughing. The tall bastard leers down at her in amusement and she can feel the burning sensation of a blush reddening her face and neck.

Then he pokes her hard with the barrel of his rifle and points it to the door, constantly jabbering away. It's obvious that he wants the passengers to leave the minibus, but Sheila's legs refuse to move. He pokes her again, harder.

Margot suddenly snaps at him:

"Leave her alone you asshole!" Her voice is low and calm but there's no mistaking the hatred in it. The tall black man steps back, his insane eyes blazing. Sheila thinks he's going to shoot them both where they stand but then the short ugly one breaks the tension with a guttural laugh. He says something to the tall one, who suddenly joins in. Then his eyes go hard again and he jabs Margot with the barrel of his gun this time. "Okay! Okay! We're doing it!" she almost snarls at him and Sheila is amazed at her friend's confidence and poise. Margot tugs her gently. "Come on, Sheila. We've got to do what he says."

She follows her towards the door on unsteady legs.

82

Outside it's still very dark, but as their eyes gradually get used to
the paucity of light Sheila can just about make out the surface of
the roadway stretching away into the blackness. All of the
passengers are ordered off the minibus, even the injured man who
staggers out with them, leaning heavily on the shoulder of the
Dutch vet. He's obviously feeling dreadful, but that doesn't stop
the tall bastard from smacking him in the guts with his rifle butt as
he passes him, Sheila notices. Whatever he's done to deserve the
beating he's had he's still pissing off that bastard a lot, she thinks.

They're shoved and pushed, almost herded, into a line by the
side of the road and as they stand there Sheila closes her eyes and
thoughts flood through her head. Is this it? Is this where my life
ends? Murdered on some fucking roadside in Egypt by men I've
never met before? She's not normally religious. In fact she's only
ever stepped inside a church at weddings and funerals, but now she
can also hear herself muttering a prayer to God to spare her. She'll
do anything, absolutely anything, if only she can live a little
longer. It doesn't matter how long – another hour, another day –
anything at all.

She hears the unmistakable sound of someone cocking a rifle
in the blackness.

ENGLAND

FIFTEEN

16th June
Heathrow Airport, London, England

The queue for arriving UK passport holders is only a tenth of the size that the queue is for non-UK nationals, but it's still taken forty-five minutes for the man to get close to the front. Even for an experienced and very well-prepared agent of MOIS, the Iranian Ministry of Intelligence and National Security, the wait has been nerve-wracking and he can feel a bead of sweat beginning to form on his brow. He knows that this is one of the tell-tale signs that could be noted by the British Border Force personnel on duty at the airport, and he knows that to reach up and wipe it away may well set off alarm bells in the minds of the officers watching and assessing the line of arriving travellers, so he does what he's been trained to do. He hides it. Well before he reaches passport control he removes a crumpled handkerchief from his pocket and begins to blow his nose rather noisily, as well as gently coughing and spluttering. Past experience has shown him that even passport controllers are human and will want to deal with him quickly if they think he's got a cold or some other bug. They won't want to catch anything off him, plus it will explain his sweaty forehead.

But he's out of luck today. The rather broad-shouldered and masculine-looking woman officer on duty at the desk is made of sterner stuff than many of her colleagues and she looks at him with cold appraising eyes as his turn comes:

"Passport, please." Her tone is clipped and unemotional.
He hands across his appropriately slightly dog-eared passport, then blows his nose into his handkerchief again. He can feel his pulse racing and his heart pounding and the sweat on his brow gets worse. She looks carefully at the photograph and his details:

"Where are you travelling from, Mr Hajib?"

He'd thought about requesting a more typically British name when he'd had his photo taken for the passport just a week ago in the French city of Marseille, but his handler had warned him that there was no way that he could pass as a completely indigenous Brit, not with his dusky skin, dark eyes and black hair. He had been advised that he'd be better passing himself off as a second or third generation immigrant from the Middle East. He had been told not to worry - that there are tens of thousands if not hundreds of thousands of people like that living in the UK now. That was easy for him to say, he had thought to himself, when it wasn't him who would be passing through a British airport where the authorities are ever-vigilant for potential terrorists arriving on their shores. He had also told him not to worry about the passport; that it was a genuine one. Apparently the Agency had someone working in the Peterborough Passport Office and she steals a few blank ones every so often. They were sure that no one would be able to spot that his passport wasn't legitimately issued by the British Authorities. That was a relief. His details had also been entered on to the passport office's computers so he was embedded in their system.

"Brussels."

It was easy to fake a husky voice as his throat was so dry with fear and apprehension.

"And how long have you been in Belgium, Mr Hajib?"

Despite the fact that he has been through many passport controls in his lifetime he is beginning to feel even more nervous now. What's with all the questions? Do they suspect me?

"About a week."

"Was it business or pleasure?"

"Purely business. I'm a salesmen for a computer-component company."

He is now sure that she is going to pull him out of the queue and hand him over to one of her cold-eyed colleagues standing nearby in the background. But then, it's all over. Her face is transformed by a friendly smile and she hands back his passport.

"Welcome home. It looks like you could do with a hot Lemsip, Sir."

What the hell is a Lemsip? he wonders.

"Yes, yes, thank you. I do feel a bit rough."

He takes his passport, having correctly guessed the meaning behind her remark and steps away from the desk. Iranian Colonel Massoud Hassan is free to join the other arrivals as they make their way to the airport's exit.

I've done it. Now the 'Great Satan' will pay for what he's done to me!

SIXTEEN

16th June
Heathrow Airport, London, England

Jonathan Harris is a field agent who has been working for the Security Service, MI5, for sixteen years. To be frank, he's never received a promotion during that time and is unlikely to receive one in the future, because he's not the brightest spark in the bonfire. However he's not brainless either. You don't get to work for the Box if you're dumb. Today his task is to follow a low-level terrorist suspect named Mehdi Arkoun, a North African man originally from Algeria, who has been resident in the UK since he arrived in England with his parents in 1996 when he was just six years old.

Arkoun has been identified by several fellow Muslims at his local Mosque as a man with radical beliefs. The informers have mentioned that he listens to local radical Muslim clerics and attends their meetings after prayers on a Friday afternoon. Close surveillance of his two-bedroomed flat in Luton has also revealed that he sometimes talks to other likely radicals on the 'Terrorist Watch List', the list of potential terrorists and their associates in the United Kingdom. During this time he has never been found doing anything that could justify his being charged with a criminal offence, but he's one of several thousand people that the Box 'keep an eye on' from time to time. Unfortunately there are just too many people in this lower risk category of the watch list for the Box to be able to justify full-time surveillance for them all, especially in these times of government austerity. Therefore Arkoun is put under irregular or intermittent surveillance which is carried out by a field agent, as well as having his telephone landline, mobile telephone line and email/Facebook/Twitter accounts etc. monitored by the

Government Communication Headquarters (GCHQ) at Cheltenham. All of his snail mail is automatically side-tracked at the local Post Office sorting office as well, and is physically checked by agent Harris twice a week, along with the mail of the other three dozen potential terrorists who are on his personal operational list and living in Luton.

Harris has been watching Arkoun on and off for the past twenty months, ever since he first became known as a possible suspect to the Box. In all of that time he has never spotted anything in Arkoun's behaviour that could be construed as even remotely suspicious, apart from some of the people that he occasionally keeps company with. Nor has there been any activity that could be interpreted as grounds for 'upping' the amount of surveillance that he warrants. That is, there has been nothing until today.

Harris knows almost everything about Mehdi Arkoun. He reads his emails and sees what he puts on social media. He sorts through his post and listens to edited versions of his telephone conversations passed on from GCHQ. He is familiar with Arkoun's friends and the people who dislike him in the local community (and there are plenty of the latter as he's a right arrogant little prick). He knows the girls he fancies and would know which ones fancy him back (if there were any…).

As far as he is concerned, there hasn't been any previous report of Arkoun paying a visit to Heathrow Airport to pick up a stranger, especially in a Ford Mondeo that according to the National Automatic Number Plate Recognition Data Centre is not registered or insured under his name. It may even be stolen but not reported as such yet. Harris had to seek the permission of his supervisor to gain access to the NADC data, but the extra hassle has been worthwhile, and he is excited about this potential new development. There are not many stimulating or rousing moments in his job, which, despite what paperback novels and the tabloids may say about it, is in fact a boring, monotonous and repetitive job ninety nine point nine percent of the time. But not today. Today Harris is on to something, he's sure. He can *feel* it in his water. Today Mehdi Arkoun is being a very naughty little boy, and unfortunately for him, today is the day that Jonathan Harris, MI5 Field Agent, has been allocated to watch him.

Arkoun is holding up a piece of cardboard with a name written on it in large letters as he waits in the arrivals hall at Heathrow. He's used a black marker pen to make the sign. Harris has to manoeuvre through the thick crowd until he's in a position where he can read what's on the board and finds that it simply says: 'Massoud Hajib'. After fifty or so minutes of waiting amongst the crowd, the passengers of a flight from Brussels finally make their way towards the barriers and one of them spots Arkoun's card and walks over to him. He is a tall, lean man of obvious Middle Eastern extraction. He's in his mid-forties and has a hard, almost gaunt face with coal-black eyes and a slightly hooked nose. The two men briefly shake hands but there's nothing friendly about the meeting, not like they'd be if it was an innocent pick up of an old friend or acquaintance. The stranger just thrusts his medium-sized suitcase into Arkoun's hand, gestures rather loftily for him to lead the way outside, and then follows a few metres behind him, his eyes roaming suspiciously around the crowded concourse.

Harris is a very experienced field agent. He doesn't follow the pair out of the arrivals lounge but instead takes a calculated gamble and rushes ahead of them via another route to the short-stay car park where Arkoun has parked his Mondeo. When they arrive at their car he has already been sitting inside his own vehicle for a couple of minutes, and is ready to pull out and follow them.

Harris keeps his head down below the level of the dashboard as they climb into their Mondeo, keeping watch on them by using the rear view mirror set at an acute angle. As soon as Arkoun settles into the driving seat he starts the engine. The stranger he's picked up has a last look around before climbing into the back of the car. This is yet another sign to Harris that the two men do not personally know each other, otherwise they'd be sitting next to each other in the front of the car. As they pull out and head off towards Luton via the M25 North, Harris remains where he is for ninety seconds before pulling out in his battered Audi A6 saloon car. As he drives along he keeps a good distance (always two or three other vehicles between them and him) and calls in again to his superior via his hands-free mobile phone set. He reports in about Arkoun's activity during the morning, and asks his boss to begin checking on a couple of things; first of all: who owns the Mondeo and whether it's been stolen or not, and secondly; the name of the stranger that he's picked up – Massoud Hajib. With the detailed description that Harris gives his boss, plus the approximate time that the man must have come through passport control, it won't take long to figure out who he is and where he's travelled from. Harris and his boss know that he probably won't have travelled under his own name if he is a terrorist, but that's the beauty of having so many closed-circuit TV cameras at Heathrow; they're bound to find one that will give them a reasonable image of the man's face. Then it will be relatively straight forward to feed that picture into the Advanced Facial Image Recognition Software back at Thames House, the headquarters of the Security Service. If the stranger is known from any file on their system, or the system of their colleagues at the Secret Intelligence Service, or in any of the police forces around the United Kingdom, including the Metropolitan Police's Counter Terrorism Command, or even in the files of the Foreign and Commonwealth Office, then they'll be able to find out who he is. If all of these sources fail to identify the man then there's always recourse to the files of Interpol and Europol in Europe, and the FBI, Homeland Security and the CIA in the States. Identifying someone has never been easier, especially now that the digital age is upon us.

Traditionally facial recognition software has relied upon algorithms that identify distinctive facial features by extracting landmarks or features, from an image of the subject's face. For example, it may analyse the relative position, size or shape of the suspect's eyes, nose, cheekbones and jaw. These characteristics are then used to do a search for other images in a database that match. However, this system has never been that accurate and unfortunately it has proved to be too easy to bypass by someone who wants to disguise their features. This can be achieved simply by wearing spectacles with thick frames that hide the eyes or putting pads into the mouth that disguise the shape of the cheek bones and the jaw line. Newly emerging trends in facial recognition now include three-dimensional facial recognition, which is claimed to vastly improve the accuracy of the system. This technique uses 3D sensors to capture information about the shape of the whole face. This information is then used to identify distinctive features on the surface of a face, such as the shape and contour of the eye sockets, nose and chin. Unlike other, older techniques, this new 3D method is not affected by the lighting that is on the subject at the time that the image is collected, and can also identify a face from a range of viewing angles, including a profile view. If it is used in conjunction with other newly emerging techniques, such as skin texture analysis, which turns an individual's unique skin lines, patterns and even spots into a mathematical space, this system can increase the performance of facial recognition by a massive twenty to twenty-five percent.

Arkoun pushes the Mondeo way over the speed limit on the motorway, topping ninety five miles per hour. Harris is faced with a hard choice at this point. Although his Audi may look battered on the outside, its engine is well maintained and has been 'souped-up' by the mechanics back at HQ. It can quite easily keep up with the speeding Mondeo. However, the motorway is not that busy and if he tries to keep up there is a distinct possibility that he'll be spotted. He knows that it's not possible for any other unit from the Box to come and help him out with his surveillance as they would take too long to get to him. The journey back to Luton (if that's where Arkoun and the stranger are going) should only take about forty minutes. So, rather than blow the surveillance at this critical stage, he decides to hang back, hoping and trusting that Arkoun will be heading back to his familiar ground and that he can pick him up later.

It is a risk of course, but it's a calculated risk that he's forced to take. If Arkoun and the stranger have even the smallest inkling that they are being tailed they could quite easily just disappear, or even worse, simply stop doing whatever they're planning to do.

SEVENTEEN

16th June
Luton, England

Unfortunately for Jonathan Harris, his calculated risk does not pay off. He does not find that Mehdi Arkoun and his mysterious passenger have gone straight back to Arkoun's flat in Luton. The MI5 agent is angry with himself at losing touch with the pair but he's not too despondent. He believes that there is still a good chance that Arkoun will turn up sooner or later; he just hopes that it will be the former. Having established that Arkoun's Mondeo is not parked near any of his normal haunts around the city, Harris begins to put his backup plans into motion.

First of all he calls his boss again and reports losing the pair. When he does this he finds out there is some useful news waiting for him; it turns out that the Mondeo has been stolen from North London. The owner was surprised to find it missing from its usual parking spot when he was contacted by the local police and asked to check on his vehicle, and it seems it could have been taken anytime in the last three days. Harris thinks it is now very plausible that Arkoun is likely to be up to no good as he's taking the chance of using a stolen car. He also learns that the security personnel at Heathrow have identified the man that Arkoun picked up. To double check the identity of the man they email a still from a CCTV camera overlooking passport control to Harris's secure IPad for him to formally identify him as the man that was picked up, and he confirms that the picture in the frame is a perfect likeness of the man. The passenger manifest of the flight from Brussels that the man arrived on gives his name as Massoud Hajib, which also ties in with the name written on the piece of cardboard that Arkoun had held up at the airport.

In order to find out more information about the man the technicians at Thames House and GCHQ are now putting the image and name through every system and bit of advanced software that they've got access to. They have also forwarded both, as a matter of urgency, to the relevant agencies in Europe and the United States, just in case the man is known to them.

Meanwhile a team has been despatched from Thames House to help Harris set up surveillance on Arkoun's flat. As soon as they arrive they will requisition a suitable flat which has already been found in the tower block overlooking Arkoun's flat. The current tenant, a little old woman living on her retirement pension, will be put up in a swanky hotel for as long as it takes at the expense of the British Government. It's doubtful that she'll mind or put up a fuss once she sets eyes on her new four-star room or has a look at the Hotel's menu and realises that it's all paid for by someone else. It'll be the first holiday she's had in years.

Once the surveillance team is set up and everyone is absolutely sure that Arkoun is not inside his flat, the tech boys will break in and set up their cameras and listening devices in every room, and then leave again. They of course will not leave a single sign that they have ever been there. Other teams will be checking out Arkoun's regular haunts and his friends and acquaintances to see if they can locate him, while liaison officers will be quietly talking to the local police force. Photographs of Arkoun and Massoud Hajib will be handed out to police officers who patrol the city, and they will be asked to keep an eye out for both of them.

The end of a very busy day sees Harris set up with a team of three other MI5 field agents in the old lady's flat. Digital cameras and camcorders are in position on tripods set well back from the window in the shadows and pointing at Arkoun's windows and the entrance to his block of flats. Flat-screen monitors showing the feed from Arkoun's flat are switched on and being recorded, even though he hasn't returned. One of the team is on his mobile, ordering four medium pizzas to be delivered, along with garlic bread and soft drinks. All that remains is for Jonathan Harris to telephone his long-suffering wife and inform her that he won't be able to go around to her sister's with her as they'd arranged weeks ago. Something has come up at work and his presence is required:

"No, love. Sorry. I don't know when I'll be home again. Kiss the kids for me will you, and say hello to your sister?"

The phone is slammed down in his ear.

Or perhaps not then? he thinks to himself.

EGYPT

EIGHTEEN

16th June
Hurghada, Egypt

John Smith is in a bad mood. After a day of getting his kit ready he had hardly got any sleep the night before. Then there had been the three hour drive from his home on the north Norfolk coast to Gatwick Airport in the very early hours of the morning. This was followed by four hours of waiting around in the airport, twiddling his thumbs while his bum fell asleep on a typically uncomfortable seat in the Departures Lounge. Then, to top it all, this was followed by the seven hour-long flight to Egypt, his long legs cramped in the confines of a seat that felt like it had been made for a dwarf, and a small one at that. And all of the time he was in the considerably frosty company of not one, but two extremely unhappy women; his partner Doctor Linda Webb and his liaison with the British Security Services, Detective Inspector Helen Wright. The atmosphere was not friendly at all. The women were looking daggers at each other and at the same time giving him the cold shoulder. As if all that wasn't bad enough, every time his eyelids had drooped closed on the long flight he'd jerked awake, his heart pounding and sweat beading his face, remembering that awful flight from The Gambia, just a few years ago. The one that had nearly killed him. *Had* actually killed him a couple of times if you want to be pedantic. For some reason he just couldn't shake the memory of his desperate hand-to-hand fight with those eight terrorists from his mind. Talk about the journey from Hell.

Now, after a hasty meal grabbed in the à la carte restaurant of the 'Sol Y Mar Ivory Suites', a business hotel in the El Kawsar District of Hurghada, he finds himself sitting in on a meeting – and it's a very fraught meeting at that. Apart from himself and Helen

Wright there are six diplomats present, two each from the British, Dutch and American Embassies in Egypt. Mike Oldport and Dwayne Huntsbringer are also with them and very, very angry.

"Just stop giving us excuses!" exclaims Oldport, his face reddening. "It's been six fucking days since our wives were taken away at gunpoint, and as far as I can tell you haven't done a fucking thing to try and get them back!"

Most of those present are sitting around a big table in a conference room on wicker chairs, though Smith and Helen are sitting off to one side on well-upholstered lounge chairs, watching the proceedings and the people present with interest.

"We'd be grateful if you didn't swear at us, Mr Oldport. We're only doing our job." It's one of the British delegation that answers him.

"Yeah, and not very well!"

The senior diplomats around the table are typical, conventional examples of their profession; middle-aged men and women in well-cut and expensive clothing, lightweight suits for the men and long skirts and blouses for the women, all in neutral colours. Helen Wright looks very different in a brightly coloured summer dress, with the hem well below her knees in deference to the Islamic religion (ninety per cent of Egyptians are Muslim). Smith can't help but notice that her calves are tanned and just muscular enough to be extremely sexy, but he tries his best to ignore them. Oldport and Huntsbringer are still in the same clothes that they had worn on the flight from England almost a week ago. They are both unshaven and looking scruffy and haggard.

Hardly surprising with the worry they must be going through, Smith thinks.

The diplomats don't look too flustered at Oldport's outspoken criticism. It is obviously not the first time that he's had a go at them.

"I can assure you that the British government, as well as our colleagues..." He indicates the other people in the room with a weary wave of his hand. "...are taking this incident very seriously indeed, Mr Oldport. As are the Egyptian security forces."

"Then why can't you find out where they've been taken? You said at our last meeting that you would be studying the satellite images. You said that there was a good chance that your analysts would be able to locate the hostages!"

"Indeed, yes. I'm afraid that it turns out that there were no satellites over southern Egypt at the time that your group were abducted."

"No satellites at all? You're kidding, right?"
This is the big American. He is answered by a woman from his own embassy:

"I'm afraid it's true, Mr Huntsbringer. Normally there would be at least two satellites in orbit over Egypt at any one time, but apparently they have all been rerouted over northern Syria and Iraq to help pinpoint targets for the coalition air strikes against the Islamic State terrorists. We've approached the Department of Defence about rerouting one back to our area but I'm afraid that even if that is allowed, it may be days before it happens."

"Shit! What about the Egyptians? Why haven't they managed to find them on the ground? They've still got helicopters flying over the area, haven't they?" The British diplomat answers this one:

"As you know, Mr Huntsbringer, it was the Egyptian police force that initially found the abandoned minibus along the Halaieb We Shalatein Highway about two hundred kilometres south of Quseer. They also found the tracks of the pickup trucks heading along a dry riverbed into the eastern desert, but unfortunately they faded after only a few kilometres. They have had two helicopters combing the desert in that area ever since then, but regrettably, they were recalled to Cairo yesterday afternoon."

"Why?"

"I'm afraid that there are a number of large civilian protests planned for today. As you know it's a Friday and the protests often begin after Friday afternoon prayers. The Egyptian security forces suspect that there may well be violent protests by supporters of the Muslim Brotherhood in the centre of Cairo, as well as in other cities such as Alexandria. They need all the resources at their disposal in case the protests get out of hand, and, I'm sorry to say, that includes those helicopters."

"I'm sure that they will return to the search once the protests are over," interjects one of the Dutch diplomats.

"Jesus bloody Christ!" shouts Mike, "It's a sodding desert for fuck's sake. Why can't they find a couple of bloody pickups in the middle of a desert? It can't be that bloody hard!"

The British diplomat sighs:

"I understand your distress, Mr Oldport, but the Eastern Desert covers an enormous area. It's over 85,000 square miles in size and I'm afraid that finding vehicles in this huge area is not as simple as it sounds. Most of the desert is not simply open sand. It actually consists of rocky areas dissected by thousands of dry wadi's – river beds. It's quite literally like looking for a needle in a very large haystack. The kidnappers have had six days in which to drive deep into the desert and we and our Egyptian counterparts don't even know which direction they're travelling in."

"But we've figured that the kidnappers are Somalis, haven't we? Then surely it's likely that they're going to move south towards their own country? That should narrow down the search area considerably."

Dwayne Huntsbringer is obviously trying his best to remain calm and to think logically and Smith is impressed by the big American, especially after reading up about his past service with the US Rangers. He'd been given a slim dossier containing as much as was known by the authorities about all of the victims of the kidnappers, as background information. Huntsbringer had been awarded a Silver Star for valour during the First Gulf War, the third highest military combat decoration for a member of the US Armed Forces. He also had two Purple Hearts, awarded for wounds received during the same conflict. Smith did not yet know the circumstances behind the decorations being awarded, but he could guess that they weren't handed out for being timid in combat.

The American lady answers him:

"That may be the case, Mr Huntsbringer, but it's also possible that they could be heading for a 'base' somewhere inside Egyptian territory. Equally they could be heading towards Libya, northern Sudan or even north-eastern Chad. As you can imagine the borders here are extremely porous, especially to someone driving in the desert and away from the roads. Perhaps they are even on foot now? We just don't know. There are far too many possibilities at this point."

"Have the bastards made any demands yet?" This is from Mike Oldport.

"I'm afraid not."

"So we still don't know why they've kidnapped Sheila and Margot and the others? We still don't know if they're terrorists or whether they're just in it for the money?"

"Again, I'm afraid not, Mr Oldport."

"What is the US government doing to get our wives back?" Hunstbringer looks directly at the lady in charge of the US mission. She looks uncomfortable for a moment, gazing around the table at the foreign diplomats, but then she seems to come to a decision:

"I can't tell you everything that we are doing, Mr Huntsbringer, as some of it is 'Classified', but I can tell you that a SEAL team has been put on alert and has already flown out to our naval base on the island of Diego Garcia, in the British Indian Ocean Territory, from their own base at Virginia Beach in the States."

She looks quizzically at one of the Dutch diplomats, who nods his head at the unasked question, and continues:

"There is a frigate of the Royal Netherlands Navy currently patrolling in the Red Sea and the Gulf as a part of the international effort targeted against Somali pirates. I'll let Mr Van Der Hootten elaborate."

The Dutchman clears his throat and begins speaking in a low voice:

"Yes, the ship in question is a Karel Doorman Class Multi-purpose Frigate, HNLMS Van Amstel. She is presently anchored off the coast of the Red Sea about fifty nautical miles from the location where your vehicle was abandoned, and she is being prepared for the SEAL team who will be transferred to her from Diego Garcia tomorrow morning."

"The SEAL team will then be on constant standby for when the kidnappers are located," adds the American lady.

"You mean that they will attempt a rescue?"

"Yes, Mr Huntsbringer. I can't say much more but when your wives and the other victims are located, *no matter where they are*, the SEAL team will be deployed to bring them safely home."

Huntsbringer muses that over for a few moments:

"Hmm. *Once they have been located.* That's the difficult bit." He doesn't seem too impressed by the plan.

"What about the British S.A.S.?" Mike asks.

"What about them, Mr Oldport?" asks one of the British diplomats.

"Well the Americans are sending their guys over and the Dutch are lending them one of their ships. What the hell are the British doing? Why aren't you sending in the S.A.S.? The British diplomat sighs again:

"I'm afraid that the British Special Forces are very understrength these days, Mr Oldport. They've not been immune from the defence cuts facing the rest of the army. As you may know the British Army is in the process of being cut from 102,000 personnel to just 80,000, which in real terms means that the Special Forces as a whole now have less potential recruits for selection. And let's not forget that they have their hands full in other parts of the world right now. They are spread pretty thinly including the terrorist hotspots of Iraq, Syria, Mali, north Uganda, etc, etc, as well as searching for 'Jihadi John'."

"Oh, I get it! They're doing more important stuff!"

"That's not it at all, Mr Oldport. We are taking these kidnappings very seriously, as we would any crime committed overseas against UK nationals!"

"Of course you are!"

After this final outburst the meeting comes to a close. It's obvious to all present that nothing else is going to be gained by going over the same ground that they've talked about in the last two or three meetings, and both Mike and Dwayne are getting more and more impatient with the lack of action on the ground.

As they are leaving the meeting Dwayne Huntsbringer approaches Smith and Helen Wright with a questioning look on his face:

"We weren't introduced to you during the meeting. Who are you two?" Smith warms to his directness and smiles at the big American, his bad mood forgotten for just a moment. It's Helen who answers though:

"We're from the British police, Mr Huntsbringer. I'm Detective Inspector Helen Wright and this is Detective Inspector John Clarke." She calls Smith by the false name that's on his current passport, courtesy of the British Secret Intelligence Service. "At this stage we're just here as observers I'm afraid."

"Hmm."

"I'm really very sorry about your wife being kidnapped."

"Yeah? So's the whole diplomatic corps, but they're not doing much to get her and the others back, are they?"

Mike Oldport joins them then. He looks worn out and completely fed up:

"This is a complete farce! We should go after the bastards ourselves. That's the only way we'll ever get Sheila and Margot back! This lot of wankers are useless!" He almost snarls at the back of the embassy staff as they leave the room. Smith looks them both in the eyes:

"You're right. That's what I'd do if it was my wife who'd been kidnapped." They look at him in surprise. "If it was me, I'd hire a four-wheel drive and go and look for them myself."

Five minutes later and everyone has left the room except for Smith and Helen Wright.

"What the hell was that all about?" she fumes at him. "What gives you the right to wind them up like that? If they try and go after the Somalis on their own they'll probably end up getting kidnapped themselves, or even worse. What are you playing at, John?"

Smith just smiles infuriatingly:

"At the moment it sounds like they've got as good a chance as anybody else to find these bastards."

"Yes, and get themselves killed doing it!"

"Nobody lives forever, Helen. Why shouldn't they have a go themselves? It's not like much else is being done to get those people back, is it?" His face is deadpan but she can see the anger flaring in his coal-black eyes. "If it was me, I'd have been on their trail days ago!"

"But they're not you, are they? They're just some poor bloody civilians who have been caught up in a mess that they're not prepared for."

Smith relents a little, but his bad mood is still apparent:

"What I don't understand is why I've been brought over here? I feel like a spare prick at a wedding." Helen colours a little at this.

She's not in the best of humours either after a very long day which has been full of bad feeling. She and Linda Webb, Smith's partner, who has also come to Egypt on Smith's insistence, have not hit it off at all and this is partly why Smith is in such a huff.

Perhaps inviting Linda along on this trip is not the best idea I've ever had? he thinks to himself. The trouble is that I promised her we'd never be parted again, not after Iran and The Gambia.

Helen sighs, also thinking about Linda's reaction to her and her own reaction back. She believes that Linda has guessed correctly that she's secretly in love with John, even though she's done her best to keep her feelings hidden. She shakes away her thoughts and tries to get her mind back to the job in hand:

"I've got another meeting in half an hour, with the MI6 section head. He's driving down from Cairo."

"I'm not invited?"

"You know what the boss said. You're to have nothing to do directly with anyone from the Firm in Egypt and I'm to act as your go-between. He doesn't even want his own people to know who you are."

"Hmmm. It's nice to be loved."

She grins at his sullen answer.

"Come on. You can buy me a drink in the bar before my meeting. With any luck I'll find out exactly why they have brought us here."

"Can I invite Linda?"

She sees the mischievous glint in his eye and punches him lightly on the arm.

"No!"

Smith laughs.

"Super."

NINETEEN

16th June
Hurghada, Egypt

Helen Wright is absolutely shattered. It's now getting close to midnight and the two previous days filled with travelling and meetings are beginning to catch up with her. However she has agreed to drop by Smith's hotel suite before going back to her own to tell him the news after her latest meeting with the Firm's head of section from Cairo.

She's a good looking woman in her late twenties, tall and slim with long blonde hair tied into a simple ponytail. Helen first met John Smith a few years ago when she had been a detective constable posted to the Serious and Organised Crime Agency in Cambridgeshire. There she had been working under Detective Chief Inspector Alan Davies, the head of SOCA, when they first heard about the disappearance of an eleven year old girl called Mary Knightly from Peterborough on a Friday afternoon. All of the police officers in the city had been put on standby and many people from Mary's local community had volunteered to help the police search for her on areas of waste ground and other green spaces in the city over the following weekend. Sadly it had all been to no avail, and Mary's dead body had turned up on Monday in a builder's skip outside a block of flats which were being demolished. She was discovered by a shocked demolition worker as he dumped some scrap plasterboard in the skip. A hurried autopsy revealed that little Mary had been sexually assaulted, raped and mutilated before she was murdered. At the time DCI Davies had argued that the Serious and Organised Crime Agency, rather than the Homicide Squad should be put in charge of the investigation of Mary's murder. The latter was already snowed under with a massive case involving a racist murder in Peterborough, so the Chief Constable of Cambridgeshire Constabulary had agreed to Davies' request.

Davies and his team of very experienced officers, including the young but extremely talented and ambitious twenty-two year old DC Wright spent the next three weeks working hard on the case. They interviewed hundreds of prospective witnesses and potential suspects and watched hour after hour of CCTV footage retrieved from shops, car parks and many other spots in the area where Mary was believed to have been abducted on her journey home from school. But they found nothing that gave them even the slightest clue as to where and how she had actually been taken, or who had been involved. The only useful evidence had been found during the autopsy on Mary's poor, badly mutilated body: the forensic lab had managed to get a clear DNA profile of her possible killer from the fragments of skin taken from beneath her nails and the fingerprints lifted from one of her shoes found close to her body were clear and in very good condition. However they were not able to exploit the evidence further as there wasn't a match for either the DNA or the fingerprints in the National DNA Database or the Police National Computer.

Their case had just about hit a brick wall.

Then they had a stroke of good luck. A national appeal for help about the case on the BBCs Crimewatch programme resulted in a host of phone calls from members of the public. Most of the calls contained false or misleading information, even though they were most probably made with good intentions. However, two separate phone calls, most probably made by the same person who wished to remain anonymous, mentioned a van driver named John Smith. The caller said that he had been seen late on the Friday evening that Mary had been abducted chucking blood-stained clothes in a bin outside his home in Coventry, seventy miles from Peterborough. A third anonymous phone call from yet another person gave the make and registration of a van spotted close to the skip where Mary's body was eventually recovered over the weekend that she had been missing. A simple computer query identified the van as one that John Smith drove for the delivery company he worked for.

Finally it seemed the net was beginning to close.

Helen Wright was with DCI Davies when he had initially visited Smith for an informal interview at his home. During their conversation they had both been convinced that he was not their man. Either that or he was the best actor that they had ever come across. Helen remembers her first impressions of Smith as a handsome, middle-aged man with sad eyes and a very quiet, self-contained, self-confident demeanour. Despite herself she had also experienced an attraction towards him, not quite sexual, but certainly physical in some sense. She had never met anyone before who had the same subdued magnetism that Smith had in abundance. It was almost as if he was a caged wild animal, and that underneath his calm exterior there lived something feral and completely untamed. Her gut feelings told her that Smith would not harm an innocent teenage girl and she went to great efforts to make sure that Davies understood her opinion. Despite this he had ordered Smith's arrest very soon after. At the time he was under a great deal of pressure from the local media and his Chief Constable to get a result, and she thought that he detained Smith as much to relieve the building tension as to cover himself in case Smith did have anything to do with the crime.

When forensics had turned up strands of Mary's hair from inside the back of Smith's van, Helen had been dumbfounded. Davies, of course, was over the moon and absolutely convinced that he had found their man through his pure and utmost skill as a detective. Unlike John Smith, Davies had an ego the size of a football field.

Eventually Smith had been put on trial at Peterborough Crown Court and the case against him had gone superbly from the viewpoint of the police and the Crown Prosecution Service. Even Smith seemed resigned to the fact that the evidence against him was overwhelming and that the outcome of the trial would result in his imprisonment at Her Majesty's pleasure for the rest of his natural life.

Then something had happened to change all of that and Helen still didn't know what that was. The very day that the verdict was to be announced, Smith had suddenly turned. He killed two civilian prison guards with his bare hands and escaped from the court building.

In the weeks that followed Smith went on the rampage, torturing and murdering the case's chief prosecutor, raiding an army centre and stealing weapons, ammunition and explosives, destroying the offices of the Serious and Organised Crime Agency in a rocket attack and blowing up the Police National Computer and National DNA Database. Finally his rampage led him to murder his trial judge, one of Helen's colleagues on the case; Detective Sergeant Henry Price, a very secretive and suspicious character from MI6, the Secret Intelligence Service, who had been assigned to the case, and eventually the former head of MI6 itself, Sir Thomas Sewell MBE. Then Smith had simply disappeared off the map, as though he had never existed. During all of this mayhem though, it had emerged that John Smith was not the simple delivery van driver that he appeared to be. He was in fact a highly-trained and extremely well experienced former MI6 agent and Special Forces soldier. He was the ultimate modern-day warrior and a cold-blooded killer.

When Smith disappeared DCI Davies had been appointed as a liaison officer to work with the Secret Intelligence Service to try and track him down and Helen, at Davies's request, had joined her. To cut a long story short, they had eventually found Smith living under an assumed name in The Gambia, a tiny country in West Africa. Smith was finally imprisoned for abducting, raping and murdering little Mary Knightly, although by this time Helen had even more serious doubts about his guilt. Helen was promoted to detective sergeant partly as a result of his capture, but of course, you can't keep a man like John Smith locked up forever. He secured his freedom from prison during a particularly daring escapade and disappeared once again, although this time he was believed to have died.

One person did not believe he was dead however. Davies just wouldn't give up looking for him and through sheer obstinacy and persistence he eventually found him living in Norway with his new girlfriend, Dr Linda Webb. However no one in the police force, the Secret Intelligence Service or the British government was keen on finding out that Smith, the pain-in-the-arse ex-SAS sergeant that had mauled the British Justice System so severely was alive and well. They ignored Davies and even laughed at him behind his back. In the end, completely disillusioned, Davies had turned to the

Iranians who he knew hated Smith probably even more than he did. They had ordered a 'Fatwa', or death sentence against him for disrupting their plans and killing the terrorists on that fateful flight from The Gambia.

This is the point where Helen Wright stepped back into the picture, as Davies told her that he was going to kill Smith with the help of the Iranians just before he left to go to Norway to get his man. Appalled, Helen had broken into Davies' office, found out where Smith and Linda were living in Norway and telephoned them to warn them that Davies and his Iranian friends were coming. Her response was in part due to the fact that by then she was absolutely convinced that he was innocent of the killing of Mary Knightly, but also because she had unwittingly become very personally involved in the case. Slowly she was falling in love with the man that she had inadvertently helped to set up and this was the first time that her feelings began to surface.

Smith survived his encounter with the Iranians and seriously wounded Alan Davies, who died a slow and painful death in the Norwegian wilderness abandoned by his new found friends. Confronting Helen in her home in England, he had agreed that he would help her with her career in return for her having saved his and Linda's lives. Over the coming months he kept his word and helped her by supplying information on an illegal child sex slave and wild animal smuggling operation run by a Nigerian campus cult in his old stomping ground of The Gambia. As a direct result of this she gained yet another promotion, this time to detective inspector.

John's influence over Helen's career did not stop there. Very soon afterwards she found herself appointed as the liaison officer between the Director Generals of both MI5 and MI6 and a shadowy vigilante group of ex-armed forces personnel apparently headed up by John Smith and known as The Brotherhood. She didn't know how she had got the job, which carried a huge amount of kudos even if it was strictly off the official books, but she was sure at the back of her mind that John Smith had had something to do with it. Smith, of course, typically denied all involvement and just smiled infuriatingly in that naughty-little-schoolboy way of his whenever she brought up the subject.

Anyway, this is how Helen ended up in Egypt acting as the go-between for Smith, the local section of the Secret Intelligence Service based in Cairo and the Director Generals of MI5 and MI6 back in the UK.

When Helen arrives at the door to Smith's hotel room it is opened by a re-vitalised Dr Linda Webb. The older woman has spent an hour in the bath and has enjoyed an unhurried meal since arriving in Egypt, while Helen and Smith had rushed to their meeting with Oldport, Huntsbringer and the embassy diplomats.

"Oh, it's *you*." Linda announces when she sees Helen. She doesn't look happy to see her. "You'd better come in. John's in the shower but you can wait for him."

"Thanks, Linda." Helen walks in and Linda returns to her seat, inviting the younger woman to sit with her on the other side of a large breakfast table. There's a moment of stilted silence before Linda sighs:

"I guess that you know that I'm not very happy?" she asks. Helen hadn't expected that.

"Yes. It's pretty obvious."
Linda sighs again at Helen's short, sharp answer.

"When John told me about you, he forgot to tell me that you're hopelessly in love with him." Her voice is cold and clipped.

"Ah," Helen slumps a little in her seat, much too tired to get into an argument and to even try and deny the truth. "That's probably because he doesn't know that I am."
Linda looks at her quizzically.

"Really?"

"Yes, really. I haven't told him and I'm not going to either."

"Hmmm." Linda's eyes search the younger woman's across the table, looking for a lie in them, but seeing only tiredness and honesty. "So he honestly doesn't have a clue that you're in love with him then?"

"He may have guessed that I have....feelings....for him, but he doesn't know that it's love. I didn't even realise myself until recently, when I'd heard that he was wounded on the Albanian job."

"Oh." Suddenly Linda reaches out and grasps Helen's hand on the table top. "I must apologise for my behaviour today then,

Helen." She smiles warmly. "I thought that perhaps something was going on between you two…I'm sorry."

Helen smiles back, flicking back a strand of sweaty hair from her face.

"No problem, Linda. And you needn't worry. As soon as I saw how John acts around you, it quashed any fantasies that I might have had about him and me. He's obviously very much in love with you."

Her eyes are deeply sad and Linda can't resist moving around the table and putting an arm around the younger woman's shoulder.

"Oh, I'm so sorry, Helen!"

Helen just laughs.

"You've nothing to be sorry about, Linda! I can see that you're a good person and you've certainly been good for John. I can see how relaxed he is in your company."

"Thanks, Helen."

At that moment Smith walks through from the bathroom suite, humming an indistinct tune under his breath. He's wearing a pair of damp khaki shorts and rubbing vigorously at his head with a towel, so he doesn't see their visitor for a second or two. When he does his face breaks into a boyish grin. Obviously his mood has lightened a little in the past hour or so.

"Hi, Helen! Sorry, love, didn't know you were here." He reaches out to the large double bed to pick up a clean T-shirt but as he does so he's pulled up short by Helen's audible gasp of surprise. "What?" he says, looking up to see that her face has gone pale. Helen is staring unashamedly at Smith's mostly naked body with a shocked look on her face.

"What?" he asks again, beginning to feel really uncomfortable now.

Helen finally draws her eyes away and looks down at her hands, a red flush slowly spreading across her face and neck. Linda looks from Helen's face to Smith's and suddenly she's giggling. Helen can't help it. She joins in.

"What's so funny?"

Smith's face is creased with a frown, not understanding anything at all now. All day these two women had been giving each other the cold shoulder and the evil eye, and now they're giggling together like a pair of schoolgirls. Women! Linda is the first to recover. She forces herself to be serious though it doesn't quite work and it's obvious that she's still giggling inside:

"I don't think that Helen's seen you without your clothes on before," she says. Smith gets another giggle from the pair as he clutches his T-shirt close to his chest as though hiding. He is really very uncomfortable now.

"So? I don't see what's so funny!" He sounds utterly defensive.

The two women look at each other.

"It's not funny really, John." Linda has finally got a bit of seriousness back into her voice. "I'm sorry, but I'm so used to seeing your body that I don't even notice all of the scars anymore. But it must have been a bit of a shock for poor Helen!"

"Ah." It suddenly dawns on Smith what the two women are talking about. He drops the T-shirt and peers down at his own chest, tucking his chin in as far as it will go. "Yeah. I have got a few scars I suppose."

"A few!" Helen almost starts laughing again. "I had no idea!" Smith grins and walks across the room to stare into a full-length mirror mounted on the wall.

He can't remember the last time he looked in a mirror, except to have a shave. He looks up and down at his reflection and is totally surprised at what he sees. He's a good six feet two inches tall and despite his age (he's in his mid-fifties), the last few months of almost obsessive fitness training have left him lean and muscular with almost an athlete's body, *almost*. For most of his life he'd weighed in at a steady twelve stone, about one hundred and seventy pounds, but then he had spent several month's recuperation at the Defence Services Medical Rehabilitation Centre after his single-handed crazy attack against the headquarters of the Albanian Mafia. His body had become soft and the good food at the rehabilitation centre had also helped him to pile on the pounds. This was probably helped along by his advancing years. Most men suffer from an attack of weight gain around their middle as they reach their mid-forties and Smith had been no exception. He felt like he only had to eat a one ounce packet of crisps these days and he'd put on a couple of inches around his waist. He had gone up to nearly fifteen stones in weight and it had been a battle ever since to reduce that back down to what he had been before.

116

He'd had to push himself hard to get his fitness back with regular runs on the beach, and long walks along the Norfolk Coastal Path with Linda as she pointed out the sometimes huge flocks of waders and seabirds, able to name every species for him.

He's now about thirteen stone and is slightly thicker around the waist than in his younger days, but at least most of it is muscle. However, he doesn't really recognise himself as he looks in the mirror. What the fuck happened to me? he thinks. Jesus, but I look old!

He leans forward to stare closely at his face in the reflection, totally zoned out now and ignoring the two women as they sit and watch him, fascinated. Bloody hell, look at those lines. I look like a crinkled piece of paper! And look at that bloody grey! It's everywhere. What happened to my black hair? Last time I looked I'm sure I had some dark hair left?

He pulls back to stare at the rest of his body with fresh eyes on the marks that the years of conflict and war have left on his body. His chest and abdomen are criss-cross by fiery red scars where the terrorist highjackers on the Gambia Flight had sliced him with their knives during that desperate fight for his life. Underneath are numerous thin white scars where the Soviet guards had cut him in moments of boredom during his interrogation in Afghanistan in the mid-eighties. They're almost invisible to the naked eye now, yet he can still feel every single bloody one of them in his memory as they cut through his flesh. His upper right arm is blemished by a long shallow and pink-fleshed furrow left by the passage of a pistol round during his attack on the Albanian Mafia, and the same fight has bequeathed him with ugly puckered wounds in his right shoulder, left arm and two on his right thigh from gunshot wounds. He twists his body so that he can see part of his back. It's just as bad as the front with more knife wounds and the exit wounds from the gunshots, but there's also about fifty small angry-looking burn scars scattered across his shoulders and lower backs. These last ones are from the Soviets in Afghanistan again, who would insist on stubbing out their cigarettes on his bare skin.

"Jesus!" he says thoughtfully. "I'd forgotten about this little lot." And what the fuck happened to the young man that I used to be? He turns to see that the two women have composed themselves and are looking a little crestfallen at giggling at him. "I'd better not go sunbathing down by the hotel swimming pool then, I'll frighten the natives!"

He grins, and suddenly they're all laughing together.

"What did you learn from the head spook then?" All three are now sitting around the table, having got over their fit of laughter.

"Well, not too much more than we learned from the embassy staff. The kidnappers are definitely Somalis. This is what local eyewitnesses in Quseer said when they were interviewed by the Egyptian police. There were at least four of them there during the kidnapping, but of course there may be more of them involved. Apart from that and the fact that the tourist minibus was found abandoned along the coast road about two hundred kilometres south of Quseer he didn't have a lot to add. The general feeling is that this is a kidnapping for money rather than a terrorist act."

"Yeah? Why's that?"

"Because the Somalis fired their weapons into the air during the kidnapping. The analysts in London believe that if they were Al-Shabaab terrorists, or terrorists from any other group for that matter, they would have gone for the maximum amount of casualties, considering the normal mode of operation for radical Muslim terrorists."

"Mmmm. I suppose that that makes sense."

"Plus the word on the streets in Mogadishu is that it's becoming much too dangerous for Somali pirates to try and capture ships in the Gulf of Aden and the Arabian Sea any more. Most ships passing through those waters now employ armed security, or at the very least they have active countermeasures such as high-powered fire hoses to prevent the pirates from boarding them. Plus the area is heavily patrolled by several navies, including the British, Dutch and Americans. The pirates are still operating in the Gulf and along the coast, but they are getting far fewer results for the amount of effort they're putting in. For the last couple of months the Firm's local assets in Somalia have been hearing whispers about the war lords shifting their emphasis from offshore attacks and kidnappings to land-based kidnappings in the countries neighbouring them.

"That's good news then, Helen. At least it means that the hostages have a high value to their kidnappers. If it had been the work of a bunch of Islamic fanatics we would probably be watching their murders on the internet."

Helen pauses before speaking again and it is pretty obvious by the pensive look on her face that she's got something important to add but for some reason is holding back.

"Come on, Helen. What's up?"

"The Firm has decided to work alongside the Americans on the job. They've been getting some pressure from Washington about working in partnership, especially as the Yanks are the ones that are providing the Special Forces for any hostage rescue that might be needed."

"You mean the SEAL team flying in tomorrow morning?"

"Yep. The boss of the Firm has informed the US State Department that we have an operative in-country and I'm afraid that the Yanks want you to work together with one of their own Central Intelligence Agency operatives."

"Christ! Do I have a choice in this?"

"Afraid not, John. This has come via the Director General of the Firm himself; you're to work with the American as your partner."

"Super."

"I'm sorry, John. I know that you'd prefer to work alone on this!"

"I'll bet that smug bastard in London is enjoying this, the fucker." Smith surprises her by suddenly smiling. "What he probably doesn't remember, unless he's reread my file recently is that I've worked with guys from the CIA before, in Colombia in the early 1980s. Shit, I even trained a load of them in Close Target Reconnaissance techniques at Fort Bragg. I liked them. They were good blokes. Have you got any information on the person who I'll be working with?"

"Only the basics, John. Apparently he's an operative with the Special Operations Group of the Special Activities Division of the CIA. Does that mean anything to you?"

"Yep! They're the guys that carry out the 'black-ops'. The sneaky-beaky deniable operations. They're the blokes I worked with before. I might even know him, have you got a name?"

"It's a guy called Robert O'Brian. Ring any bells?"

"No." Smith can't hide his disappointment. "I knew a guy called O'Brian in the group but he wasn't a Robert. Do we know anything about him?"

"Apparently he's an ex-SEAL. He served for eighteen years in the US Navy, sixteen of them with SEAL Team Six. He sounds a bit like you, John. They told me that he's been on over four hundred combat missions and has been decorated fifty times!"

Smith grins.

"What did you tell the Yanks about me?"

"Just that your name is John Clarke and that you're an agent in the Secret Intelligence Service."

"That'll piss them off, the nosey bastards. They'll want to know a lot more than that! Let's hope that this bloke O'Brian is all that he's cracked up to be, eh? He sounds like he might be useful."

"Well, I hope so, because he's arriving in Hurghada tomorrow morning at eight."

"Super."

ENGLAND

TWENTY

17th June
Luton, England

Jonathan Harris is standing in the front room of the old lady's flat, his eye pressed firmly against the viewfinder of the Canon EOS 6D digital SLR camera with his fingertip hovering over the shutter button. The 300mm lens gives him an excellent view of the front door of Mehdi Arkoun's flat across the road. The young Muslim Luton man has his back turned to Harris as he fumbles with his door key, but the MI5 field agent shoots off a few frames anyway, just to provide images for continuity if it ever comes to court. Arkoun finally gets the door unlocked and pushes it open, turning for just a second to get the attention of the person sitting in the front of a car. It's parked just out of Harris's view and that of his colleague Jenny Sanderson to the side of him who is handling another camera, this one set to record on Full-HD video. Harris presses his finger firmly down and the camera whirrs away as it takes nine frames per second, the 11-point autofocus system capturing Arkoun's face in perfectly sharp detail.

Another of Harris's colleagues is walking along the road outside, a small radio microphone attached to the collar of his lightweight summer jacket and an earpiece hidden away inside his ear.

"The car is a red Citroen C5, registration: alpha mike zero six foxtrot uniform tango. I've got a semi-clear view of the passenger, but I can't tell whether it's definitely Tango One, over."

"Roger that, Tony. For fuck's sake ensure that he doesn't make you, over." Harris's voice is calm but there's no denying the undercurrent of excitement in it.

123

"Willco. No problem. I'm going into the newsagents. I'll be out of view in ten."

"Roger that, Tony. Jen, get that registration sent off and checked please." Harris watches Arkoun as he stands inside the entrance hall of his flat, holding the door open as a figure walks quickly over from the car and steps past him to move inside. He has his finger on the shutter but the man doesn't turn and doesn't show his face. "Bollocks! Did you get anything, Jen?" he asks the woman on the video camera.

"No sorry, John. Nothing. The bugger didn't show his face at all."

"Ah, bugger!"

Harris is now in a quandary. The identity of the stranger that Mehdi Arkoun had picked up at Heathrow the day before has been confirmed by the advanced facial recognition software, and been relayed to him and his team earlier that morning. He now knows that this is the real deal. The man is a highly-placed Iranian intelligence agent, and Harris's team have been given the go ahead to ask for whatever resources they need to find him, and discover what he's doing in the United Kingdom, no matter what the cost. Other teams are being brought in as well; one to cover the rear of Arkoun's block of flats and a couple of mobile teams with two motorbikes and three different vehicles to follow him and his guest wherever they go. They even have cooperation from the local boys in blue, who are providing armed cover for the surveillance teams. Despite what you may see in the cinema or on the television, MI5 field agents are not normally cleared to carry firearms on the streets of Britain. Luckily it's a team of Bedfordshire Police firearms specialists that Harris has worked with before and he knows them quite well.

Harris is thrilled that Arkoun has finally turned up at his flat. He's using another car now and this one is probably stolen as well. And the Luton man isn't on his own either. Harris is hoping against hope that it's the Iranian who's accompanying him.

After a few minutes of waiting to make sure that Arkoun and his friend don't come straight back out of the flat, Harris calls his superior on his mobile.

"Well? Is it him? Is it the Iranian in Arkoun's flat?"

"I can't say for sure, boss. It might be. None of us had a good view of his face, though whoever it is, he's about the same age and build as our man."

"Have you got any feed from the inside of the flat?"

"Yes, boss. We've got two cameras fitted; one in the lounge and one in the kitchen, but the sod seems to be staying put in the entrance hallway for some reason. I can't make any sense of it unless he's going to be coming back out again soon. The hall is the only room in the bloody flat where we haven't got any audio either. We can hear indistinct sounds of talking in the hall with the mikes that we've fitted in the other rooms but we can't make out what's being said."

"Shit. I'll try and set up a direct line from you to the technicians here, so that they can listen in in real time. They'll be able to boost the sound so that they can pick up what's being said but it's all going to take time to get set up."

"Let's hope we get something more soon, boss. Surely the guy can't spend all of his time in the hallway? Hold on. Something's happening, boss. I can hear Arkoun shouting now."

"What's he saying?"

"No idea, boss. It's in Arabic, I think. Unfortunately both Jenny and I speak Russian not Arabic." There's a long pause as Harris listens intently to the sound of loud shouting coming over the live feed. Then there's a sharp, loud bang. "Fuck me! That's a gunshot, boss! I'm sure of it!"

"Okay. Get the firearms officers in there, John!"

"Roger that!" Harris keeps the line with his boss open while he gets on to the radio to his armed backup team that is made up of the two Specialist Firearms Officers from Bedfordshire Police: "Tim? Phil? We've heard a gunshot in the target's flat! You're weapons free and clear to make a forced entry!"

"Roger, John. We're moving now." Risking a look out of the window Harris can see the two figures of the policemen jumping out of the rear of the Vauxhall Vivaro van parked up the road and sprinting towards the front door of Arkoun's flat. Both of them are helmeted, wearing modular Osprey body armour, with ceramic trauma plates slipped into pouches covering their chest and backs, and brandishing Heckler and Koch MP5SFs, the single-shot semi-

125

automatic version of the world famous sub-machine gun issued to their police force.

As the two coppers slow down and cautiously begin to cover the last few metres to the door of the flat, weapons held in the ready position and fingers creeping on to triggers, Harris finds that he's holding his breath in deep suspense.

In the next moment Harris and Sanderson are thrown backwards like a pair of rag dolls, slamming into the rear wall of the room at huge velocity as the window in front of them disintegrates, showering them with thousands of slivers of glass that slice and dice them into bloody pieces. The massive shock wave from the explosion rips across the street, travelling at hundreds of miles per hour, rocking the whole building to its very foundations with its force and buckling the tarmac of the street outside. The heat wave that follows the blast a micro-second later is so hot that it melts the plastic of the surveillance equipment in the room, causing it to bubble and spit and run in tiny rivulets. The curtains and soft furnishings in the room, as well as the clothes worn by the two field agents, instantly burst into flame as the intense flash of heat touches them. Dust and debris fill the air in a choking mass and then the sound of the explosive blast hits like a solid wall of noise.

Not that it matters to Jonathan or Jenny though.

They're already dead.

TWENTY-ONE

17th June
Downing Street, London

The Prime Minister David Cameron brings the emergency meeting in the Cabinet Office Briefing Room (COBR) to order:

"Good evening, ladies and gentlemen. I'm sorry that the Foreign Secretary cannot be here with us today but I'm afraid that he's on a plane somewhere over the Atlantic at the moment, on his way back from a meeting of the G8. He has been informed of the events that have led up to this meeting, and I will be keeping him up to speed as things hopefully progress further." He peers at the top ranking individuals who have gathered for the meeting, all of them seated around a large table.

Sitting to his left is the London Metropolitan Police Commissioner; next to him is the Commander in charge of SO15, the Counter Terrorism Command of the Met, followed by the Chief Constable of Bedfordshire Police. Next around the table is the Home Secretary, looking distinctly unhappy, and after her are the Director Generals of MI5, the Security Service and MI6, the Secret Intelligence Service. The last person at the table is the Director of UK Special Forces.

Seated behind each of these people away from the table are little groups of flunkies and aides. Everyone in the room has a sombre expression on their faces, reflecting the seriousness of the whole situation.

"Perhaps we should start with you, Chief Constable?" The Prime Minister looks at the head of the police force in Luton, the Chief Constable of Bedfordshire Police, a middle-aged woman with long blonde hair severely tied back to frame a pale face beneath her hat. "Perhaps you'd like to bring us up to speed on this dreadful incident?"

She coughs a little to clear her throat:

"Thank you, Sir." Then she shuffles a pile of papers lying on the table in front of her, trying to get her thoughts into order before speaking. "As you all know, at eighteen minutes past one this afternoon, an explosive device detonated in Brook Street, central Luton. We don't yet know how many casualties there are as a result of the explosion, though we do know that at least two police officers from Bedfordshire Police, two operatives from the Security Service..." she inclines her head to nod at Sir Andrew Lowe, the chief of the Box, who nods back at her in acknowledgement. "...and at least three civilians have been killed. There are also several dozen other injured civilians who are being treated in Luton and Dunstable Hospital, and a few of these have life-threatening injuries." She pauses and looks around the other people at the table.

"The explosion appears to have originated inside a flat belonging to one Mehdi Arkoun, a young Muslim man who has been on the Terrorist Watch List for some time. His flat was under surveillance by the Security Service at the time of the explosion and the two police officers from my force who were killed were on scene as armed backup to these surveillance teams."

"Arkoun was followed by one of my field agents as he picked up another person arriving at Heathrow from Brussels yesterday," Sir Andrew interjects. "Our agent was unable to follow them directly to the suspect's flat for fear of compromising himself, and it appears that they did not return there last night. We do not, at this time know where Arkoun and the person he picked up at the airport spent the night."

"Do we know if they were in the flat at the time of the explosion?" asks the Home Secretary, her voice sharp and accusing.

"No. Unfortunately the building where the explosion occurred is still considered to be unsafe, and as yet we haven't been able to ascertain whether anyone was inside the suspect's flat during the explosion. We do know that Arkoun and a second person arrived at the flat a short time before, and that the sound of a gun-shot was picked up by the surveillance equipment, but we do not know if that other person was the same man that Arkoun picked up at Heathrow, or whether they had left the flat before the bomb went off. Unfortunately the field agents who have the answers to these questions were the two that were killed."

"Who is this other man? Have we identified him yet?" This comes from the Prime Minister, who is obviously trying to sound like he is still in control of the meeting. He is trying to instil confidence into a meeting where most of the people present including himself feel completely out of their depth.

"Ah, that's where it gets really interesting. If you don't mind I'll hand you over to Sir Hugh?"

The chief of MI5 indicates his colleague, Sir Hugh Metcalfe, the Director General of his sister agency; the Secret Intelligence Service. Sir Hugh smiles back at him.

"Thank you, Sir Andrew. *Interesting* is a very apt word in this case." He leans back from the table and mutters quietly into the ear of one of his aides. The aide promptly opens a box-file and withdraws a stack of papers. Then he begins to pass the papers amongst the other aides positioned in the outer ring around the table, who then pass the papers inwards to their own respective bosses.

"The top sheet is a still photograph of the man that this Mehdi Arkoun picked up from Heathrow Airport yesterday, taken from CCTV at passport control. As you can see, the photograph is very clear and we have been able to pass it quite rapidly through our 3D facial recognition software." He pauses for a moment as though drawing out the drama, and the Home Secretary gives a very audible sigh at his quite obvious theatrics. "This man's name is Massoud Hassan and as far as we are aware, he is a colonel in the Iranian Ministry of Intelligence and National Security."
For a moment there is a buzz of muted but excited conversation around the table as this news is taken in and digested.

"An Iranian?" asks an incredulous David Cameron. "Are you saying that this man is a spy working on behalf of the Iranian government?"

"That's impossible to confirm at the moment, Sir. If you look at the second sheet on the papers handed to you, you will see a brief summary of the man's service. I'll go over the main points for you." He looks down at the sheet before resuming to speak:

"The first time that we came across Hassan's name is in a number of documents that we secretly obtained relating to the Iranian government's infamous massacre of political prisoners in 1988. Apparently Hassan was a corporal in the army of Iran at that time and his regiment systematically tortured and then executed men and women who had been arrested for holding views that were contrary to those of the Iranian government and Ayatollah Komeni, especially prisoners who supported the opposition parties such as the People's Mujahedin of Iran, Fedaian, and the Tudeh Party. The exact number of prisoners who were executed during this purge is unknown, but the opposition parties in Iran claimed that it was as many as thirty thousand."

There are a few sharp intakes of breath around the table at this.

"From the official documents that we have obtained it appears that Corporal Hassan was an enthusiastic participant in these interrogations and executions. This seems to be the case because he was hand-selected for service in a naval commando force called the Takavar after his regiment ran out of victims to kill about five months later. As a member of this commando force he would have been thoroughly trained in military skills including sub-aqua diving, parachuting, weapons, unarmed combat, land warfare and close quarter combat etc. etc.. They are not strictly classed as Special Forces, and I suppose that their nearest equivalent in the British Armed Forces would be either the Parachute Regiment or the Royal Marines." At this point Sir Hugh looks across at Brigadier Clarkeson, the Director of UK Special Forces for confirmation of his supposition. The Brigadier nods his head in agreement.

"At the end of his Takavar training Hassan would have served a six-month probationary period with an active combat unit, before becoming a fully-fledged commando. According to a copy of his service evaluation which we obtained with many others from a source that we had in place inside the Iranian Ministry of Defence at the time, he did so well during his training and probationary periods that he was commissioned as an officer with the rank of first lieutenant. As you can imagine this was when we started to be very interested in how his career would progress, along with several hundred other officers in the Iranian Army who we thought might be of interest to us in the future." He smiles at his colleagues. "It's Standard Operating Procedure for the intelligence agencies of most countries to keep a tab on the higher-ranked military personnel of potential enemies," he explains.

"Anyway, it appears from what little we have been able to glean that Hassan went on to serve with distinction in several conflicts, but most especially while operating with the Kurds against Saddam Hussein's regime in northern Iraq. Apparently his team specialised in small-unit raids involving sabotage, assassination and hostage-rescue, and they were really rather good."

"In 2001, Hassan volunteered to be transferred to the Quds Force, a special unit of the Iranian Revolutionary Guards, with the rank of captain. The Quds Force had been formed during the Iran-Iraq war and is considered to be one of the finest Special Forces units in the world today, with extremely talented personnel. Their main objective is to train and equip foreign Islamic revolutionary groups in the Middle East. From the information that we have, which I'll admit is rather patchy, it appears that most of Hassan's period of service with the unit was spent training and helping the Shi'a death squads in Iraq."

"The next official mention that we have of Hassan does not appear until 2007 in the national newspaper, the Tehran Times, when an official press release mentions that he was transferred to the Ministry of Intelligence and National Security, known as MOIS, with the rank of major. This ministry is Iran's leading intelligence-gathering agency. It also has a covert arm that is reputed to recruit potential terrorists and plan international terrorist attacks, and is under the direct control of the Supreme Leader. As you know, this is currently the Grand Ayatollah Ali Khamenei, and he has more power in Iran than the President of the country."

"At this point our information on Hassan more or less dries up, apart from news of his official appointments. In 2010 he was appointed as the military attaché at the Iranian Embassy in Oslo, which as we all know from watching the Bond movies means that he was there as an undercover intelligence officer." He chuckles indulgently at his own feeble joke, then carries on quickly when no one else joins in: "Two years ago he was expelled from Norway and sent back to Iran in disgrace. We don't yet know the official or the unofficial reasons for his expulsion, and our colleagues in the

Foreign Office are presently talking to their Norwegian counterparts to try to get more information on why he was sent home. All I can say at this point in time is that the Iranians do not normally look upon such 'failures' as being sent home in disgrace with any ambiguity. Diplomats and intelligence operatives who are expelled from other countries are usually dealt with quite ruthlessly, either being imprisoned for a long period of time or summarily executed. These punishments are normally extended to their close family members as well. It is very unusual for these people to ever surface again, so why Hassan is now on the loose in the United Kingdom, I can't say. Perhaps we will be better informed as to his intentions when we find out why he was deported from Norway?"

At this point there is an interruption to the proceedings as a messenger enters the room and beckons to one of the SO15 (the Counter Terrorism Command) Commander's aides, who promptly goes to the door to collect a single sheet of paper from the messenger, which she then hands to her boss. Commander Vaughn quickly reads through the message.

"Ladies and gentlemen." The very experienced and quite senior police officer raps the table with a knuckle to get their attention. "I'm afraid that I have some particularly bad news. This is the preliminary report from the bomb squad's forensic team at the scene. It appears that the explosive used in the device detonated in Luton was a form of Semtex known as Variant 1A, which apparently is particularly powerful with at least three times the explosive capacity of normal plastic explosives, such as PE4 or C4." He pauses to look around the table, making sure that everyone understands the true meaning of his next words:

"Even more worrying than this though, is that the explosive charge was 'shaped'."
Most of the faces of those present look grim as they think about the implications of this news, All except the Prime Minister.

"I don't understand, commander. What does 'shaped' mean, and why is it even more worrying for us?"
The top anti-terrorist policeman tries to hide a brief look of irritation at the ignorance of the politician, then he takes a deep breath and answers:

"A shaped charge is an explosive charge that is adapted to focus the force of the explosive's energy, Sir."

"Yes? So what commander?"

"Look at it this way, Sir." interjects Brigadier Clarkeson, speaking slowly in his best 'how to explain something to an idiot' voice. "In a normal explosion all of the energy from the blast is thrown out fairly evenly around it. But in the case of a shaped charge the blast's energy is thrown out in a specific direction only, rather like aiming a shotgun."

"Yes, I understand that Brigadier, but why is it more worrying for us?"
His face is creased by a frown.

"Because it means, Sir, that the whole thing is more likely to have been premeditated, rather than say, just an accident. You know, the explosive device going off when it wasn't meant to."

"Yes, I agree with you, Brigadier. It may also mean that the device was placed in such a way that it was meant to kill the Security Service people across the street in their observation post." This is from the commander of SO15.

"Which means that the terrorists knew my people were there and were watching them, and they cold-bloodedly took them out!" from Sir Andrew.

"Ah. I see."
Finally the Prime Minister loses his frown as understanding dawns.

"Yes, Sir. If it was this Iranian colonel who set off the explosion, then he has probably been aware of our surveillance since he was picked up by Arkoun at Heathrow, which in turn leads me to suspect that he has escaped from the scene somehow and is still on the loose." This from Sir Hugh.

"You don't think he's a suicide bomber then?"
Sir Hugh nearly chokes on his laughter:

"Hassan? A suicide bomber? I don't think so, Sir! He's more of the type to strap the belt on to somebody else and give them a slap on the back!"

"Oh dear."

"Which begs the question, Sir Hugh; why would a full colonel of Iran's secret service be sneaking into the UK? Why not just come here on a diplomatic passport as part of their embassy staff?"

Sir Andrew looks thoughtful. "We have to assume that he's here with a definite purpose in mind."

"Perhaps he's after a high-level target of some sort?"

"A bombing? Or an assassination? Perhaps he's here to murder Iranian dissidents living in the United Kingdom?"

"That's entirely within the realms of possibility, given Iran's clear hatred of dissidents. But it would have to be a very high priority target for the Iranians to risk their government being compromised, especially after they have just made this very public nuclear agreement recently with the United States? Why would they risk losing all of the international goodwill that they've just gained? Perhaps he's here to assassinate the Foreign Minister?" Sir Hugh can't resist twisting the knife: "Or perhaps he's after you Prime Minister?"

"Oh dear."

"Indeed, Sir."

TWENTY-TWO

18th June
Thames House, Millbank, London

It's not usual for the Director General of the Secret Intelligence Service to visit the headquarters of its sister organisation, the Security Service. In fact no one can remember it ever happening before. Therefore the whole building is buzzing with the news and with speculation as to why he's here. As Sir Hugh Metcalfe is escorted by security personnel through the corridors of Thames House, numerous staff members find sudden excuses to be in the same area of the building, stating that they have a message for so-and-so, or need to meet with so-and-so in order just to catch a glimpse of the big man. A man whom many of them think of as the enemy.

Sir Hugh, for his part, can imagine what's going on in the minds of the people around him, and he can feel the bitterness and jealousy that he knows is lurking beneath the brief smiles of welcome. The Firm and the Box have always been huge rivals and they have never been keen to share information with each other when it could be to their advantage not to, even if that sometimes means that the security of the UK is compromised. He accepts this state of affairs as a long-standing tradition, therefore the invitation to have a private lunch with Sir Andrew Lowe inside the headquarters of MI5 has come as a bit of a shock to him as well.

When he finally arrives at Sir Andrew's office, he's welcomed inside by the Director General's Personal Assistant, a motherly-looking rather frumpy woman in her late thirties:

135

"Please come inside, Sir. Can I take your coat?"

He hands her his expensive camel-hair overcoat and she disappears into a side room. He then walks across the plush carpet to where his host is sitting smiling behind a rather large polished oak desk.

"Ah, Sir Hugh! Welcome, welcome." The Director General of MI5 is in his early fifties, quite tall but slightly portly in build with greying hair cut in an old-fashioned short-back-and-sides style. He steps around from behind his desk to shake Sir Hugh's hand and indicates a comfortable looking sofa and chairs to one side of the office. "Would you like a tea or coffee?"

"Coffee, please," he answers, sitting himself down in one of the chairs. Sir Andrew joins him, sitting in a matching chair with a low coffee table between them.

Sir Hugh has never been one to beat about the bush. Even in his former role as the Metropolitan Police Commissioner he had never been known for his tact. Now he comes straight to the point:

"Why have you invited me here, Sir Andrew?" He waves his hand around to indicate the large office. Sir Andrew raises his own hand to forestall any other conversation as his PA steps back into the room.

"A coffee for Sir Hugh please, Mary and a mint tea for me I think."

"Certainly, Sir. Coming right up."

The woman bows her head in acknowledgement and disappears back into her own office, quietly pulling the door closed behind her.

Sir Andrew smiles at his colleague:

"I'd trust Mary with my life," he says. "But not with anything that has to do with John Smith!"

Sir Hugh's face drops.

"John Smith! What the hell's going on? I understood that you wanted to talk about this Iranian character who killed a couple of your field agents, not that bastard Smith?"

Sir Andrew grins at his colleague's anger. Ever since they had both been kidnapped by Smith and his group of ex-forces vigilantes calling themselves The Brotherhood just eight months before, both Sir Andrew and Sir Hugh had not spoken the man's name out loud to each other. This is despite the fact that they had come to an agreement with Smith and The Brotherhood that had given them

136

both a huge chunk of the credit for taking down the Albanian Mafia in the UK.

Both men stay quiet as Mary brings in their drinks on a tray and places it on the coffee table.

"Thank you, Mary. That will be all for now. Please make sure that we are not disturbed."

"Certainly, Sir." After she withdraws again into her own office Sir Hugh leans forward, his eyes angry and his lips drawn back:

"What the fuck is going on, Sir Andrew? Why the hell do I feel as though the roof is going to start tumbling in on our heads?"

"Ah, that would be because I've mentioned John Smith." Sir Andrew grins. "He always seems to have that effect on people!"
Sir Hugh flops back into his seat with a sigh. He stays still and quiet for a moment but then obviously makes up his mind about something. He leans forward again, his voice low:

"After our little meeting with Smith and his cronies, I spent some time digging into Smith's past with the Firm."
He pauses as though he's already said enough.

"Please go on, Sir Hugh. We are friends and there is nothing that you can say about the Firm's past dealings that will shock me. Besides I've read Smith's autobiography in the Sun, so I doubt that there's anything too surprising there."

"Mmmm. The trouble is that everything he says in his autobiography appears to be true, dammit, though it took me a long time to get to the bottom of it, I can tell you! Some of the older members of the Firm seem to have been having problems with their memories and it took a few swift kicks up their arses to get them to talk to me, even if I am their boss!" He sips at his coffee, giving himself a chance to calm down a bit. "It appears that Smith first earned his spurs with the Firm as an agent operating in the Rhodesian Army in the late 1970s, after that country had declared unilateral independence from Britain. Apparently he did a good enough job. It was information from Smith that allowed us to give that bastard Mugabe warnings about several attempts on his life, not that he ever proved to be grateful!" Sir Andrew nods his head in agreement. Robert Mugabe, the long-time President of Zimbabwe, is well known for his hatred of the British.

"After the war in Rhodesia ended, Smith worked for us again on a number of highly successful jobs, including the capture of a huge arms shipment due to be delivered by the Libyans to the IRA and a year-long operation delivering those same arms to the Mujahedeen fighting the Soviets in Afghanistan."

"It sounds like he was quite a successful agent?"

"Mmmm. I suppose we could say that about him." Sir Hugh sounds reluctant to give Smith any praise. "But then it all went to pot. He was captured by the Soviets in Afghanistan and underwent three months of interrogation. Eventually he was swapped for a low-level Russian operative and brought back to Britain in disgrace."

"Disgrace?"

"Yes! He had let the side down by getting himself captured, the bloody fool. It was lucky that the whole thing didn't blown up in our faces! Imagine the political fallout there would have been if our operations against the Soviets in Afghanistan had been made public?"

"Ah, yes. I doubt that our political masters would have been very happy about that."

"Too bloody true! Luckily for us the Russian spy that Smith was swapped for had also been up to some very newsworthy things, so the whole sordid affair evened itself out. The Russians kept quiet about our digressions and we kept quiet about theirs."

"That should have been the end of Smith's operations with the Firm. All of the psych assessments at the time stated that he was emotionally and mentally damaged by his ordeal, almost beyond repair. The man was an utter and complete bloody mess!"

"Then why did the Firm ever use him again?" Sir Andrew asks, genuinely curious.

"Baroness Thatcher, God Bless her, poked her bloody nose in, that's why. Do you remember the hotel bombing in Brighton in 1985?"

"Of course. The Provisional IRA very nearly killed the British Prime Minister! But what has that to do with Smith?"

"Nothing directly. It appears that dear old Maggie was so angry at the attempt on her life that she ordered one of my predecessors, Sir Thomas Sewell, to form a very secretive unit within the Firm."

"Ah, of course, I remember now. What was the unit called again?"

138

"The Increment." Sir Hugh almost spits the name out. "So much for bloody secrecy!"

Sir Andrew smiles gently and lays a hand on his colleague's arm.

"Don't fret so, Sir Hugh. This was all before your time."

"Mmmm. Anyway, Smith was the first one to be recruited by the Increment."

"But why? I thought you said he was in a complete mess after his interrogation by the Soviets?"

"Apparently. That was exactly *why* he was recruited. It was judged that his mental state at the time was ideal for us to use him as a bloody assassin."

"Dear God!"

"Don't blame him, Sir Andrew. Blame dear old Maggie and Sir Thomas!"

"No wonder the man hates us so much."

"That's only half of it. Smith went on to murder an awful lot of people for us, ranging from terrorists in Northern Ireland through to ex-British soldiers who were hiring themselves out to the drug cartels in Central and South America."

"To cut a long story short Smith totally flipped out in the end, and Sir Thomas had no choice but to discredit him and get him banged up for life. After all, he would have spilled the beans if he hadn't."

"Yes, I understand that of course, but it was very distasteful to frame Smith for the rape and murder of a young teenager, all the same."

"Needs must, Sir Andrew. Needs must."

"Yes, I suppose so."

"Anyway, as we know, Smith escaped during his trial and went on that bloody rampage. Not that it all went his own way though, as we eventually recaptured him and he was imprisoned for life. Then of course he engineered his escape from prison and faked his own death. At that point he had totally disappeared from the minds of both the Firm and the Increment until he emerged again at the head of The Brotherhood, and made his deal with the pair of us."

"It's a hell of a story!"

"Yes. And thankfully most of the general public and our political masters think that it's a load of old hogwash! Thank God!"

"Amen to that, Sir Hugh!"

The two men, possibly the most powerful two men in the entire United Kingdom, subside for a while and finish their drinks as they contemplate the past and how it almost went completely wrong for their respective agencies. Finally Sir Andrew shakes himself from his thoughts:

"I spoke to the Foreign Office early this morning." He pauses while he puts down his teacup. "They have heard back from their contemporaries in the Norwegian government, and they have given me some very interesting information about our Iranian friend Colonel Massoud Hassan."

Sir Hugh looks confused:

"What has this got to do with Smith? Why...."

Sir Andrew forestalls another question with a raised hand.

"Patience, Sir Hugh. All will be revealed." His colleague grunts in frustration, but nevertheless he sits back and listens. "It appears that Colonel Hassan was arrested for murder by the Norwegian police a few years ago." He sees the questioning look on his colleague's face. "No, it was no one special, just a local Lutheran priest at a village church in southern Norway, in a place called Flatdal Kyrkje. However, the colonel was deported from Norway for his involvement in the murder and sent back to Iran in disgrace."

"Yes, yes. We know that he was disgraced!"

"Ah, that's very true. But what we didn't know was that the good colonel had also possibly been involved in an operation against a certain Australian lady called Dr Linda Webb, who was living in Norway at the time."

"So?"

"So, I managed to track down the Norwegian policeman who had originally arrested Hassan...." He looks up his name on a sheet of paper lying on top of a manila file on the coffee table. "His name is Lars Gundersen. He's retired now, but at the time of the case he was an inspector in the National Criminal Investigation Service of the Norwegian Police.

140

What he had to say to me was very interesting indeed. He was never able to prove anything, but he believes that a British policeman was somehow involved with the Iranian and his hunt for this Dr Webb, a man by the name of Detective Chief Inspector Alan Davies. Apparently this Davies character was the same senior policeman that had originally arrested John Smith regarding the murder of the young girl; the murder that he had been framed for by the Firm." He looks across the table at Sir Hugh, almost accusingly, but the head of MI6 just shrugs his shoulders as if the framing of an innocent man isn't at all important in the grand scheme of things. Sir Andrew decides not to pursue the point any further, after all, where would it get him to antagonise his so-called colleague? He carries on: "Later, this Davies was seconded to the Firm and was tasked with trying to find Smith when he escaped the country after he murdered one of your predecessors, Sir Thomas Sewell, the very man who set up the Increment. This all took place before you took over the Firm of course."

Sir Hugh has become more intent now.

"Go on. This may become interesting."

"DCI Davies eventually located Smith when he was lying in hospital at death's door after taking on those terrorists aboard the 'Gambia Flight'. It was his work that led to Smith being imprisoned.

The Norwegian police inspector also informed me that DCI Davies had been found murdered in Norway, at the same time and in the same general area that Hassan had been arrested, and he thinks that the two events are somehow connected, although he has no idea how or why. But what he told me after this is where everything definitely becomes more interesting. Apparently the Norwegian police found some fingerprints at Dr Webb's cottage in Norway. Inspector Gundersen had the fingerprints checked through Interpol and guess who they belonged to?"

"Smith by any chance?"

"Absolutely correct! He couldn't do anything about it of course, as Smith had already been reported dead - he died in an 'accident' in a British prison."

"So what about this Webb woman? How is she involved with Hassan and Smith?"

"Well, it appears that Dr Linda Webb was the surgeon who operated on Smith when he was dying in hospital!"

"Bloody hell!"

"Exactly! I've made further enquiries about Dr Webb and it appears that she is now cohabiting with Smith in north Norfolk. She is his mistress!"

"Okay. It's all starting to make sense now, except for one thing: what the hell is the connection between this Iranian colonel and John Smith?"

"I think I might have the answer to that one too. I also spoke earlier to Nina Robbins."

"Nina Robbins?"

"Yes. She's the poor girl that we put in charge of our joint desk to hunt down Smith and The Brotherhood for us."

"Ah, the red herring...."

"Precisely....of course she has no idea that we are using Smith as a trouble-shooter now, nor that we are in fact in touch through Detective Inspector Wright with The Brotherhood, and working with them."

"A necessary subterfuge to keep the other law enforcement agencies off our backs."

"Indeed. Anyway I asked Miss Robbins to give me an abbreviated run-down on her progress to date and on the information that she has gathered on Smith, and that's when it all became clear to me!"

"So?"

"When Smith killed those terrorists on board the Gambia Flight, the Iranian Supreme Leader issued a Fatwa, a death sentence on Smith. There's a half a million pound reward on him."

"Of course. We know that."

"But, if I remember correctly, Smith informed the two of us last year that he had paid an undercover visit to Tehran, and that he had ended up killing the head of the Iranian Ministry of Intelligence and National Security."

"So he did."

"Perhaps, just perhaps, this Colonel Hassan has been sent to the United Kingdom to hunt down John Smith?"

"Excellent! With any luck he'll manage to do it and we'll be rid of the bastard once and for all!"

"I agree. Smith is a potential thorn in our side, even though he is ostensibly working for us now. However, there is an inherent danger in all of this."

"And that is?"

"If it becomes public knowledge that Smith is still alive and that he is now working for us, it will be the end of our careers."

"Ah."

"Exactly; 'Ah'."

"Well, I don't imagine that you've gone to the trouble of inviting me here and not have a solution to this problem in mind?"

"Very true. First of all we must make every effort to keep any mention of a connection between this Hassan and Smith totally secret and just between the two of us."

"I agree entirely."

"Secondly, we have to do something to negate both of these problems, the Iranian and Smith."

"Some sort of direct action?"

"Not necessarily, at least not yet. If we are right then either Hassan or Smith will meet their end when the two run into each other, and despite Smith's record I wouldn't necessarily bet on him winning. This Iranian looks to be a useful character too."

"With any luck they'll both kill each other!"

"That would be ideal, but I wouldn't bank on it. I think that we need to monitor this situation as it develops very carefully, and we should be equally careful about the amount and content of information that we feed to our colleagues in the government."

"Yes. It is imperative that no one finds out about our involvement with Smith, and that we don't incriminate ourselves in any way."

"Of course." Sir Andrew sighs. "It's a shame really. I quite like Smith."

This is met with a snort of derision from Sir Hugh:

"You do? I can't stand the cocky bastard!"

"I'd noticed." He sighs again. "Now that we've agreed I'm beginning to feel hungry. There is a very good delicatessen not too far from here. I thought I'd send Mary out with an order. Do you fancy that?"

"Yes, I'm famished."

"Okay, I'll call her…"

TWENTY-THREE

18th June
Thames House, Millbank, London

Nina Robbins is very nervous as she is guided into the Director General's office by Mary, the DG's Personal Assistant. Like most of the staff in the building she's heard about the unusual visit paid by the chief of MI6 to her own boss earlier that day, and is afraid that that visit may have had something to do with her and her 'desk'. After all, hers is the only unit operated jointly between MI5 and MI6, with personnel from both services under her command. Her anxiety is not helped by the fact that the motherly-looking Mary is not acting at all friendly towards her as she has done in the past whenever she's been summoned in front of the great man. She hopes that that isn't a bad omen.

As she enters the large plush office she sees that Sir Andrew is seated behind the polished oak desk, his head tilted down as he reads something in front of him. She quietly pads across the deep pile carpet until she's standing in front of the desk, but Sir Andrew still doesn't look up at her. He is totally engrossed in his reading. Eventually, Nina clears her throat to attract his attention and her boss finally deigns to look up.

"Ah, Nina. Thank you for coming to see me so promptly." She notices that although his face is cheerful, the smile on his lips has not got quite as far as his eyes, which remain cold and appraising. She is also aware that he neither stands up to greet her nor offers her a seat on the comfortable chairs to one side of the room, as he has always done in the past. She feels increasingly tense with every passing second.

"That's okay, Sir Andrew. I was in the building when I received your request for a meeting."

144

She hopes that she sounds more confident than she is feeling.

"Mmmm. I know." Finally he leans back in his chair, looking a bit more relaxed. "I've had a talk with Sir Hugh this morning about your desk." I knew it, I'm for the chop! "As you will have heard, we have suffered a very real tragedy with the loss of two of our field agents in the bombing at Luton." What the fuck does this have to do with me?

"Yes, Sir. It's very sad."

"Of course. It also means that every available resource we have is being diverted in order to find the man who killed them."

"Yes, Sir." What else can I say?

"Exactly how many agents do you have working on your desk, Miss Robbins?" For a second she's taken aback by the quick change of subject.

"Twenty-two, Sir, including myself and Rebecca Harris, my second-in-command. Eleven from the Box and eleven from the Firm."

"I know that we have spoken about this recently, but remind me. Exactly how many members of this vigilante group known as The Brotherhood have you managed to get convicted?"

"None, Sir." Her reply is no more than a hoarse whisper.

"Speak up, Miss Robbins! How many did you say?" In contrast Sir Andrew's voice is growing louder and angrier.

"I said 'none', Sir," she stammers. "But I did explain that the information we supplied to various police forces around the country led to fifteen people being arrested for vigilante crimes, Sir, including GBH and attempted murder!"

"Yes, you did. But none of the fifteen suspects were even charged for the crimes, were they Miss Robbins?" His voice is dripping acid now.

"No, Sir. No, they weren't."

"And why was that, Miss Robbins? Remind me again, will you?"

"Because the evidence was lost, Sir."

"Lost by whom?"

"By the police, Sir. Or by my desk."

"Your desk?"

"Yes, Sir. The evidence was either lost by the police or lost whilst in transit from here to the police forces involved in the different cases, Sir."

"In all fifteen cases?"

"Yes Sir."

"Mmmmm. Not a very good record of achievement for you, is it Miss Robbins?"

"No, Sir."

She looks down, thoroughly ashamed.

"It appears that The Brotherhood may have many more fingers in a wider range of pies than either of us expected, eh? Perhaps even in your own desk?" Her head comes back up at the softening of the Director General's tone. "I believe that you have two teams carrying out covert surveillance on John Smith's sons?"

"That's correct, Sir."

"Have you had any results?"

"No, Sir."

"Have you come across anything that even remotely suggests that Smith is still alive and that he is a part of The Brotherhood? Apart from the initial intelligence that we were given by our agent Martin Fisher?"

"No, Sir. Nothing at all."

"Mmmmm." He taps a finger against his chin as he sinks into deep contemplation for a minute. Nina stands absolutely still, hardly daring to breath. She knows that whatever her boss says next may well lead to the end of what was promising to be a good career for her in MI5. "Having talked at some length with Sir Hugh about this, he is graciously letting me take the decision on what to do with your desk. Despite the fact that you have had no success whatsoever, I am inclined to believe that this may not be due to incompetence on your part. I think it may be down to the feelings of some of our ex-military personnel who seem to favour what The Brotherhood is doing to punish criminals and prevent wrongdoing in our society - a response that appears to be echoed even in the corridors of power in parliament. Therefore, I cannot entirely blame you for this. You will remain in charge of your desk, and Miss Harris will remain as your second-in-command." Nina feels a rush of relief and struggles not to show it on her face. "However, I am going to cut your manpower. How many field agents are involved in the surveillance on Smith's sons?"

"Eight at any one time, Sir. Though I swap them around as much as I can to prevent them becoming complacent and sloppy, Sir."

"I see." Again he taps a finger against his chin as he calculates what to do. "I am reallocating eight of your people, Miss Robbins. I need every agent that I can find if we are to catch the man who killed our colleagues before he kills again. That will leave you with twelve field agents."

"Thank you, Sir." It could be worse, a hell of a lot worse!

"I strongly suggest that you continue with your surveillance of John Smith's sons. Twelve agents should be enough to be able to swap the teams around a bit and give them some time off." He stares at her intently. "If there is even the slightest hint that Smith is still alive, or even that someone else may be looking for him or attempting to contact him through his sons, I want to know about it instantly. Do you understand Nina? Instantly!"

"Yes, Sir!" What the fuck is all this sudden interest in Smith?

"Okay, you're dismissed."

She almost runs from the room before he can change his mind.

EGYPT

TWENTY-FOUR

19th June
Hurghada, Egypt

Smith's first meeting with the American CIA agent Robert
O'Brian turns out to be hard work. On the surface he looks and
acts like a gung-ho Yank working for the CIA. The ex-SEAL is a
short, stocky guy with a buzz-cut who wears sun-glasses and
chews gum all the time. Smith cannot initially figure out whether
O'Brian's outward appearance is a deliberate show intended to put
people completely at their ease because they think that he's a
knob-head, or whether it's designed to really piss them off. Either
way, Smith is secretly impressed with how cool the man appears.

Robert O'Brian, on the other hand is not impressed by Smith,
or at least not by his age. The first words that he utters when they
meet are:

"Jeez. You're a bit over-the-hill for this game, aren't yer
fella?"

"You're no spring chicken yourself, mate," is Smith's instant
angry retort.

"I'm not even forty yet, fella, but you, what are you? Sixty
plus?"

"Not quite yet."

"You can't be far off it though. Am I right?"

"Mid-fifties, mate."

"Really? Jeez. All I can say is that you must have had a hard
life, fella!"

"Cheers."

"Are you sure that you'll be able to keep up?"

Smith looks the American up and down, noting the strong defined
profile under his tropical shirt, his flat stomach and his short

powerful-looking legs. The man looks fit enough, though a little heavy with muscle, which in Smith's opinion looks good, but is not much of an advantage for a foot soldier. After all, all that muscle is just extra weight to carry around. Smith smiles.

"I'll manage somehow, mate."

The American grunts in reply. Then he asks:

"Are you ex-S.A.S.?"

"None of your business, mate."

"Okay, fair enough. But you are ex-army, right?"

Smith nods at this one.

"I'm ex-Navy myself."

"I know, mate, but I'm sure you'll get over it in time."

"Hhmmmm. I can see that we're not going to get on very well, are we, fella?"

"I guess that just about sums it up, mate."

"Hhmmmm."

"You've said that once already."

"Hhmmmm."

Despite their differences and the American's annoying habit of coming straight out and saying out loud what he's thinking, as they start to work together, Smith finds himself liking O'Brian's wit and dry sense of humour more and more. He's also impressed by the man's professionalism. He's not sure whether the feelings are reciprocated though. O'Brian appears to be a man who is not easily impressed.

Not long after Smith's and O'Brian's first meeting, Dwayne Huntsbringer and Mike Oldport decide that they've waited long enough for official action. It's been almost ten days since Margot and Sheila were kidnapped, and despite assurances from their own government representatives, not a lot has happened. No satellites have been re-directed over Egypt to try and locate their loved ones, as they're all too busy over Syria and Iraq where they are helping the coalition forces to locate and then bomb the hell out of the Islamic State militants. Even the Egyptians appear to be far more concerned with trying to keep the internal peace of their own country than helping two foreigners find their kidnapped loved ones. Plus their own air force are now totally focused on bombing the IS militants in Libya in revenge for the beheading of twenty-one Egyptian Coptic Christians back in January. Apart from the deployment of the US SEAL team to the Dutch naval vessel on patrol in the Red Sea, nothing appears to have happened.

Extremely fed up with the lack of positive action, Huntsbringer and Oldport elect to go after the Somali kidnappers themselves. They travel north to Cairo and begin to put the word out in the bars and restaurants there that they're looking for a small team of mercenaries to help them.

Of course the British, American and Dutch governments are not very pleased at this turn of events and they try to dissuade the two men from their chosen course of action. In reality though there is little that they can do to stop them in a foreign country. The Egyptian authorities are staying quiet about the whole thing, perhaps glad that the problem is being taken out of their hands. They have enough on their plate keeping the Muslim Brotherhood in check, and now they have the very real fear that IS will begin to target Egyptian cities with suicide bombers or gunmen. The whole region appears to be sinking into turmoil and a small group of kidnapped tourists is not very high on anyone's agenda at the moment.

O'Brian is more than a little pissed off with Smith when he finds out that the Brit may have been the one to give Huntsbringer and Oldport the idea of going after their wives themselves, but Smith just gives him one of his infuriating smiles when the American confronts him about it:

"Good on them, is what I say, mate. Nobody else is doing fuck all to help them."

"I've been ordered to join them, covertly of course. I put you up for the job but apparently Huntsbringer and Oldport know your face already and think that you're a British police detective." Smith does his best to hide a look of smug satisfaction, but fails miserably. The American grins then continues:

"So I asked my bosses to talk to your bosses and it's been agreed that you will be going along as my back-up. Out of sight of the damn cowboys of course."

Smith's face falls. He has a good idea what this means; spending day after day in the heat and dust of the Eastern Desert until they find the kidnappers, or not as the case may be.

"Super."

TWENTY-FIVE

21st June
Mojo's Lounge and Bar, Sarayat El Gezira Street, Cairo, Egypt

Mojo's Lounge and Bar is a very moody place. The lighting is muted with lanterns placed high up on dark walls glowing down softly on to the wood furnishings and dark red drapes hanging around numerous booths and alcoves. It's located on the top deck of the 'Imperial Boat', a large ex-river cruiser anchored permanently on the Nile and just one of the dozens of floating restaurants on cruise ships based along that section of the world-famous river. With its open air atmosphere and fabulous views of the Nile amid the backdrop of the city's lights, it is a comfortable, inviting and rather exotic location.

However, Smith and Helen Wright are not here to enjoy Cairo's nightlife. They're sitting tucked away at a small table in a corner booth, hidden by a series of heavy curtains hanging around the booth to afford them privacy. The waiters probably think that they're acting like a normal pair of romantic westerners on holiday, but they're not. As they tuck into their Mahshi hamān, an Egyptian speciality which is basically grilled pigeons stuffed with rice and herbs, and sip wine as they gaze into each other eyes like star-crossed lovers, they are also listening into the conversation that is going on about thirty metres from them at another table through the small wireless receivers hidden deep inside their left ears.

The dialog they are interested in is happening at a table in another larger booth, and there are five men sitting around it. Dwayne Huntsbringer and Mike Oldport both look tired and worn out. Their clothes are crumpled and stained and both of them have several days growth of stubble on their chins. Their eyes are tired

154

and have dark bags of skin beneath them, testifying to their many nights of broken sleep. Sitting on the opposite side of the table from the two friends and nursing cold beers in tall glasses are three other men. The first is the American CIA agent, Robert O'Brian (though he has of course introduced himself under the false name of Robert Carling) and it is he who is wearing the hidden microphone so that Smith and Helen can listen in.

Dwayne Huntsbringer looks up from the slim laptop sitting on the table in front of him to look at his fellow North American. Just for once O'Brian has removed his shades and his startlingly pale blue eyes look back into Dwayne's with no hint of guile or dishonesty.

"So, you say that you're an ex-SEAL, Mister Carling?"

"I am an ex-SEAL."

"Okay. You'll understand that we've got to be sure that you are who you say you are, and that you're going to be able to help us?"

Huntsbringer looks at the other two men as well as O'Brian as he speaks.

"Of course, that's not a problem, Mister Huntsbringer. But you're an ex-Ranger yourself aren't you, Sir? You'll understand that men like me don't carry around testimonials. What I did in the SEALs, even the fact that I served in the SEALs is classified information."

"I understand, Mister Carling. However, all servicemen know about the history and organisation of their units. After all, it's a part of our training and our culture, isn't it? So I'll just ask you a few questions to set our minds at rest, if you don't mind?"

"No, Sir. You go ahead."

O'Brian smiles.

"Good. When did you join the US Navy?"

"Eighteen years ago."

"And you served in the SEALs for....."

"Sixteen years."

"What have you been doing since?"

"Since I left the navy? Let me see....a bit of this and a bit of that. I've kept my hand in, you might say, taking on small freelance opportunities such as this one."

"Anything that you care to tell us about?"

155

"No. I don't think so."

"Okay." Huntsbringer types a query into the internet on his laptop, which is operating on the restaurant's Wi-Fi signal. He quickly reads through the Wikipedia entry for SEAL Team Six. "Can you tell me the name of the first commanding officer of SEAL Team Six?"

O'Brian smiles again at this one.

"It was before my time, but that would be Richard Marcinko. He was in command from 1980 until 1983, which was a little unusual as naval officers typically held command positions for a duration of only two years at that time."

"When was SEAL Team Six officially disbanded?"

"1987."

"What is the name of the unit that succeeded it?"

"Well Jeez, everyone still calls it SEAL Team Six of course, but its official designation these days is the 'United States Naval Special Warfare Development Group' or 'DEVGRU' for short, and it's a component of the Joint Special Operations Command." Huntsbringer types in another query: 'Weapons used by SEAL Team Six.' The Wi-Fi's a little slow but it soon comes up with a list of entries. He chooses one at random from near the top of the page: americanspecialops.com, and browses through.

"Have you ever done any sniping during your time in the team?

"Yes."

"What weapon did you use?"

O'Brian eyes almost mist over with pleasant memories.

"Jeez, I had a lot of choice over weapons in those days, but my personal favourite is the McMillan TAC-338 Sniper Rifle. It weighs 11 lbs, has a barrel length of 26.5 inches, and is fed by a five round magazine. It's chambered with a .338 Lapua Magnum round that is designed to engage soft targets out to longer ranges than other cartridges, such as the .300 Winmag for instance. My personal best distance at taking out a target with the McMillan was two thousand metres, but I heard tell that a compatriot of mine, Chris Kyle – you know, the famous 'American Sniper' killed a bad guy at two thousand one hundred metres in Iraq with the same weapon." He smiles again at Huntsbringer. "Is that detailed enough for you, Sir?"

Dwayne glances sideways at Mike. Their eyes meet and he nods.

"He appears to be genuine." O'Brian snorts softly to himself at this. "You're in, Mister Carling."

Dwayne turns to the second of the three men sitting opposite. This guy is a small slender Egyptian, with dark eyes that seem very large in proportion to the rest of his face and a very dark, almost black skin. He is dressed casually in jeans and an open-necked shirt but he gives an overall impression of neatness and compactness.

"I don't understand why you're here, Ibrahim? I know that you own the camping and diving safari that we were booked on for our vacation, but we're looking for soldiers to help us, preferably from Special Forces." The Egyptian turns his large dark eyes on to Dwayne and the American can almost feel the intensity of the man's emotions through them. He speaks in perfect English without any trace of an accent, in short clipped sentences:

"There are two reason why I'm here, Mister Huntsbringer. The first is that you and your wives, plus the other tourists who were kidnapped by these Somali scum came to my country expecting to have a peaceful vacation. That this despicable crime has happened to you is a blot on my personal integrity. I am *shamed* by it!"

"You don't have to be, Ibrahim," says Mike gently. "It was none of your doing."
The Egyptian bows his head in acknowledgement.

"It is kind of you to say so. Nevertheless. I own the company and I feel a certain amount of responsibility for what has happened to you." Mike is just about to interrupt again, but Ibrahim silences him with a raised palm. "Please let me continue, Mister Oldport. My second reason for coming here is that I too am an ex-Special Forces soldier. I served in the Egyptian Army for twelve years in the 616th Marine Commando Battalion of the 153rd Special Forces Regiment as a specialist member of an Underwater Demolition Team. I was a part of the Sa'ka Forces.

I saw active combat against the Iraqis in the First Gulf War, just like you, Mister Huntsbringer. After I left the service I made a small fortune working as a deep sea diver on the North Sea oil rigs which is why I was able to set up my own diving and safari company, but I have never forgotten the hard lessons that I learned as a Marine Commando, and I am still an excellent shot and very, very fit."

Dwayne nods to show he understands and pauses for a moment to type in another query to google: '153rd Special Forces Regiment'.

The third entry down on his screen is the Wikipedia entry for the Egyptian Army. Huntsbringer clicks on it and then scrolls down through a long list of the army's structure until he comes to 'Special Forces Corps'. The 153rd is listed as a Special Forces Regiment/Group, but there's no direct link to it, so he clicks on the Special Forces Corps hyperlink that's in blue font. This brings him to another Wikipedia page entitled: 'Sa'ka Forces'. He scrolls down and finds an entry for the 153rd Regiment which includes a mention of 616th Marine Commando Battalion. It's pretty obvious to him that Ibrahim is on the level, but he throws in a random question anyway:

"Can you tell us what Sa'ka means, Ibrahim?" He has a slight problem pronouncing the word but the Egyptian smiles, understanding what he means.

"The origin of the name, which means 'Thunderbolt' in English, is taken from a military unit that was established over three thousand years ago by Ramesses the Great, the most warlike and powerful of all the Pharaohs. It is now the Egyptian Army military unit to which all of our Special Forces belong." Ibrahim leans forward with his hands flat on the table. His voice is calm but his eyes are angry: "I am an Egyptian. This is *my* country and these...." He gestures around the lounge. "...are *my* people. You will need me to help you. Can any of you even speak Arabic?" O'Brian is the only one to answer:

"I can speak a little Arabic, but not Egyptian Arabic."
The small Egyptian simply shrugs his shoulders to emphasise his point.

"Thank you, Ibrahim." Both Dwayne and Mike look at each other again, and both of them nod emphatically. "You're in." Dwayne turns to the third and final man sitting on the other side of the table.

"Mister Frank Robinson?"

"Yeah. That's me, mate." The third man is tall and lean, almost skinny. His face is long and pale-skinned, and his teeth are too large for his mean-looking mouth. His hair is cut close to the scalp in a buzz-cut like O'Brian's and he speaks with a broad cockney accent.

"So, you served in the Special Air Service Regiment?"

"That's right, mate. Eight years in the S.A.S."

At this point Mike takes over the questioning. He's read a few books on the S.A.S., and fancies himself as a bit of an expert on the subject of the British Army's most famous Special Forces Regiment:

"So what was the regiment that you started out in when you joined up?"

"The Paras. Four years, before I took selection."

"Which battalion?"

"The Second."

"What squadron did you join in the S.A.S.?"

For a moment Robinson falters in his quick fire answers:

"D Squadron."

"Which troop?"

"Seven Troop; freefall."

Mike looks pointedly at Dwayne who types in: '7 Troop, SAS' as a query on his laptop. There are lots of entries listed for a book entitled: 'Seven Troop' written by Andy McNab. Without clicking on any of them it's plain from the writing beneath the entries that 7 Troop is in B Squadron. Suddenly the Wi-Fi connection drops off, leaving a frozen screen. Dwayne sighs and pushes the laptop to Mike keeping the screen hidden from the English man. Mike bluffs it out:

"Forgive me if I'm wrong, but Seven Troop is actually in B Squadron, not in D?"

The cockney answers rather too glibly and quickly:

"That's right. Sorry, mate. I meant to say B Squadron. I got transferred to D Squadron later when I was posted to Afghanistan. My mistake, mate."

"Hmmm. You've told us that you served in the First Gulf War. What did you do there?"

"I was in 'Scud Alley', wasn't I, mate. Did for all of them Scud Missile launchers that were aimed at the Jews." He can see that neither Mike nor Dwayne are looking too convinced, so he steps it up a gear. "Have you heard of John Smith?"

159

"No, I can't say that I have, Mister Robinson." For a moment Mike can't place the name.

"You must have. He's the geezer who killed all of them terrorists on that flight from Africa a few years ago!"

"Oh, *that* John Smith, of course. What about him?"

"Well, I worked with him, didn't I. Him and me were muckers." He crosses two of his fingers. "Close as this we were."

"So?"

"So? Only the best fucking Special Forces soldier there ever was, and me and him were mates, weren't we?"

"Like I said Mister Robinson; so what?"

The cockney sighs with desperation.

"Look, mate. I can handle meself in a fire-fight, alright!"

Dwayne looks across the table at O'Brian, whose face is giving nothing away, and then sideways at Mike. Mike shrugs and leans across to whisper in his friend's ear:

"These are the only guys who have come forward, Dwayne. It wouldn't hurt to have another gun with us, would it? Even if he's not entirely kosher?"

Dwayne looks back at Robinson for a minute.

"Okay. You're in."

The English man sighs in relief.

"We need to talk about your terms of service," says Mike. "We're both well-off, but we're not rich. We can only afford to pay each of you two hundred pounds."

"What? A week?" This from the cockney.

"No! Two hundred pounds a day. That's all we can afford."

The three men nod at this, accepting.

"What about insurance?" asks Robinson.

"Insurance? I don't understand?"

"In case we're killed or badly injured. What will you pay out if we don't come back or come back but with bits missing?" The cockney laughs nervously.

"Ah, I see. How would, say, twenty thousand pounds sound to you?"

"Make it thirty?"

"Okay. Thirty thousand it is. Does everyone agree?"

Both O'Brian and Ibrahim nod in the affirmative. Dwayne speaks up again:

"We need to talk about the operation, but first we need to get hold of some weapons. Any ideas?"

Ibrahim smiles.

"Don't worry about weapons, Mister Huntsbringer. I have a half-brother who is an officer in the Egyptian police force. He can get us all of the assault rifles and ammunition that we will need, for a price of course."

"Great. When can you set it up?"

"I will talk to him tonight. We should be able to collect the weapons tomorrow morning."

"Great!" Dwayne claps his hands together. "Now, let's talk tactics……."

Thirty metres away, tucked up in their booth, John Smith and Helen Wright have had good reception throughout of the men's brief conversation, hearing every word as clearly as though they were sitting right next to them.

Helen looks across enquiringly when Harry Robinson boasts about knowing Smith, but he only grins back at her and shakes his head, mouthing the words:

"I've never met him before; he must be a wannabe." He makes the universal sign for a 'wanker' with a flick of his wrist.

Helen smiles back at him, leaning in close to the ear that is not fitted with a receiver and whispering:

"I'll check up on him through the Firm." Her breath feels hot on Smith's ear and the caress of it on his skin sends a slight tremor through his body.

Helen senses the tremor rather than feels it and she glances up and sees that Smith is staring into her eyes. Immediately he snatches his eyes away, as though he has been caught in a naughty act, and quickly picks up his glass of wine, taking a long drink from it. Helen feels a shaft of deep warmness in her loins at her nearness to Smith, and quickly pulls away herself, taking a deep gulp out of her own glass, her hand shaking slightly. For a moment both of them are too embarrassed to say anything, then the spell is suddenly broken as they hear through their earpieces that the group of conspirators is breaking up and going their separate ways for the night.

Within five minutes the American agent is the only one of the five that remains in the lounge. He goes to the bar for a drink.

A few minutes later, Smith and Helen, their meal finished, also head for the bar, sitting down on bar stools next to O'Brian, whom they both greet as though he's an old friend that they haven't seen for ages, just in case someone, anyone, is watching.

"Jeez. That was a bit tense." He smiles at them, his shades firmly back over his eyes. "I'll get the Company to check out that Ibrahim character. What about the English dude?"

"No worries. Helen will be on to it as soon as we get back to the hotel."

"They're planning to move out in three days' time, once we've got all of our supplies together. Huntsbringer has hired two Land Rover Discoverys and the Egyptian is supposed to be supplying the weaponry. I take it that you will be trailing us somehow?"

"Yes, mate. You know that offer of equipment that you made before dinner?"

"Yes?"

"I'd like to take you up on it. If I ask my own people for the amount of kit that I'll need, it'll take two months before it gets here and I'll have to sign a thousand bits of paper before they hand it over. I'm guessing that your boys on the frigate will have everything I need?"

"Sure, no problem."

"How about delivery?"

"I'll arrange a helo to drop the stuff off down at the coast. Just give me a day and time when you can pick it up."

"Great. How about the morning after tomorrow? That'll give me time to get down there, plus it'll also give me time to zero in the rifle while I wait for you and the others to arrive in the area."

"That's fine. I'll set up the drop as soon as I get back to my room. Will seven a.m. do you?" Smith nods in the affirmative. "Perfect. I'm guessing that we'll start our search at the spot where the kidnapper's vehicles left the main road and they dumped the minibus." The stocky American sips his cocktail, looking across at Smith he changes the subject flawlessly:

"Are you sure you'll be able to handle an M82 at your age? It's a seriously powerful weapon." Smith searches the American's face for a tell-tail sign of humour, but can't spot anything. Either

162

the man is very, very good at hiding his emotions, or he really does have his doubts about Smith's age and abilities. Either way, Smith decides not to rise to the bait.

"Jeez mate, I'll manage somehow." He still can't resist a sarcastic answer though. "If you get into a spot of bother in the desert, I'll do my best not to shoot you by mistake."

The Yank looks back at him, his face wooden and his eyes cloaked by the sunglasses. He answers in a dry voice:

"I'd sure appreciate that, fella."

Helen can sense the tenseness between the two men, and she feels her anger growing.

"Will you two grow up! The last thing we need on this job is a pissing contest between you two schoolboys!"

They both look at her in surprise.

"Roger that."

"Jeez, okay. Helen."

"Good!"

There's an uncomfortable silence for a moment, which is eventually broken by O'Brian:

"You know, it's funny that that fella Robinson mentioned John Smith, the S.A.S. guy..." Both Smith and Helen tense up at the American's statement, but he doesn't seem to notice, as he's too caught up in his memories. "...my dad once worked for the Company. When we saw that Smith had killed all of them God damn terrorists on that African plane, my dad told me that he had once worked with the guy years ago, down in Colombia. Apparently this Smith had been attached to my dad's unit and he'd got to know him quite well. He said that they'd had a great time once in Bogotá, but he wouldn't tell me what they got up to."

Helen looks over the American's shoulder at Smith, but his face gives nothing away.

"Why is it that everyone goes on about this bloody Smith character?" Helen asks, intent now on not looking at Smith.

"Well, my dad is an ex-marine. He did three tours of Nam before he went into the agency, so he knows his stuff, and he says that Smith was the best God damn soldier he had ever known, on either side of the Atlantic. Coming from my dad that is mighty praise indeed!"

"Is your father still alive?" Helen asks.

163

"My dad? Sure, he's sixty eight years old and still as fit as a fiddle!"

"What's his first name?"

"Daniel. But everybody always called him Danny. Why do you ask?"

"No reason. Just being polite."

TWENTY-SIX

21st June
Four Seasons Hotel, Giza Street, Cairo, Egypt

Helen Wright's room on the fifth floor of the Four Seasons Hotel is smart and elegant, and thankfully the almost silent air conditioning unit is efficiently keeping it a lot cooler and humid than it is outside in the North African night. Smith sighs as he sips at a cool beer he's just pinched from her refrigerator.

"What was all that about with O'Brian?"
Helen looks over at him naively. She's just plonked down herself down on the edge of the big plush double bed.

"All what with O'Brian?"

"Don't come the innocent with me, my girl." Smith tries to look stern, but after a second or two he can't help smiling. Obviously he's just too mellowed out after an excellent meal and a few glasses of wine, and all at the UK government's expense. He could get used to this life. "You know what I mean, pumping the Yank for information about me."

"Oh that." Helen smiles back, relaxed herself. "I just wanted to know why everyone I talk to thinks you're such a great hero." Smith snorts.

"Don't be daft! There's nothing bloody heroic about me! All the real heroes that I've ever known are dead. I'm a survivor, nothing more."

"Sure. I believe you, John." She decides to change the subject slightly: "Did you know him? O'Brian's dad I mean."

"Yeah. I didn't realise he was his dad though. Danny was a good bloke."

"Was it during that time you mentioned before, when you worked with the CIA?"

165

"Yep. That was a long time ago though. Must have been...."
He pauses to think and have another sip of beer. "Jesus, it must have been early in 1984! Over thirty years ago. Bloody hell. I was in the SAS at the time, and I was sent over to cross-train with the American Green Berets, their Special Forces – sort of equivalent to the SAS, at Fort Bragg in North Carolina. In hindsight though I don't think they really needed me; it was just a way for my boss to get rid of me for a few months. I was a bit of a square peg in a round hole in those days and I don't think my colonel ever knew what to make of me or what to do with me."
He laughs at this.

"Anyway, I was sent there to train the Green Berets in Close Target Reconnaissance skills, which was my specialised patrol skill at the time." Helen frowns at this so Smith explains: "CTR is when a small group of soldiers sneak up right close to the enemy, often into their actual positions, to gather intelligence. The trick of it is to get in and out without anyone knowing you was ever there."

"It wasn't just soldiers I ended up training though. There was also a small group of guys from the Special Operations Group from the Special Activities Division of the Central Intelligence Agency in amongst them. These guys were all ex-army or marines, like O'Brian's dad, and they carried out most of the cloak-and-dagger sneaky-beaky 'black ops' stuff for the Company. I liked them. They were quietly-spoken and totally unassuming, quite unlike the Special Forces guys, but by fuck they knew their stuff."

"So how come you ended up working with O'Brian's dad in Colombia if you were just there to train them?"
Smith looks slightly embarrassed at this.

"Ah. You see I was young and a bit gung ho in those days, Helen. I sort of invited myself along on their first few missions. I justified it to my own bosses and the Yanks by saying that I wanted to polish up their training 'on the job' so to speak."

"You mean that you *volunteered* to go to South America? You volunteered to step into another war that had nothing whatsoever to do with you? You, who's always telling me that you're not a hero and that you've always tried to avoid any fighting of any kind?"
Helen finishes in a 'holier than thou' voice with another innocent look.

166

"Okay! Okay! Like a said; I was young and stupid!" He holds up his hands. "But remember that Colombia was the centre of the cocaine trade in those days. A trade that was worth something like twenty billion dollars a year to the Colombian cartels, but which caused untold misery to the poor buggers that abused the stuff in the States and over in Europe. It was important to do our bit."

"Mmmm. Please go on."

"There's not much more to tell. I was only in Colombia for just over a week and I helped the CIA guys take out one of the leaders of the Cali cartel, and we did a few Close Target Recce's on a couple of small DMPs – Drug Manufacturing Plants, hidden deep in the jungle. Then I helped them plan out the follow-up attacks to be carried out by the Colombian anti-narcotics police, with a little back-up from the CIA and the Drugs Enforcement Agency guys on the ground. End of story."

"What about Bogotá?"

"Bogotá?"

"Yep, O'Brian mentioned that you and his dad had 'a great time in Bogotá'. What was that all about?"

"Ah, yes, Bogotá. Well, that's another story...."

TWENTY-SEVEN

25th April 1984
Embassy District, Bogotá, Colombia

At first the short and stocky ex-US Marine and CIA operative, Danny O'Brian and the tall lean British Army sergeant, John Smith, didn't hit it off that well ('like father, like son'). O'Brian was an old school Irish Catholic American who judged the British to be a brutal occupying force in Northern Ireland suppressing a Catholic majority in the province. To Danny, the men of the Provisional Irish Republican Army were genuine heroes; freedom fighters. To Smith (who by this time had spent a total of twenty-one months fighting the Provos across the water, and another two months undercover in Cyprus, where he had helped to put a stop to a large arms shipment on its way to Northern Ireland from Libya), the IRA were indiscriminate killers and nothing but cowards.

When they were off-duty the two men argued incessantly about the conflict in Northern Ireland. So much so that they drove away the other members of the CIA's team who were being trained by Smith. The two men's vocal quarrels would send the others heading off and preferring to drink with the Green Berets who they were sharing the course with when they hit one of the many bars in Fort Bragg.

Despite the fact that their views about the 'Irish Problem' differed so much, the two men did have a lot in common. Both of them had spent the formative years of their careers fighting overseas for their respective countries in 'dirty' wars. The American had been in Vietnam, where he had served three tours with the marines, the last two with the 3rd Force Reconnaissance Company. The English man had been in Rhodesia, where he had served in some of the most famous anti-insurgent regiments in the world, including the Selous Scouts and the Rhodesian Special Air Service Regiment. Gradually, over time, they began to acquire a grudging respect for each other, though they could never agree about the problems in Northern Ireland.

Smith, in particular impressed the American with his professionalism and his reconnaissance skills, but also with the easy way that he passed on those skills to his trainees and the fact that he never stinted in trying to get the most out of them. Danny O'Brian, for his part, impressed the hell out of Smith by applying himself to everything that he did with one hundred and ten per cent effort and dedication.

By the time the seven-weeks of intensive training came to an end, O'Brian and Smith were the very best of friends and trusted each other implicitly, much to the amazement of everyone on the course who had heard them arguing together almost from day one. It was not surprising therefore that at that juncture, even though the official training was over, that Smith bluffed and bullied his way into accompanying the boys from the Special Operations Group into Colombia. and that Danny O'Brian made sure that he would be attached to his team. A week of operating in a hostile environment and sharing life-threatening dangers together meant the two men became even closer. They were inseparable.

It was in this setting that Smith's last two days with the Americans was to be spent Resting and Recuperating in possibly the most exciting city in the world at that point in time; Colombia's capital – Bogotá.

Bogotá, located high up on a plateau in the eastern Andes, had a population of over five million people in the 1980s. It also had one of the highest rates of murder anywhere in the world, with literally tens of thousands of people murdered every year. The vast majority of these crimes were drugs-related. It gave the impression of a modern-day city that had been transported back into the Wild West, with gun-toting criminal gangs and policemen everywhere on the streets, and they were often indistinguishable from one another. The gangs were made up of macho young men who sported long curved-down moustaches, always carried guns and had a very short life expectancy. The law was represented by the national security police of the Departamento Administrativo de

Seguridad, abbreviated to DAS. These guys numbered in their thousands, wore cheap suits and shades all the time and were armed with a variety of weapons, though the favourite tool of their trade was the Mini-Uzi, a smaller civilian version of the famous 9mm Uzi submachine-gun, but with the same firepower as its larger military cousin.

Originally set up in July 1960, DAS had many responsibilities within Colombia, including arranging security for state institutions, politicians and civil servants, providing judiciary police services, internal and external counter-intelligence, working with the US Drug Enforcement Agency in the war against illegal drugs and even immigration control, including issuing visas. Unfortunately by the early 1980s DAS was riddled with small-minded men making a fortune in back-handers from the drug producers and dealers, mainly due to the massive amounts of money that could be earned by anyone who was on the side of the drug's cartels. They were about as corrupt as any police agency anywhere in the world could be.

At the same time, as a direct result of all the murders the pot-holed, rubbish-strewn, sewerage-stinking streets of Bogotá were the home of an estimated ten thousand orphan street kids who made their dwelling wherever they could – under bridges, in culverts and sewers and in the municipal parks. These homeless and parentless kids had to beg or steal to make enough money to eat, or else they scavenged off the food thrown into the bins at the back of restaurants and shops. They never washed and were filthy, had long matted hair that never saw a comb, skin black with ground-in grime and a stink that made the hairs in your nostrils curl. These street kids were known in Spanish as los desechables, which means 'the disposables' in English.

Often there would be so many of these street kids that they would drive trade away from some areas of the city with their constant petty thieving, pick-pocketing and begging. When that happened the local traders would get together and hire one of the numerous 'death squads' to come in and thin out the numbers of the kids. Many of the DAS officials ran lucrative side-lines as members of these death-squads. They would pull up at night-time in their official pickup trucks, round up a few dozen los desechables and gun them down in cold blood, often in full view of

170

civilians or even policemen. They just didn't care. In fact nobody in the whole city seemed to care much about the fate of the kids. The bodies would be thrown into the back of the pickup, loosely covered with a tarpaulin and transported out of town where they would be sold to one of the many pig farms dotted around the outskirts of the city. The pig farmers would dispose of the bodies quickly and efficiently by chopping them up with chainsaws and feeding them to their pigs. The pigs of course, would in turn be made into sausages or pies and that's why very few people in the know would ever eat anything made out of pork in Bogotá.

So this was the city that the unlikely friends Danny O'Brian and John Smith found themselves in, on their last weekend together. They were staying in the Cosmos Hotel and on their first night out they decided to go out on the town to sink a few beers, both of them carrying concealed hand guns shoved down the waistbands of their jeans, a .45 M1911 pistol for Danny, and a 9mm Browning Hi-power for Smith. *Everyone* went armed wherever they went in Bogotá, especially at night-time.

They spent the evening hitting a few bars, had a steak for their evening meal (deliberately avoiding the ham), and watched a Formula One Grands Prix race on a TV screen in a nameless joint somewhere deep within the Embassy District of the city.

By the end of the evening they'd each sunk about half a dozen Budweisers and Heinekens. They were merry, but nowhere near drunk and incapable. They bought a couple of bottles of Tequila in yet another bar and headed back to the Cosmos, intending to drink themselves silly close to their pits so that they wouldn't have far to travel when they'd had enough. It was on the way back as they were stumbling through a dark street only lit by the moon (there were no street-lights in Bogotá), that they heard gun-shots nearby.

TWENTY-EIGHT

25th April 1984
Embassy District, Bogotá, Colombia

Even before the sound of the multiple gun-shots had faded away both men had thrown themselves on to the ground, drawn their respective semi-automatic pistols, discarded their bottles of Tequila in the dirt and rolled to either side of the narrow street seeking cover. Luckily there was no one in sight or they might have become the recipient of a couple of quickly aimed rounds from the two wound-up, reactive men. Instead, there was just the sound of raucous laughter coming from around a corner in front of them, followed by the unmistakable sound of another burst of fire from a Mini-Uzi.

"Fuck!" Smith said.

"Shit!" echoed O'Brian.

The two men slowly and cautiously regained their feet, dusting off their jeans. However they were unwilling to return their pistols to their waistbands.

"What the fuck's going on?" Smith whispered to his friend.

"God knows."

They looked at each other in the semi-dark and couldn't help grinning.

"Shall we have a look?" asked the American.

"Sure. Why not?"

Smith and O'Brian were both in their prime and at the peak of their careers. They were confident that they could handle whatever was waiting for them, and they were both still young enough to be idealistic.

They walked slowly forward down the street with its pools of dark and murky shadows, pistols held loosely two-handed in front of them, ready to react to any threat instantly. Another burst of sub-machine gun fire erupted from around the corner, this time accompanied by a high-pitched squeal of absolute terror. The squeal was abruptly cut off in mid flow by a single gun-shot that sounded like it came from a pistol of some kind.

The two men instinctively slowed down as they reached the corner.

"Are you up for it?" whispered Smith. The American just nodded in the affirmative without answering. "Ready?" Another tense nod. "Go!" They threw themselves silently around the corner, just as they had on numerous exercises together back in Fort Bragg, Smith high and O'Brian low, both with pistols thrust out and ready to pour death at anyone who looked even remotely threatening. The sight that met their eyes was enough to curdle the blood in their veins.

There were four Colombians, easily recognisable to the friends as members of DAS, not just because of their cheap suits and the fact that they were wearing sunglasses (even though it was night time and dark), but because they were also wearing the white arm bands that they had learned that DAS officers routinely used to identify themselves. Three of the men were holding Mini-Uzis in their hands, though they were also attached by long slings sloping down from their right shoulders. The fourth man's sub-machine gun was hanging down his back from its sling, while he held a semi-automatic pistol of some sort in his fist. But it wasn't the men or the guns that instantly sickened the Brit and the American, it wasn't even the line of kids kneeling in front of them, with hands on their heads and looks of absolute terror on their filthy snot and tear-streaked faces. What instantly turned their guts was the pile of dead kids that was visible on the back of a pickup truck a few feet away. It was hard to tell their ages because of the dirt and their malnourished bodies but they couldn't have been older than just seven or eight years of age. They were smothered in blood, and even in the dark there was the loud sound of a hundreds of flies buzzing around their corpses and the smell of faeces and urine was thick in the air. Smith and O'Brian, both of whom had seen plenty of gruesome sights during their careers found themselves gagging at the sight and stink of the dead kids.

173

They never knew what alerted the DAS officer to their sudden appearance around the corner. Was it one of the kids looking in their direction with a startled expression on their face? Was it a slight sound? Perhaps a scuffle as they moved in the dirt or a chink from some loose change in their pockets? Or was it just some sort of instinctual warning that made him half turn around and see them. It the long run it didn't really matter.

Both of them fired at the same time. Smith, in the' high' position, put two 9mm rounds into the face of the man who had turned. He then followed up by putting another two into the back of the head of the man to the right of him. O'Brian, in the 'low' position, concentrated on the targets to the left, just as he had during their numerous exercises together, blasting huge holes in their turning heads with his canon of a pistol. In less than five seconds the initial contact was over and the four Colombians were dead.

They stepped forward cautiously, taking short steps and examining the darkness to make sure that there were no more enemies around. Despite being excellent shots, they then kicked the bodies in their groins to make sure that they were definitely dead, pistols at the ready to put more rounds into them if needed. No man can fake death while being kicked in the bollocks - it's a physical impossibility.

In the silence of the street, the line of kids remained still and quiet. They did not know whether to stay put or to run from this new horror that had appeared before them. Even in the dark the two men could see that their eyes were huge with the terror they were feeling.

Satisfied that they had taken out the Colombians cleanly O'Brian turned to Smith:

"Shit. Now what do we do? We've killed some cops!"
Smith grinned, the madness of combat still blazing in his coal-black eyes.

"I suggest we do what one shepherd said to the other shepherd."

"What's that?"

"Let's get the *flock* out of here!"
Smith turned to the kids, waving his arms about:

"Vamoose kids! Go on, fuck off. It's your lucky day! Skedaddle!"

They skedaddled, disappearing into the darkness as fast as their skinny filthy legs could take them. Smith turned to O'Brian:

"Don't worry about this, Danny. These fucking murdering, bastard scum deserved everything they got, mate."

"I agree, John."

"Let's never mention what happened here ever again."

"That's a deal!"

"Super."

The two men followed the kids into the darkness. They retrieved the bottles of Tequila as they headed back to their hotel, hugging the dark shadow of the sides of the streets as they went. Of course they were hoping that they wouldn't run in to another group of DAS officer's hell-bent on revenge, or that they wouldn't be arrested for murder before they could leave the city. Yet they were also fully prepared to sell their own lives dearly if either option happened.

21st June
Four Seasons Hotel, Giza Street, Cairo, Egypt

"Ah, yes, Bogotá, well that's another story...." Smith smiles at Helen, her sheer beauty almost taking his breath away. "But I'm afraid it's not one that you're ever going to hear, love. I'm off to bed, got an early start in the morning!" And with that he heads towards the door, half of his mind in the present, and half of it back on that filthy street in Bogotá, remembering the terrified looks on the faces of those los desechables, and wondering what became of them. Did they live long and learn to prosper? Or did they just end up in the hands of yet another death squad? He will never know.

But there is one thing that he does know and that he is absolutely convinced of; what he and Danny O'Brian had done on that night so long ago had been the right thing to do, and he would do exactly the same again tomorrow if he was given the chance.

Fuck them, those murdering bastards got exactly what they deserved!

TWENTY-NINE

25th June
Halaieb We Shalatein Highway, 200 km south of Quseer

John Smith has spent much of his life acquiring the tools of his trade from the stingy, cost-cutting, penny-pinching UK Ministry of Defence. Therefore when he receives the first-class, top-of-the-range, no-expenses-spared kit that is dropped off for him in the Eastern Desert by a US Blackhawk helicopter crew from the Dutch Frigate, HNLMS Van Amstel, he cannot quite believe his eyes. It's manna from heaven and like having all of his Christmases rolled into one. He even manages to silently tolerate the barely comprehensible southern USA accent of the SEAL who delivers the supplies with a barely suppressed smile of joy while he is going through it with him. Smith is like a small boy set loose in a toy shop full of goodies, and they're all his to play with. At least for now.

The first toy is a brand-new Polaris Sportsman MV850 all-terrain vehicle (ATV). It's a low-profile sand-coloured four-wheel drive military-grade ATV with an 850cc 77hp 4-stroke twin-cylinder engine and electronic power steering. As the SEAL shows him around the vehicle he points out the infra-red lights, the all-steel exoskeleton, the large storage racks in front of and behind the driver which can carry 272 kg of kit, the comfortable-looking centrally-located moulded seat, the roll-bar, the fixed front winch, underbody full-length skid-plate, large capacity 44.5 litre fuel tank, and best of all; the 'Terrain Armor' tyres. These tyres are of a revolutionary new design, being non-pneumatic and built to sustain combat-level damage without compromising functionality or mobility (or so the SEAL tells him). The tyres are built to absorb the roughest terrain possible and multiple impacts, including gun

176

shots and the shrapnel from explosions, and are not subject to flats, cuts, rips or tears like traditional off-road tyres. Basically they look normal with deep treads on the rim, but without side-walls. The interior of the tyre is constructed of a polymeric web - it looks like a bees comb made of individual hexagonal cells - that you can see through. They are so tough that there is now no requirement to carry a spare tyre on the vehicle, leaving room for more useful cargo.

The ATV is supplied with a small off-road trailer which has a 680 kg load capacity, the same Terrain Armor tyres and is loaded with numerous toughened-plastic fuel and drinking water containers that look a little like old-fashioned jerry cans. As the SEAL tells him, there's enough fuel on the trailer and on the ATV to drive the heavily-laden MV850 for eight hundred miles at its top on-road speed of fifty-two miles per hour, though a lot less than this if the vehicle is constantly driven off-road over undulating terrain. There is also a large container of US Army MRE (Meal, Ready-to-Eat) ration packs as well as other useful kit such as a one-man bivvie and desert camouflage nets.

"We weren't told whether you require vegetarian, Kosher or Halal ration packs, Sir. So they're all standard. I hope that's okay?"

Smith waves his hand in the affirmative, too busy bending down and peering through the web of the tyres, amazed at the obvious and simple design. Then what the SEAL has said hits him and he looks up into his earnest face:

"You mean to say that you have vegetarian ration packs?" he asks, dumfounded.

"Of course, Sir."

"Amazing."

He bends down again to try pinching the tough tyre rims with his fingers. The SEAL coughs to get Smith's attention and drones on, leaning over the ATV's complicated driver's instrumentation panel containing a speedometer, tachometer, odometer, trip meters, hour meter, clock, diagnostic indicator and fuel gauge:

"You'll notice, Sir, that there is also a GPS fitted to this vehicle. If you have to abandon the vehicle for any reason, just press this little green button here and we'll be able to locate and

retrieve the vehicle at our convenience. Please do not forget to press the little green button, Sir."
Smith smiles politely and nods.

As shiny as the ATV is, there is something else that grabs Smith's attention even more; the weapons.

The first one is an old, rather battered, bog-standard Chinese-produced AK47 assault rifle with a folding metal butt and a wooden stock. Standard fare for any operator everyplace in the world. Though the Kalashnikov as it's often called is basic in design, it's a reliable and robust workhorse of a weapon. But it's not the AK that grabs his immediate attention. In fact it's a small green box stencilled with 'Mk 23' in yellow lettering. He looks at the SEAL:

"Is that what I think it is?"
The SEAL retains the same earnest-looking dead-pan face he's had all along.

"That depends on what you think it is, Sir?"
Smith ignores the subtle sarcasm of the warrior directed at what he thinks is probably a typical spook.

"A Heckler and Koch Mk 23 semi-automatic handgun?"
Despite himself the SEAL is amazed that this spook knows what the weapon is:

"Yes, Sir. That's correct. This is a Mk 23 Model 0 SOCOM (Special Operations Command) .45 Pistol, fitted with a sound suppressor and a Laser-aiming Module ahead of the trigger guard."
He tries to keep the pride out of his voice, but fails miserably.

Smith reverently opens the lid of the green box. Inside, in a foam-moulded mounting lies what most people would think of as an ugly block-shaped pistol. But to Smith it is beauty personified. He lifts it out gently, turning it in his hands to peer at it from every angle.

The Mk 23 is considered to be a match-grade pistol, which means that it is precision made to a very high standard with quality materials. It is capable of producing a two-inch diameter group of hits at a range of twenty-five metres in the hands of a skilled marksman. For a handgun this level of precision is exceptional - almost unheard off - unless it's a competition weapon. The Mk 23 also has exceptional durability in harsh environments, being both waterproof and corrosion-resistant, which makes it highly suitable for use by Special Forces around the world, though sadly it is not offered as a standard weapon in the British SAS. The .45 rounds held in a twelve-round detachable magazine are low velocity but still have considerable stopping power. They are able to knock a man off his feet at thirty metres, unlike many handguns of a similar size.

"I nicked one of these once, in Slovenia. I think it was one of the first of these little beauties to be produced by HK back in the early nineties," Smith says quietly, almost to himself, "but I never got to fire it in anger. I'd been issued with a P228 SIG Saur, but some twat of an informer had tried to double-cross my team so I had to take him out. It was his Mk 23 that I nicked. I dropped the P228 in a river." He laughs for a second but then his eyes lose focus and his facial muscles tighten up as he remembers his all-too brief operation in Slovenia in June 1991, during the ten-day long war of independence. "I had to bury one of my blokes there." What was his name? Fuck, I can't remember.
The SEAL mellows a little more as he recognises the look on Smith's face, before straightening up and getting back to business.

"Can I just show you the Barrett Light Fifty, Sir? The helo pilot doesn't want to stay on Egyptian soil longer than he has too. He wants to get me back to the ship ASAP, Sir."
Smith shakes himself free of his reverie and his memories.

"Yeah sure, mate." He puts the pistol back in the box and closes the lid, then turns to the big rifle resting on its bipod. "Don't worry about an induction though. I've fired this weapon before, son."
The SEAL is even more impressed. Not many spooks know how to handle an anti-material weapon like the Barrett M82, let alone have fired one?

"Okay, Sir. The ammunition for it is in the trailer, Sir. There's one hundred and twenty rounds for the Mk 23, six hundred rounds for the AK47 and two hundred more for the Barrett."
Smith whistles.

"I think that'll do me, mate, though with any luck I won't have to fire anything except the zeroing rounds. You boys can have all the fun this time when we locate the fucking Somalis!"

"I can live with *that*, Sir."

179

The SEAL grins for the first time since hitting the ground and begins to make his way back towards the waiting chopper, which still has its rotors turning, but then he turns with a questioning look on his face.

"Yeah? What's up, son?"

"The guy you buried in Slovenia. Did you kill him?"

Smith laughs harshly.

"No, mate. The silly twat got his head blown off by accident in a fire-fight between the Slovenians and the Yugoslavians!" The SEAL grins back at him, starts to turn away but then turns back again, impulsively pulling something from his pocket as he does so.

"Here you go, Sir. This is for you." He holds out his hand and in it is a scabbarded knife. "This is *my* SEAL knife, Sir, and I'd appreciate it back when this mission is over." It has a black powder-coated, seven-inch-long, partly-serrated blade and a glass-reinforced nylon handle with a raised diamond pattern to prevent slippage. "This knife is not just given to *anyone*, Sir. You have to *earn* it. It has undergone one of the most extensive testing and evaluation programmes ever undertaken on any weapon by the US Army." Smith is too stunned by the simple but telling gesture to do anything but reach out and take the knife. "Like you say, Sir. With any luck you won't need it. But should you find yourself in the position where you *do* need this knife, Sir, it won't let you down!" With these last words the American finally turns and runs towards the chopper before Smith can think of anything to say.

Within seconds the man has climbed aboard and the rotors start to turn at an increasing rate. The Blackhawk takes to the air. Smith stands with his head bowed and one hand raised to shield his eyes from the sand whirling about from the chopper's downwash. With his other hand he keeps a tight grip on the SEAL knife.

THIRTY

25th June
Twelve kilometres from the Halaieb We Shalatein Highway, 200
km south of Quseer

Smith drives away from the coast along the dry bed of a wadi
meandering through the sand and smooth rocky landscape of the
Eastern Desert. The ATV is very easy to drive and holds the
uneven ground very well, but it isn't long before he realises that
his muscles will take some time to get used to sitting on it. Already
his thighs and ankles are beginning to ache from the constant
pressure needed to keep himself in the seat and he guesses that it
will probably be a another few days before his muscles fully adjust
to the new type of activity.

He searches for and eventually finds a spot that is perfect for
what he intends to do. It's a valley with a straight level bottom just
over two kilometres long, surrounded by low-lying rocky hills.
There has been no sign of human life at any point on his twelve
kilometre journey into the desert and he knows from the aerial
photographs that he has studied of the area that there is little
likelihood of running into or being heard by anyone. The bulk of
human activity in this part of Egypt is confined to a very narrow
strip of land bordering the long coast of the Red Sea. The desert
itself is basically uninhabited.

He parks up the ATV at one end of the valley, groaning a little
from the ache in his legs as he dismounts. The Heckler and Koch
Mk 23 is strapped securely into a custom-made holster on his right
thigh. The AK47 is sitting loose in a canvas scabbard angling
forward along the side of the ATV and in a position where he can
grab it quickly and easily should he need to, a little like the way
that cowboys used to carry their Winchester rifles in the old Wild

West. The Barrett M82 is covered with a loose cotton cloth to keep the dust and sand off it and is clipped into an open stand right behind his seat where it can also be grabbed within seconds. The scabbard of the SEAL knife is strapped upside down to his Personal Load Carrying Equipment (this used to be simply known as 'webbing' before it became customary to give every little piece of kit a long highly technical-sounding name). It's attached to a yolk strap on the left side of his chest and the knife is held in position in the scabbard by a strong clip. Smith is dressed in a worn set of desert camouflage combat trousers, shirt and bush hat, the only items that he bought with him from the UK apart from his superb Meindl Desert Fox Boots. With all of his weaponry and shiny new kit Smith is feeling on top of the world and ready to take on anything. It's been years since he has experienced this much freedom on an operation and he is revelling in it.

He pulls the big M82 from its stand, feels its weight in his hands for a minute to get used to it and walks forward a few metres until he finds a level spot with a good clear view along the full length of the valley. Then he settles it down on to its bipod on the ground.

The original M82 was designed and developed by an American called Ronnie Barrett in the early 1980s. It has gone through various changes and modifications since those early days and the model that Smith is armed with is the Barrett M107A1, which was released to the armed forces of the world in January 2011. It is designated by the US Army and the Marine Corps as a 'long-range sniper rifle' but is mostly used in a anti-material role rather than against human targets. It fires the same .50 (12.7mm) round that was developed for the M2 Browning machine gun. This large calibre round is capable of cutting a human being in two, but can also be used for a variety of other applications. If fired into the engine block of a vehicle for example, such as a Land Rover or a truck, it will very abruptly prevent that vehicle from ever travelling again. It has also proven itself useful in destroying parked-up aircraft and even downing low-flying helicopters. The Helicopter Interdiction Tactical Squadron of the US Coast Guard has also exploited it to disable the engines of the fast boats that are used by drug smugglers. It is such a powerful weapon that snipers have used it to take out targets positioned *behind* walls made of brick or concrete blocks.

The rifle itself is semi-automatic and is fitted with a ten-round capacity detachable box magazine. The M107A1 weighs just 12.4 kg, which is significantly lighter than the original M82. Its overall length is 145cm, so it's not a small rifle, but the barrel length makes up 73.7cm of this and gives an effective range of almost four thousand metres, which is two miles eight hundred and fifty-four yards. Of course, hitting a man-sized target at this extreme range is almost impossible, even for the most experienced sniper. However, if your target is something as big as a small building or a truck, hitting it even at this range shouldn't be a problem and the large-calibre round will still do its job of penetrating and disabling whatever it strikes.

John Smith is a vastly experienced sniper. He first learned his trade on the British Army's six-week-long Sniper Course in sunny Sennybridge in South Wales, way back in 1982. In the late 1980s he further improved his skills on the US Army's Special Operations Target Interdiction Course and the thirty-five day Special Forces Sniper Course at the John F. Kennedy Special Warfare Centre at Fort Bragg in North Carolina. He knows that in order to hit a target at long distance the weapon has to be zeroed in.

Smith walks out to the other end of the valley from the ATV and chooses a large flat-faced rock that is in clear view from where he's parked the vehicle. Using a small paint pot and brush he's brought with him just for this job he hand paints a rough white circle of about a metre and a half in diameter, then adds three more increasingly smaller circles inside it, finishing off with a painted disc in the centre which is about 10cm across. He then walks slowly back towards the ATV counting his paces as he goes to give himself a rough idea of the range to the rock, which works out at about two thousand three hundred metres. By the time he gets back to his start-point the paint on the rock is bone dry thanks to the heat of the sun. This *is* a desert after all.

Smith lies down beside the Barrett Light Fifty (as the Americans call it), pulls it into his right shoulder until it is snug and tight, and then flips down the caps on the Leupold Mark 4 Long Range/Tactical 4.5-14x50mm M1 riflescope mounted on to the rifles optics rail, and looks through it. He gently turns the non-fast adjustable eyepiece until the rock at the end of the valley comes into focus (even though it looks pretty small at this range) and then tightens the locking ring. After that he turns the magnification adjustment ring until the scope is at its full magnification and the white painted circles on the rock now look a lot closer than they did previously. Next Smith cocks the rifle by pulling back the handle and letting it go forward under its own steam (this action grabs up a round from the top of the magazine and pushes it into the chamber), then he looks through the scope again and centres the cross hairs on the small white disc at the centre of the target. To make sure that his body position is as comfortable and in-line with the target as it can be he closes his eyes and relaxes his stance. Then without opening his eyes he tenses again and pulls the rifle into the direction of aim in his shoulder. Only now does he open his eyes again and is happy to find that the target is still visible through the rifle's scope. Following this he takes three deep slow breaths which oxygenates his blood and at the same time allows him to relax and 'feel' the rifle in his hands. He takes another deep breath, lets half of it slowly out, stops and gently squeezes the trigger.

The recoil from the Barrett is considerable, pushing the rifle back into Smith's shoulder with a lot of force. However he is expecting it and already knows it won't be as bad as what you might expect from such a large calibre weapon. Most of the recoil is soaked up by the barrel assembly, which moves inward towards the receiver against large springs when a shot is fired. In addition the weapon's heavy weight and the large muzzle brake at the end of the barrel soak up a lot of the recoil so that overall it's quite manageable once an operator gets used to it.

He follows through by letting out the rest of his breath and simultaneously gently releasing the trigger, carefully watching the fall of shot through the scope. The huge .50 round chips off a large piece of the rock just above the outer circle in line with the target's centre. Smith sighs contentedly. It's going to be a long morning sighting in this baby, but I'm going to enjoy every minute!

After taking five carefully-aimed shots, Smith turns the elevation adjuster on the scope which with any luck will make the next rounds fall lower on to the centre of the target. However, even after making this adjustment his aim is still off by about half a meter, so he fires another full set of five rounds and then readjusts the scope again. He's fortunate that there is no breeze, so he doesn't have the added complication of adjusting his aim for windage as well as elevation. His next and final set of five shots all hit or closely bracket the tiny white aiming disc on the rock and Smith is thoroughly pleased with himself. You've still got it, lad!

Finally he covers the rifle and its scope in the piece of cloth that keeps the dust off and gently replaces it into its stand behind the driver's seat. The stand grips the rifle in two thickly padded steel-sprung jaws, not just to prevent it from falling out every time the wheels of the ATV hit a rock, but also to stop the rifle scope from being jarred and losing its careful zeroing.

Next up he pulls the AK47 from its scabbard on the side of the ATV, adds a couple of full magazines to the pouches on his lightweight webbing, and walks forward. There is no way that the AK will ever have the accuracy of the Barrett and be able to match its range, but it still needs zeroing at about six hundred metres to get the best out of it. And then there's the Mk 23! Great stuff!

Smith is one happy man. He is very comfortable and at ease working with the weapons to get them to perform at their best.

ENGLAND

THIRTY-ONE

28th June
On a train somewhere between Marylebone in London and
Birmingham New Street

Massoud Hassan shifts uncomfortably in his seat. British trains are
a new experience for him, and though the seats on the Chiltern
Railways train are fairly wide and comfortable, he just can't get
used to seeing the British countryside zooming past at high speed
through the window while he has nothing to do but twiddle his
thumbs. Plus his wound is still hurting him, and he suspects that it
may be infected.

It's been eleven days since he killed that fool Arkoun, but he's
still angry at the incompetence of the man. Hassan had spotted the
British intelligence agent as soon as he had walked into the
Departures Lounge at Heathrow to meet Arkoun. The agent had
even made brief eye-contact with him, which is a definite no-no
when conducting covert surveillance. When he had confronted
Mehdi Arkoun about the presence of the intelligence officer during
their subsequent drive from the airport to Luton, Arkoun confessed
that he had spotted nothing untoward. That was the moment that
Hassan had decided that he would dispose of Arkoun at the earliest
possible opportunity. He did not need helpers who were so inept.

During the drive to Luton Hassan had kept a careful eye on the
rear-view mirror and was confident that they were not being tailed.
He imagined that the intelligence agent must be reasonably sure of
their destination, certain enough to stay well back out of sight and
risk picking them up later on the route. Therefore Hassan ordered
Arkoun not to take him to his own home, but to drive further on so
that they could find a small motel or something similar to book
into for the night. It was then that the stupid Britisher had informed

him that the weapons and explosives that had been gathered for this mission were all stashed in his flat. How stupid could the man be? Hassan was fuming!

They had booked into a small bed and breakfast that they found in a side-street on the outskirts of Luton, and spent the night there while Hassan tried to decide how he was going to handle the situation. He had a number of choices, but none of them were perfect. The first was to abandon the weapons and explosives, kill Arkoun as soon as he could and make contact with the second person on his list of British Muslim contacts. This was not an ideal option as he did not know if the weapons and explosives could be replaced, or how long it would take even if it were possible. He was impatient and tired of inaction. He wanted his fitting revenge and he wanted it now, not in six months or a year's time!

The second option was to risk going to Arkoun's flat and picking up the kit. Again this was not without its down side. In fact it was positively dangerous. Without doubt the British intelligence services would be watching the flat and there was a good chance that when they saw Hassan and Arkoun moving several heavy items from the flat to the car that they would pounce straightaway and arrest them both. If he was arrested with fifty pounds of plastic explosive and enough small arms to supply half a dozen terrorist cells, he would spend the rest of his life in a British prison (even if he ratted on his own country's intelligence ministry and traded vital information to the British). He had spent enough time in prison already. He would never voluntarily go back, even if a British prison was probably only a shadow of the brutal Iranian prison that he had been released from.

The third option was to abort the mission entirely. He could try to disappear in Britain, or be brave and inform his superiors in Iran that he had been compromised, but both of these choices would mean that his extended family in Iran would be executed in recompense for another failure. He dismissed this idea even before it formed fully in his mind.

Massoud Hassan found himself in this unenviable situation because of a former British Army sergeant called John Smith, who was known by the Iranian government as the 'Great Satan' after he had ruthlessly slaughtered eight Iranian-sponsored Arab terrorists

190

on a flight from The Gambia to London a few years before. The terrorists had been aiming to crash the airliner into Buckingham Palace in a copycat scenario of the Al Qaeda attack on the twin towers in New York. At the time all of the Royal Family were in the palace for the birthday celebrations of Her Majesty the Queen, so the entire British royal dynasty would have been wiped out in one fell swoop. However Smith had stopped the terrorists in their tracks and saved the day. As a consequence of his actions a Fatwa, the legal pronouncement of a death sentence in Islam, was handed down upon Smith by Ayatollah Akbar Hashemi Khomeini, who had been the Supreme Leader of the Islamic Republic of Iran at the time.

Hassan was serving as an undercover intelligence agent with the Iranian Embassy in Oslo when information came to light that Smith was living in Norway. He and a team of Iranian Special Forces soldiers initially attacked Smith's house in Stavanger but he hadn't been at home. Eventually they tracked him down to a small farmhouse in Flatdal, in Telemark, but somehow Smith had been forewarned of their intended mission. He and his girlfriend managed to elude Hassan's team and disappeared into the Norwegian wilderness with the Iranians hot on their heels.

A cross-country chase ensued in which Smith had killed one of his Iranian pursuers and badly injured another. He also fatally wounded the British policeman, Detective Chief Inspector Alan Davies, who had supplied the information about Smith's location to the Iranians and been dragged along on the mission. Davies later died of his wounds in the wilderness.

Smith and his girlfriend had somehow escaped unscathed but the Iranians had been rounded up and captured by the Norwegian Police. Of course, Hassan had had diplomatic immunity so he hadn't been charged by the Norwegians, but he had been deported.

On account of his failure Hassan had been flown back to Iran in disgrace. There he had been stripped of his rank of colonel and sent without trial to the notoriously tough Evin Prison, located at the foot of the Alborz Mountains in north western Tehran. The prison is known as the 'University of Evin' because of the high numbers of political intellectual prisoners that it holds. He had been incarcerated in Section 209 of the prison, the section that was run by his former masters in the ministry of intelligence. His cell

191

was just four by five metres in size, with two small metal-framed windows placed too high up on the wall to see anything out of them but the beautiful blue sky. There was no bed. He slept on a blanket on the ground with nothing to cover him during the intensely cold nights except the same thin prison uniform that he wore throughout his days. He had no idea of the fate that had befallen his family after his disgrace, but he guessed that his wife and three sons were no longer living in their luxurious apartment in Tehran. They were most probably jobless and destitute and having to beg on the streets to find enough to eat. That was the normal punishment for the families of failures in the Iranian regime.

Prison had been tough, even for an ex-Special Forces Commando. There had been beatings by the vicious, brutal prison guards almost every day, poor food and never enough of it to keep his strength up, and he was constantly kept in solitary confinement. There had been many times when he was in despair but one thing kept him going. That was the thought that somewhere Sergeant John Smith was living as a free man. Hassan's heart ached with the hope, as remote as it was, that one day he would be released from his imprisonment and would be given a second chance to hunt down the English man whose laughing face incessantly filled his daydreams and his nightmares.

Then, six months ago, he had been dragged from his cell and taken to an interrogation room where his old general had informed him that he would be released and given another chance. At first he thought that he was hallucinating! But then he'd realised that Allah, the Most Beneficent, and the Most Merciful, must be looking down upon him in favour. His new task was to travel covertly to the United Kingdom and then find and kill the 'Great Satan' in as public a way as possible. If he succeeded he would be restored to his rank of colonel and his family would be back by his side and they would be whole again. He would even, or so they had promised him, be able to claim the half a million pound bounty that had been placed on Smith's head when the Fatwa was handed down upon him.

During the intense briefings that followed Hassan's release (and while he was working slavishly to return his body to the peak of fitness that he had enjoyed before his nightmare incarceration in Evin Prison), he came to realise that something had happened to

192

make his government sit up and pay even more attention to Smith than they had before. It must have been something very big indeed, whatever it was, because suddenly he found himself offered the entire resources of the Ministry of Intelligence and National Security to aid him in his quest to kill Smith. This included unprecedented access to all of the assets that Iran had been covertly building up over the last three decades in the United Kingdom, including not only caches of weaponry and explosives, but also the British Muslim sympathisers who had been radicalised in the name of Iran. Mehdi Arkoun had been one of those assets kept in secret readiness by the Iranian government, though disappointingly to Hassan, he was an incompetent one.

So while Hassan lay unable to sleep in the bed and breakfast on the outskirts of Luton he had decided on a fourth option. In the morning he ordered Arkoun to take him back to his flat. It did not take Hassan long to locate the covert observation post overlooking Arkoun's flat, and an even shorter amount of time to use all of the Semtex plastic explosive in the cache to make a crude shaped charge and cram it into a steel bucket which he aimed at the window across the road. Unfortunately, Arkoun had had second thoughts about setting off the explosives when he realised what the Iranian was doing, and had foolishly tried to stop him. Apparently he knew and was friendly with other people who lived across the road and who would doubtless be caught up in any blast. He argued with Hassan that there might be a better way, perhaps a non-violent way of dealing with the surveillance, and the argument turned into a brief tussle in which Arkoun managed to pull a knife and had stabbed Hassan in the lower stomach. Hassan had thrown the British Muslim against the hallway wall and beat him unconscious with half a dozen short sharp blows of his hands and feet. He had staunched the flow of blood leaking from his own wounded abdomen with the shirt that he ripped from Arkoun's back, sorted himself out a small selection of hand guns and sub-machine guns from Arkoun's cache, which he slipped into a large black holdall, then set a timing device on the explosives to detonate five minutes later. As he made his way to the relative safety of the back of the flat, facing away from the direction that the shaped charge would blow, he shot the unconscious Arkoun at point-blank range in the head, just to make sure that he wouldn't survive the blast.

When the Semtex exploded it took out the entire front of both Arkoun's flat and the building across the street where the intelligence operatives had their observation post. It also happened to kill the two armed police officers that were just about to force an entry through the front door after hearing the gunshot inside.

Hassan, despite being half-deafened and badly disorientated by the effects of the massive blast protected himself from its backlash by hiding in the corner of the kitchen at the rear of the flat behind an upturned table. In the total confusion and chaos that immediately followed the explosion he gathered his wits enough to slip away. From there he had made his way to another British contact that was on hand for him and his mission; a white liberal college lecturer whose sympathies lay with the cause of the poor, abused and oppressed Muslims in Britain. The lecturer was in his mid-fifties, gay and lived alone in a smart two-bedroomed house in the suburbs of Luton. Hassan got him to telephone the college where he worked and report in sick with a bad case of the flu, so that they would not expect to see him for at least a week. The poor man was very excited to be actively helping the cause at last, but on the other hand absolutely terrified of the Iranian secret agent so obviously devoid of emotion who had landed unannounced on his doorstep. He helped Hassan by cleaning and bandaging his knife wound as best as he could with the contents of a household first aid kit. He then cooked him a meal of chicken and roast vegetables which the Iranian tucked into as though he was starving and hadn't eaten for a week.

He didn't even hear Hassan as he crept into his bedroom later that night. He tried to struggle as he woke up with Hassan's strong fingers around his throat cutting off his airway, but he didn't have the strength to struggle for long. His death in the end was relatively quick and painless.

Hassan stayed hidden in the lecturer's house until the food in the kitchen ran out. Meanwhile he had used the lecturer's landline to call yet another contact on his list, this time in Birmingham. He is now on his way to hook up with this next contact.

194

THIRTY-TWO

28th June
Holmwood Road, Small Heath, Birmingham

Massoud Hassan's next contact is a Muslim railway worker. His name is Arash Ghorbani and he has lived in the United Kingdom since February 1979. He was given political asylum after he had fled his home following the deposition of Mohammad Reza Pahlavi - the former Shah of Iran by Ayatollah Khomeini and his revolutionary guards.

Arash had been a young nineteen year old third lieutenant in the Shah's army on 8th September 1978. His platoon was one of the many which were on duty in Tehran's Jaleh Square, facing a religious demonstration of thousands of people peacefully protesting against the Shah's rule. Martial law had been declared in Iran only the day before and the soldiers had already ordered the crowd to disperse. The huge mass of people had ignored the instruction to disband and move away and was squashed forward against the nervous troops. At this point a number of professional agitators opened fire on both the protesters and the real soldiers. Some of them had been trained in Palestinian and Libyan camps and a number were indistinguishable from the soldiers as they were dressed in the uniform of the Shah's army. Absolute chaos ensued with the army opening fire on the protesters. At the time it had been reported internationally that thousands of innocent people had been massacred by the soldiers, but later investigations showed that it was actually less than a hundred. Nevertheless, the incident became known as 'Black Friday' in Iran and was one of the pivotal events that would lead to the Shah's overthrow a few months later.

The backlash against the army officers who had been in Jaleh Square on that fateful day had been brutal. Many had been exposed by the Ayatollah's supporters in the army and they had been slaughtered by roaming gangs of the fanatical revolutionary guards over the following weeks and months. However Arash had been lucky and managed to escape from Iran with his wife and two daughters. Unfortunately he had had to leave his parents and three brothers and their young families behind.

In 1984 MOIS, the newly formed Ministry of Intelligence and National Security in Iran arrested the members of Arash's extended family. They executed his parents and imprisoned his brothers and their families in - ironically - Evin Prison in Tehran, the same prison where Massoud Hassan had recently been incarcerated. At the same time MOIS agents found and approached Arash in his new home in Small Heath, Birmingham and gave him a blunt ultimatum. If he was willing to become a covert 'sleeper' agent in Britain for the new Iranian government, his brothers and their families would be released from prison. If he refused to work for them then they would all be tortured and then executed. Additionally, Arash and his wife and daughters would be assassinated in England. The ex-soldier who had previously thought that he was safe in the United Kingdom, quickly realised that he had no choice. Even if he chose to sacrifice his brothers he wouldn't be able to find anywhere in Britain where he could hide from the vengeful agents of the Ayatollah's regime and they would seek him out and kill everyone who he held dear. Reluctantly he agreed to their proposal.

As it turned out, it seemed to have been a good choice and had not even been that much hassle to him. Since the 1980s, Arash had lived an almost normal life, finding a good, steady, if somewhat boring job as a middle manager in British Rail. He had retained his position when the company was transferred to Central Trains in 1997 after British Rail had been disbanded, and then to its successor London Midland in 2007. Over the years the extent of his involvement in Iranian affairs had been minimal despite the fact that he received a modest stipend of five hundred pounds a month; his home had been used as a safe house for MOIS operatives a few times and he had once been tasked with transporting a large amount of explosives to a house in south London.

However in 2010 his comfortable quiet life changed when he had been visited by a frightening man from the Iranian Embassy who wore a dark suit and had cold and calculating eyes devoid of emotion. He informed Arash that he was now tasked with recruiting young people from the local Muslim population and forming them into an eight-man covert operational cell. The ex-soldier was dismayed and had almost refused to cooperate. Anticipating that Arash might not be happy with his new job, the Iranian had shown him photographs of his two daughters dropping off their children, his grandchildren, at school. At the same time he told him in no uncertain terms that the lives of his daughters and his grandkids were totally in his hands. If he refused to help the Iranian government they would all die, but only after being abused by the men who would eventually kill them. Arash, predictably, capitulated.

Over the next five years he steadily sought out the unhappy young men who attended his local Mosque, those who were dissatisfied and disfranchised with their lives in what they saw as a Godless Britain, and gradually gathered his group together. The members of the cell had all, in turn, travelled singly or as pairs as tourists to Iran where they had been secretly trained by a special unit of the Quds Force in the use of weapons, explosives and other terrorist activities.

When Arash had received the call from Hassan the previous evening and the Iranian agent had given the correct code phrase in order to establish his authenticity, Arash had been horrified. Deep down he knew that his normal everyday life in Britain was about to come to an horrible end and that he would at last be paying the ultimate price for having been present on that fateful day in Jaleh Square in Tehran so many years ago.

He was right.

197

THIRTY-THREE

1st July
Holmwood Road, Small Heath, Birmingham

Superintendent Mark Reynolds has been a senior detective in the Metropolitan Police for as long as he can remember, or so it seems to him at times. For the past fifteen years he has been a member of the elite group of men and women which have fought terrorism on the streets of the United Kingdom. In his first appointment he was attached to SO12, the world-renowned British Special Branch, but in 2006 the Special Branch had been amalgamated with SO13, the former anti-terrorist Branch, to form SO15, or the Counter Terrorism Command and he had been transferred there.

Mark has done well in his career, heading up the units that have been responsible for the arrest and conviction of eleven people committing or conspiring to commit acts of terrorism who are presently serving out sentences of a combined total of sixty-eight years. Currently he is involved in cases where another twenty-two people that are charged with terrorism-related offences, including conspiracy to murder and conspiracy to cause explosions are awaiting trial. Mark is a superstar.

However there is one particular job that he is working on where Mark Reynolds feels as though he is always one step behind and playing catch up. He has been assigned by the commander of SO15 to arrest and bring to justice the Iranian intelligence colonel Massoud Hassan, but this is proving to be a long hard job, probably the hardest of his whole career so far.

He began his investigation in the aftermath of the bombing in Brook Street, in Luton, on the 17th June, just fourteen days ago. Two police officers from Bedfordshire Police, two operatives from the Security Service and three members of the public died when the bomb had gone off. Seventeen other civilians had been injured, two of them an old couple who had been walking along Brook Street. The couple were still critically ill in Luton and Dunstable Hospital and had both lost limbs. It was touch and go as to whether they would eventually be added to the death toll for the outrage.

On top of this carnage one other person had been found dead at the scene of the bombing. A young Muslim man called Mehdi Arkoun who had owned the flat. In his case though, he hadn't been a victim of the bomb as it was clear from the forensic evidence, i.e. the big hole in his head, that he had been shot by his accomplice before the explosive device had detonated.

A nationwide alert for Massoud Hassan had already been in place for several hours before Reynolds was put in charge of the case, but it had proven to be fruitless; there were a handful of reported sightings but these had turned out to be false alarms and a waste of time. The Iranian just seemed to have disappeared off the face of the earth.

It was not until yesterday that Reynolds had been given his first solid lead as to where the Iranian colonel had disappeared to. The clue, unfortunately, was in the form of a strangled body belonging to a university lecturer in Luton. The man had phoned in sick to work with suspected flu several days before (coincidently on the same day as the bomb went off in Luton) and had not been seen since. Luckily for Reynolds, another man who worked with the lecturer (and who later admitted to being a former gay lover of his) had visited his flat to see if he was okay and had become very suspicious when he hadn't answered his door. He called the local police who at his insistent urging that something must be very wrong indeed, had broken into his flat and found the lecturer's dead strangled body in bed.

This event would not normally have been brought to the attention of the Superintendent from SO15 except that a piece of torn notepaper was found in the subsequent search of the flat's communal bins which had the name Mehdi Arkoun written on it together with the terrorist's address. This appeared to be Massoud Hassan's first mistake and provided a tenuous link between the two disparate incidents. It was enough of a connection for the Scenes of Crime Officers to undertake further investigations which revealed more evidence in the bins including blood-stained bandages. The blood on the dressings matched that of the blood stains found on the blade of a knife retrieved from the hallway of Arkoun's flat.

When this connection was made Reynolds had immediately ordered the lecturer's phone records to be sent by email to his own iPhone. It transpired that only one call had been made in the past week, to the house of a man living on Holmwood Road in Small Heath, Birmingham. A man whose name, when checked against the electoral register, turned out to be Iranian. A man named Arash Ghorbani.

Reynolds had then politely asked the dedicated Counter Terrorism Unit of the West Midlands Police Force to place a car at the end of the street where they could keep an eye on Ghorbani's house, while he gathered his own team together in Luton in preparation for a speedy helicopter trip to Birmingham. Meanwhile the Counter Revolutionary Wing of 22 Special Air Service Regiment in Hereford, who always have a troop of men on immediate standby were activated and were now already on their way to Small Heath to rendezvous with Reynolds.

At last, things seemed to be moving quickly in the right direction.

At three o'clock in the morning the S.A.S. assaulted the house of Arash Ghorbani, bursting in through the roof and the rear bedroom windows while their sniper team covered the front and back of the house. Normally this job would have been undertaken by the police themselves, but with Hassan's background as an Iranian Special Forces Commando it was deemed appropriate and safer for the British Special Forces to take on the role of attackers. As it turned out they would have been better off just breaking the door down.

Colonel Massoud Hassan was not in the house.

Arash Ghorbani and his wife were found tied up in the bathroom. Both of them had had their throats expertly cut.

The trail had grown cold once again.

THIRTY-FOUR

1st July
Downing Street, London

The Prime Minister brings the emergency meeting in the Cabinet Office Briefing Room (COBR) to order:

"Good afternoon, everyone. I've called you all together this afternoon because of recent events regarding the Luton bombing. Plus I believe that we have some new information on the man that we believe is responsible."

He looks quizzically across the table at the Foreign Secretary, who smiles and nods his head in confirmation.

"Yes, Prime Minister."

All of the usual representatives are present in the briefing room: the Metropolitan Police Commissioner; the Commander in charge of SO15, the Counter Terrorism Command of the Met; the Chief Constable of Bedfordshire Police; the Home Secretary; the Foreign Secretary; the Director General of MI5, the Security Service; the Director General of MI6, the Secret Intelligence Service, and the Director of UK Special Forces. There is also a very nervous Superintendent Mark Reynolds of SO15 in attendance. He's anxious because this is the first time in his very long career that he's been called upon to address such high ranking officials about an investigation that he is running. On top of this he just wishes that he had something more positive to say about how it's all going. His boss Commander Vaughn, doesn't help matters when he says:

"Can I introduce Superintendent Reynolds to you, Prime Minister? He's in charge of this case."

The Prime Minister looks over at him:

201

"Good afternoon, Superintendent. I hope that you bring us some good news?"

Reynolds shakes his head, deciding to bite the biscuit straightaway:

"I'm afraid not, Sir. After tracking down Hassan to Small Heath in Birmingham, I'm afraid that the trail has gone cold again."

"Mmmmm." The Prime Minister is not the only person around the table looking unhappy. "I understand that he has killed again?"

"Yes, Sir. We found the bodies of two people in Birmingham. Both had had their throats cut."

"Charming!" mutters the Home Secretary.

"Indeed, Madame Secretary. My officers are still running in-depth background checks on his most recent victims, but I can tell you now that they were both Iranians that fled that country when the Shah was deposed back in 1979."

"So they were dissidents then?" this is from the Metropolitan Police Commissioner. "That would tie in with the theory that this Hassan character is in the UK to assassinate Iranian dissidents."

"It would, Commissioner, except that the Foreign Office is now in receipt of a communique from the present government in Iran that may shed new light on Hassan and the reason that he has come to the United Kingdom. If I may, Prime Minister?"

The Foreign Secretary looks smugly pleased with himself.

"Of course. Please carry on."

The Foreign Secretary snaps his fingers at an aide sitting just behind him and obediently the aide stands up and starts passing papers around the table, one per person.

"What you are reading now is a reply that we have received from the President of Iran, in response to an urgent query that the FCO sent to him regarding former Iranian Colonel Massoud Hassan immediately after the bombing in Luton. As you are probably aware the UK does not currently have an embassy in Tehran, so we were forced to send the query via the Swedish Embassy, which protects our interests in the country. It's a rather long-winded reply, but the gist of it is that our Colonel Hassan is no longer working for the Iranians, or in their interests. According to President Rhouhani, Massoud Hassan had been imprisoned in Iran for 'anti-government activities' after being deported by the Norwegians from their country. Apparently the colonel has since escaped from prison and has left the country. The President has been kind enough to share his latest intelligence regarding Hassan with us: former Iranian Colonel Massoud Hassan is now a terrorist with allegiance to the so-called Islamic State!"

EGYPT

THIRTY-FIVE

2nd July
Somewhere in the Eastern Desert, Egypt

Ibrahim al-Busiri is proving himself to be an excellent tracker, which is hardly surprising as he was born and raised in the Eastern Desert. Ibrahim belongs to an ethnic group known as the Bisharin which is part of the Beja nomadic peoples. His family home is located in Gebel Elba National Park, a huge area of over thirty-five thousand square kilometres of mountainous desert wilderness on Egypt's southern border with Sudan. Before leaving his home as a restless teenager to seek his fortune as a soldier in the Egyptian Army he had been a fisherman and a hunter, specialising in tracking down the flocks of wild Barbary Sheep which, at that time, could still be found on the slopes of Gebel Shendodai, Gebel Shendib, Gebel Shellal and Gebel Elba.

However, even the best tracker in the world would find the task of following the route taken by the Somali kidnappers and their victims problematic. The first difficulty is the amount of time that has expired before the rescue team actually set out on the Somalis' trail; some fifteen days in total. A hell of a lot of sand can be shifted about by the wind in fifteen days. The second problem is the composition of the desert itself, which is mostly rounded rock worn smooth by the wind, with deep sand only accumulating in sheltered hollows or across the occasional flat pans making the task of tracking very challenging.

The going has been very slow indeed, as Ibrahim walks in front of the two Land Rover Discoveries. His eyes are constantly looking down as he carefully scans each foot of the ground in front of him. It is only his exceptional skill that has kept them going, yet even then they have still followed the occasional false trail which has necessitated long detours. Often the only signs he can find are the dried wads of chewed qaad spat out over the side of their pickup truck by the kidnappers. Qaad is known as khat in many parts of the world and is a plant that is chewed for its stimulant effect and is highly addictive. The last few wads have been slightly damp inside when Ibrahim breaks them apart, a sure sign that less time has passed since they've been spat out compared to the first wads that they found when they started out on the trail. He interprets this as a positive indication that they are slowly catching up with the Somalis.

Another reason for their slow progress is their constant need to be vigilant, though they've still covered an average of about twenty kilometres a day since they've started, working almost non-stop from dawn until dusk each day. The last thing that they want or need is to stumble straight into the kidnapper's camp. Therefore one of the team is always out in front, on foot and a long way ahead of even Ibrahim. This person's job is to watch the landscape ahead for any sign of habitation or human activity. So far, a whole week into their operation they haven't seen hide nor hair of people anywhere. The desert is entirely empty except for the haunting calls of birds and a pair of jackals that have been shadowing them, no doubt eating their leftovers whenever they break camp.

It's not only jackals that have been following them though, as Ibrahim pointed out to O'Brian on their fifth day out. He had joined the ex-SEAL as they enjoyed a brief swallow of tepid water at an afternoon stop, well out of earshot from the others:

"Someone is following us." He spoke quietly, nodding towards their rear. "I have seen two small clouds of dust behind us in the last four days."

O'Brian looked at him over the top of his water bottle as he took another sip, his eyes hidden behind his obligatory shades.

"Maybe it's just a dust devil. You know how the wind sometimes kicks up little vortexes of sand in this rocky terrain." The Egyptian's large dark eyes were piercing as he looked back at O'Brian.

"No, I don't think so. Dust devils, as you call them, usually go straight up into the air and then disappear as quickly as they appear. These dust clouds have been drawn-out smears on the horizon, made perhaps by a vehicle. I should inform the others. Perhaps we can lay an ambush for whoever it is?"

He made to move back to the Land Rovers but O'Brian laid a strong hand on his arm.

"Don't do that, Ibrahim."

The Egyptian turned back to look at him, his face questioning.

"Why not?"

The American refused to be drawn.

"It's probably nothing, like I said – just *dust devils*."

O'Brian emphasised the last two words quite strongly and Ibrahim couldn't fail to understand the implication. He stared for a moment before speaking again:

"I have had the feeling since we began this task that you have not been entirely on the level with the rest of us, Mister Robert. There is something about the way that you handle yourself, an *assurance* you might call it, that doesn't sit well with your story of simply being a mercenary and being here only because of the money."

"Jeez, Ibrahim. You're an excessively suspicious guy."

"Mmmmm. We shall find out in the fullness of time, no doubt."

"So what about the dust-devils? Will you tell the others?"

"No. I will keep it between the two of us for now. Perhaps they are friendly, these devils of yours?"

"Probably."

John Smith is not feeling very friendly at the moment. His arse is sore due to the constant bucking of his ATV over the rough rocky terrain, and his back aches. While the rescue team under Oldport and Huntsbringer have been travelling mainly along fairly level dry wadis, he has had to keep to the higher, rockier ground where he can keep an eye on the small convoy and keep the amount of dust that he creates due to his movement to a minimum, though he's aware that he hasn't always managed to do the latter. There have been a couple of occasions when he has had to make a choice between skirting large areas of deep sand and losing sight of the team, or trying to keep within a good distance from them in case they get into some sort of trouble, as unlikely as trouble might seem in this God-forsaken wilderness. A handful of times he has taken the chance and driven very slowly through smaller patches of sand, hoping against hope that no one will notice the dust he inevitably kicks up.

Out of the corner of his eye he catches a brief glimpse of movement and quickly twists his head to find that it's just a bird that has fluttered up on to a rock ledge. It's strikingly handsome, a little smaller than a thrush and coloured jet black over all of its body apart from a pure white crown on its head and a white underside to its tail and rump. I'll have to remember this one for Linda, he thinks. I reckon it's a wheatear of some sort but no doubt she'll know which one! Thinking about Linda lets his mind wander pleasantly for a minute or two as he continues his slow drive forward along the base of a small cliff.

Smith has had a lot of time to think over the past week, and he knows from past experiences that this is not normally good for him; he has too many bad memories that tend to rise to the top whenever he doesn't keep himself busy. However, this time it's not been too bad and his thoughts have been fairly mellow. Perhaps it's down to the sheer vastness of this desert and its raw, harsh beauty, or perhaps it is just the endless vigilance he's been keeping. Every step of the way he has had to be aware of what the team is doing ahead of him and where it is, where their route is taking them over the ground so that he can figure out his own route so that he can keep them in sight, and all of the time of course he is aware of the desert around him. It can be mind-bogglingly boring out here surrounded by nothing but rock, sand, sky and the ever-present sun, but he knows that he must not let down his defences for even a second.

He wipes the sweat off his forehead and checks his GPS. Their journey so far has taken them about a hundred and fifty kilometres in a south-westerly direction from the point where they started to track the Somalis, which was about two hundred kilometres south of Quseer. This places them around ten kilometres from the border with Sudan in an area which Smith has been warned about in his briefing by Helen Wright, passed on from the section head of the Secret Intelligence Service in Egypt. Apparently the precise border between southern Egypt and northern Sudan has been disputed for a long time by the two countries, with both claiming large chunks of their neighbour's land. Though God knows why? It's just empty nothingness as far as I can see! he thinks to himself. The porous nature of the border and the vast wildness of the terrain makes it a very good place for smuggling operations to be conducted, and the gangs of smugglers (which include various factions run by Egyptians, Sudanese, Eritreans, Ethiopians and of course Somalis), are a highly territorial lot who are armed with everything from ancient revolvers and muskets through to modern heavy machine guns, and they are not afraid to use them if they believe that their territory is being hi-jacked.

Smith gets a sudden feeling of dread as he spots a dust trail half a dozen kilometres to the south. It appears to be heading directly towards the rescue team two kilometres in front of him. He quickly reaches down and kills his engine, then pulls a pair of binoculars from their dust-proof case which is taped to the dashboard of the ATV. The dust cloud is too far away for him to see any detail, though he guesses that there's probably more than one vehicle driving very fast as the dust cloud is growing in size even as he watches it approach. He swiftly switches his view to the rescue team. He can just see the top of their vehicles in a wadi, moving much more slowly and on a collision course with whoever is coming towards them. He can't see any sign that they've noticed the problem yet, but then realises that they probably can't see the dust like he can as he's much higher up.

He sighs. Shit! I hope it's not that dickhead Robinson who's on point! goes through his mind.

THIRTY-SIX

2nd July
Somewhere in the Eastern Desert, Egypt

In the principles of disaster, Murphy's Third Law states: In any field of scientific endeavor, anything that can go wrong will go wrong. In army speak this translates to: 'If in any given situation, something can possibly go wrong, it invariably will'. And so it is that Frank Robinson, the one potential weak link in the rescue team put together so hurriedly by Oldport and Huntsbringer, is of course the man who is on point duty at this moment in time.

He's ambling along well ahead of the rest of the team, head down and silently cursing his colleagues who seem to have guessed that he was never in the S.A.S., and that his story is all bullshit. He's also mentally having a go at the hot sun that's burning down on the back of his neck, his sore feet, why the fuck have we got vehicles if we don't sit in them? and the fucking dust and sand that gets just about everywhere.

Frank is what's technically known as a 'wannabe'. It's not as if he hasn't done his time in the forces, or even that he hasn't survived one or two 'contacts' with unfriendlies who were shooting at him. It's just that, for some reason even he can't explain, this is just not enough for him, and so he's made up half of his life story to make out to others that he's this incredibly heroic ex-Special Forces soldier.

In fact Robinson served twice in the British Armed Forces, the first time for a three year period as an infantryman in the Royal Welch Fusiliers, and then for another eight years as a member of the Royal Air Force Regiment, where he reached the lofty rank of Lance Corporal. As a fusilier he had been with the Royal Welch when they had been part of UNPROFOR (the United Nations

Protection Force) in Bosnia in May 1995 during the Yugoslav Wars, as they became commonly known. During this time the regiment together with other UN troops from participating nations had been given the task of defending the mainly Muslim city of Goražde. However, their orders had been only to 'deter attacks' against the city which had previously been declared a 'safe haven' for non-combatant Muslims by the UN, and they were massively under-equipped and poorly armed to do even that. When well-armed soldiers of the Army Republika Srpska (the Bosnian Serb Army) ignored the UN ultimatum and proceeded to attack the town completely without warning, the regiment managed to hold them off for a time, but was then driven into underground bunkers. Unfortunately about three hundred and fifty UN troops, including thirty-three fusiliers (one of which was Robinson) were captured and held hostage by the Bosnian Serbs until a relief force of Muslim Serbs arrived on the scene and fought off the attackers and freed the hostages. Although little of this desperate fight was reported by the Western media, the Royal Welch Fusiliers were credited with saving the inhabitants of the city from being massacred by their spirited defence. Later five gallantry awards and seven Mentions in Despatches were awarded to members of the regiment but Robinson was not among the recipients and he left the army a year later. He had lost his pride and his belief in his own ability when the Serbs disarmed him and his fellow fusiliers and then treated them as though they were nothing. It had even hurt to be rescued by the other Bosnians. From that moment on he had been left feeling inadequate, frustrated and guilty that he had not been able to fight back. His self-confidence was shot to pieces.

This attitude remained with him on civvie street and after a couple of years of being unemployed and dossing around Frank had joined the Royal Air Force Regiment. The regiment, known as the 'rock apes' to everyone else in the forces had been formed in 1942 with the sole purpose of providing close defence of RAF airfields. Robinson served peacetime postings in the UK and the Falklands Islands, and had then completed one operational Herrick tour in Afghanistan, but even here he had never had the opportunity to redeem his confidence or prove again that he could fight. He had then tried and failed to be selected for the RAF Regiment Flight that was being formed for a new unit called the

Special Forces Support Group. During all of this latter period of service he did not manage to recapture his belief in his own ability or redeem his dignity. He finally left the forces and had not been able to settle into anything in civvie street, moving from one poorly-paid manual job to another. Meanwhile his imagination and his war stories had grown out of all proportion until he had been found out as a liar at his local Royal British Legion Branch. He had been on a Remembrance Day parade, wearing a black blazer with a S.A.S. badge on its chest pocket, a sand-coloured S.A.S. beret on his head and a chest full of medals (two full rows of them) which he had not earned. One of the branch members had confronted him in public about why he was wearing a Korean War medal while he was obviously way too young to have served during that campaign (1950-1953). He had been booed off the parade and reported in the local paper. In abject shame he had immediately moved town to get away from a possible prosecution for wearing medals he wasn't entitled too, and to escape the vilification of his former friends in the legion.

For the previous two years he had found himself lost and unable to focus. He tried to find something to motivate him, to help him regain his self-respect and dignity. He thought it would help by getting in the thick of it again and seeing more action. He tried becoming a mercenary; a soldier of fortune. However to his abject horror and shame he had instantly been spotted as a 'wannabe' by every mercenary outfit that he had approached. That is until now, when even he knew that he had only been taken on because Huntsbringer and Oldport had been in a hurry and desperate for anyone who would volunteer for their crazy rescue mission.

Now Robinson is regretting his impulsiveness very much indeed. It had been okay the first few days out in the desert. He had been excited at the long-awaited prospect of action and hopeful in his own mind that he would have no trouble in acting valiantly when the time came. He had even regaled the others with the made-up stories of his past exploits in the S.A.S., but after a couple of minor slips where he had got his story wrong it had gradually dawned on them that he was full of bullshit and slowly Robinson had withdrawn into a sulky silence whenever he was with them.

Seven days into this adventure the novelty has completely worn off and Robinson is wishing that he'd never become a part of

214

this bloody stupid operation. There is just too much hot sun, sand, dust and bloody rocks and he's fed up with the wankers that are his so-called comrades-in-arms. He's seriously considering nicking one of the Land Rover Discoveries while it's his turn to be on stag at night, and getting back to civilisation. The only thing that has stopped him so far is that he doesn't have a clue where he is and which way safety and civilisation lies. He hasn't paid any attention at all during the teams daily conflabs to what has been said. He knows secretly in his heart of hearts, despite being hopeful that he really is a great hero, that if he nicked a vehicle and drove away he'd probably get lost in this bloody desert and die of starvation.

He really is a useless twat.

It's Dwayne Huntsbringer, driving the lead vehicle a full one hundred metres behind the despondent and useless Robinson as he plods along (with his thumb up his arse and his eyes down) who is the first to spot the approaching dust cloud ahead of them. He immediately stops and shakes the dozing figure of his friend Mike Oldport:

"Shit! We've got company coming!"

Mike looks out of the dust-covered windscreen, wide-awake in less time than it takes him to sit up fully.

"Fuck! Where the hell is Robinson?"

"He's up there on the right." Huntsbringer points to the Brit as he continues to plod over the rocks above the gully with his head down.

"Why the fuck hasn't he spotted anything?"

Dwayne just shakes his head in disappointment.

Meanwhile, the small figure of Ibrahim in front of their vehicle has also halted on hearing the Land Rover stop, and is shading his eyes against the glare of the midday sun to look forward. As soon as he spots the dust cloud that is rapidly approaching them he turns back and walks quickly to the Land Rover. By the time he's got there he's been joined by the American ex-SEAL who had been driving the second vehicle just behind Huntsbringers. He too can see the problem:

"Get out of the vehicles and arm yourselves, quickly!"

O'Brian immediately takes command and none of the others even think to argue with him. "Get up in the rocks over there." He points to the high, rocky side of the wadi, but it's too late. Just as Huntsbringer and Oldport begin to exit the Land Rover, the cloud of dust, mostly hidden from them until then around a blind turn of the dry riverbed, suddenly billows into the air right in front of them.

A large three-axle truck painted in bright red and yellow rumbles around the corner and screeches to a halt as the driver suddenly sees the two Land Rovers blocking his way. Sand spurts high into the air as the wheels lock and the truck skews off to one side to miss them by just a few metres. Behind it is a white pickup truck that also slams its brakes on, skidding through the loose stand and jerking to a complete stop just in front of them. Seconds later, a horde of shouting, jabbering black men spew from the vehicle's cabs and the open back of the pickup, angrily pointing the muzzles of their AK47s at the shocked rescue team.

Pandemonium ensues. The air is filled by the huge cloud of thick dust and sand thrown up by the vehicles as they braked dimming the brightness of the noon-day sun. The Americans, Brit and Egyptian are roughly pushed and shoved against the side of their Land Rover and their weapons are grabbed from their hands and thrown away. At least eight black Africans, dressed in worn and ripped jeans and dirty T-shirts, brandishing their assault rifles into the faces of the rescue team, continue to shout and scream angrily, their spittle splashing on to their captive's skin. Punches are thrown and shins are kicked, and more than one of the Africans aims his weapon into the air and fires off a round.

Ibrahim tries to speak to them in Egyptian, then quickly switches to Sudanese as he sees that no one understands him, but it doesn't make one bit of difference and he is soon smacked in the mouth with a rifle butt. At the command of the tallest of the Africans the foreigners are forced to their knees and their hands are violently pulled upwards on to the back of their heads while more kicks are aimed at their bodies.

Suddenly it goes quieter as the leader of the Africans begins to strut up and down in front of the line of kneeling men. The rest of his men stop shouting as he quickly fires questions at the captives. When Ibrahim answers him in Sudanese the man obviously does not like what he says as he leaps forward and launches a huge kick into the Egyptian's side that sends him sprawling into the sand. He turns to his men and screams an order. They step back from the line of captives and bring the muzzles of their rifles down to point at them, cocking their weapons with a harsh metallic sound that makes the team members cringe.

Robert O'Brian is the only one of them whose eyes are not inextricably drawn to the barrels of the assault rifles facing them. Instead he looks up at the rocky hills that lie behind their direction of travel, hoping against hope that he will see a glint of sunshine reflected off a rifle's scope.

Jeez! Now would be a great time to show me what a great shot you are, John! he thinks to himself.

But there's no sudden gunshot and no reflection of the sun. He and his team might as well be on their own out here in the empty desert, hundreds of miles from civilisation and about to be murdered by a gang of smugglers. He wonders if anyone will ever find their bodies after it's all over.

THIRTY-SEVEN

2nd July
Somewhere in the Eastern Desert, Egypt

As soon as Smith realises that the rescue team made up of Huntsbringer, Oldport, O'Brian and the others has not seen the oncoming threat indicated by the approaching dust cloud, he motors his Polaris Sportsman MV850 All Terrain Vehicle up a sharp incline in order to reach the top of the cliff behind him. The 850cc engine screams as he revs it to its maximum to stagger up the seventy degree slope for a distance of about sixty metres. Once he's over the lip and on the top of the cliff he turns left and heads across a boulder field. He knows he must decrease the distance between himself and the team if he is to provide any effective support, but he also knows that he must keep his height advantage as well. He bounces over the boulders at a dangerously high speed, pushing the vehicle to its limit. Fortunately the Terrain Armor tyres are still doing a good job of minimising the effects of the constant jarring. He drives for a further five hundred metres before the boulders begin to get too big even for the ATV to negotiate. At this point he slams on the brakes, grabs the big Barrett M82 rifle from its clamp behind his seat and slides off the ATV, leaving it with its engine still running. He looks out to his left but finds that he can no longer see the rescue team's vehicles or the cloud of dust that was approaching them.

"Shit!"

Hurriedly he again looks around the top of the cliff and sees that about a hundred metres in front of him there appears to be a smooth piece of rock around the size of a car jutting out. He takes off at a quick jog, jumping from rock to rock and then leaping on to the top of other larger ones pushing his way forward. The sun beats down on his head and shoulders with a fearsome heat, sweat pours down his face and makes his hands slippery. His breathing is harsh in a throat as dry and rasping as a sheet of sandpaper. Once or twice he almost drops the big, heavy and cumbersome rifle, barely managing to retain his grip. By the time he reaches the flat rock and flings himself down on top of its surface, his legs feel like rubber and his heart is pounding away in his chest like a fifty calibre machine gun. The rock is as hot as an oven shelf and burns at his body through his desert combats but he ignores the intense discomfort and frantically gets the rifle ready to fire while his eyes, stinging with sweat, desperately search the landscape in front and below him.

Ibrahim tries to speak to the smugglers again in Sudanese:

"We not smugglers! We looking for Somalis! We want to kill Somalis! We not your enemies!" He tries desperately to persuade the smugglers not to kill them. He's almost sure that they're Sudanese and not Somalis, but not one hundred percent, so he prays as he talks. "We have money! Do not kill us and we will pay you!"

For the first time the leader of the smuggler's interest seems to be aroused. He asks in Sudanese:

"Money? Where is money? Is it in your vehicles?"

Ibrahim shakes his head, knowing that if he says yes the smugglers will simply murder them and take the money anyway.

"No! We have plenty money in our hotel in Quseer! We will pay you plenty money not to kill us!" The leader of the smugglers laughs at this, a sneer on his face, and suddenly Ibrahim knows that their last opportunity to convince the smugglers not to shoot them has gone. He bows his head and begins to pray to himself quietly, determined to die well in front of these savages.

The leader of the smugglers laughs harshly again and utters a sharp order to the members of his gang. In response they raise the barrels of their AK47s and point them at the heads of the captives.

Robert O'Brian watches them closely and can see their finger triggers begin to tighten and their muscles stiffen in anticipation of the recoil as they fire. In his mind he damns them and John Smith to hell.

Smith pulls the M82 tight into his right shoulder until it is snug, then flips down the caps on the riflescope mounted on to the rifle's optics rail with sweaty fingers and looks through it. He looks up again and stares out over the landscape, acquiring the rescue team's precise location about two thousand metres away in his mind's eye. Then he lowers his head again to stare through the riflescope, bringing the target to bear in the scope cross hairs. He gently turns the non-fast adjustable eyepiece until the face of one of the smugglers springs into view and is clear and in focus. Then he tightens the locking ring and turns the magnification adjustment ring until the scope is at its full magnification and he can almost pick out the individual hairs on the man's face. This guy obviously never shaves and has a wispy beard covering his chin. Smith refuses to hurry. He can see that the men are going to fire soon and kill their captives but hurrying will only make him miss. If he misses then O'Brian and the others will have no chance at all. He cocks the rifle, pulling back the cocking handle and letting it go forward under its own steam, looks through the scope again and centres the cross hairs lower down on the right side of the smuggler's chest. He takes a deep slow breath and lets it out again, slowly, then another, and then another. He can feel his breathing coming back under control after the mad dash to the firing point. His chest is no longer going up and down, in and out like a bellows. He takes another deep breath, lets half of it slowly out, stops and gently squeezes the trigger.

THIRTY-EIGHT

2nd July
Somewhere in the Eastern Desert, Egypt

Dwayne Huntsbringer is full of fear, not for himself but for his wife, and for Mike's wife too. He's faced death before but never like this, not when there is so much at stake for the one person in the world that he loves above everything else. If he dies here and now Margot will have no one to look out for her, no one to get her away from the Somali pigs that have taken her. He curses himself for not seeing the danger until it was too late.

Mike Oldport surprises himself. Unlike Dwayne he's never been in a life-threatening situation like this, yet just like Dwayne his mind is not full of fear for himself as his last moment comes. It's full of thoughts of Sheila. How will she escape the kidnappers without his help? Who will pay the ransome? What will become of her? He could cry out with frustration at the unfairness of it all.

Ibrahim al-Busiri continues to pray silently to himself. His mind is calm. He has lived a good life. He has always helped those less fortunate than himself, giving alms to the poor and even sharing the meat on his table with those who had nothing to eat. He is a good Muslim and he is sure that he will soon be in paradise. He's only sorry that he couldn't help the innocent tourists who have, to his intense shame, been kidnapped in his country by the Godless Somali sons-of-dogs.

Robert O'Brian is also calm. His eyes are searching the faces of the men in front of him, flitting over their weapons, looking for even a second's passing weakness that he can take advantage of. He's not afraid of death. He sincerely believes in his own God, but his God helps those who help themselves. If he has a chance, even a very slim one to fight, then he will. His mind calculates the

221

distances and the odds. He tenses himself to act. The leering African in front of O'Brian pulls the butt of his AK47 into his shoulder and almost places the muzzle of the weapon on the bridge of O'Brian's nose. The American see his finger trigger tensing as it pulls back.

The African disintegrates before his eyes in a shower of blood and guts that drenches O'Brian and almost blinds him for an instant - he doesn't even have the time to blink before the thick hot liquid sprays into his face. Smith's first round cuts the African in two but it doesn't stop there. The angle is perfect and the half-an-inch diameter forty-two gram Browning Machine Gun slug goes straight through the first target, cuts the man next to him into two pieces as well and then goes on to slam through the rifle butt of a third African before burying itself in his lungs, hurling his body a full three metres to the side from the sheer impact.

It's only as the last body hits the ground that the subsonic sound of the Barrett M82 is heard, sounding like a loud clash of thunder in the ears of the Africans and the rescue team alike. Everyone present is stunned into immobility. Then another round takes off the head of the smuggler leader in a further spray of blood, snot and gore and his body slides to the ground with a wet sound.

Suddenly everyone is moving and screaming. O'Brian flings himself sideways, knocking the kneeling form of the Egyptian next to him to the ground, simultaneously shouting at the others to get down.

Another African takes a BMG round in his chest. His body is hurled off its feet and slams into the side of the big red and yellow truck, the round travelling right through him and thunking into the metal with a loud clang as it penetrates the side.

The Africans are in full panic mode now. They've completely forgotten about the white men and the Egyptian who were kneeling in front of them. Two of them raise their AKs and fire off a stream of rounds around them, not aiming at anything because there's nothing to see, just blasting off in absolute fear. Their rounds zip off harmlessly into the air. Another smuggler turns and runs back towards the cab of the pickup, flinging his rifle aside in his terror.

A BMG round takes out one of the men shooting, entering through his right shoulder and exiting out of the left side of his chest. His body falls one way while his head and shoulders fly off in another direction, leaving a fine red mist floating in the air where he had stood a split second before. The other African drops his rifle and runs towards the pickup, his face and body covered in a red slime of blood sprayed on to him from the dead body of his comrade. A round takes him in the middle of his back, flinging his corpse hard against the radiator of the pickup.

By now the last African still alive has opened the pickup door and leapt inside. He fumbles to turn the key and switch the ignition on. The .50 calibre round takes him straight through his open mouth and his head simply explodes. One second it's there, the next it's gone. The round, travelling at two thousand eight hundred feet, or eight hundred and fifty-three metres per second shows no detectable reduction in speed at the resistance caused by the back of his skull. It just carries straight on through the back seat and the rear floor of the pickup, burying itself three feet deep into the compacted sand and rock particles of the wadi's floor.

Then everything is silent except for the faint patter of droplets of blood landing on the sand like fine rain, and the hissing of the pickup's radiator where the slug that took the penultimate African entered and then finally disintegrated inside the engine block.

O'Brian's the first one to move. He leaps to his feet from where he had been covering the body of Ibrahim with his own, wipes the already thickening gore from his eyes and face and scuttles across to pick up the nearest abandoned AK47. He cocks it to make sure that there's a round in the chamber and systematically begins to move around the area checking that each and every one of the Sudanese smugglers is dead and accounted for. Once that gruesome task is done he flings open the door to the red and yellow truck to make sure that no one is hiding inside.

Only when he has finished his check and he is absolutely sure that the wadi is entirely clear of any live enemy does he allow himself to slump down, strangely exhausted. He feels like he's just run a marathon, or two.

Jeez! That was a close thing!

Fuck me, but that guy can shoot!

Smith also feels as though he has run a marathon. He releases his grip on the Barrett M82, finding that his hands feel like claws, he had been holding it so tightly. He lowers his head and closes his eyes.

It has only taken him twenty-five seconds to fire off the six rounds and kill those eight men, all at a range of about two thousand metres. Despite the advanced recoil suppression of the Barrett his shoulder aches from the backward slamming of the big rifle. His closed eyes have stars in front of them from the intense concentration and his ears are ringing from the noise of the rounds going off.

Fuck me I need a drink, he thinks searching for the water bottle pouch on his webbing. Finding it he rips open the top cover and pulls out the bottle. It is then that the reaction hits him. He tries desperately to twist off the top of the water bottle but his hands start to shake badly, preventing him from getting a grip on it and his whole body is wracked by violent shudders. He gives up and flips over on to his back. Even through his closed eyelids he can still feel the sun burning down on his retinas at the back of his eyes. He lifts a shaking hand and covers his face with his forearm to keep the sun off for a minute or two.

He tries desperately to empty his mind, to clear it of the awful images he has just seen through his riflescope but he can't. He doubts whether he'll ever rid himself of them.

Some things never change.

The worst moment for him had come just after he'd killed the last African in the front of the pickup. Briefly he had caught a movement in the edge of the scope and instantly swung the barrel of the M82 around to face this new threat. His finger had just been tightening on the trigger when suddenly he realised that it wasn't the enemy whatsoever that he had in his sights. It was Frank Robinson. He had eased off the pressure, having been only a hair's breadth away from plugging the man.

Frank Robinson was surprised at his response to the events that had just happened. He'd been so intent on his own dark thoughts that he hadn't spotted the approaching vehicles until they were almost below him, at which point he had shouted an incoherent warning to the rest of the team and had thrown himself down to the ground and out of sight. He had no idea that his warning shout had been drowned out by the roar of the smuggler's big truck and that the others hadn't heard it.

The smugglers had not seen him on the rocks above the dry riverbed as they had been too intent on not smashing headlong into the Land Rover Discoverys when they had suddenly appeared in front of them. From the rocks Frank had a fine view as they screeched to a halt and tumbled out of their vehicles and then forced his colleagues down on to their knees at gunpoint. At this point Frank could easily have just slunk away and hidden in the rocks, waiting until it was all over and emerging only when the smugglers had moved on. But he didn't. Instead Frank felt a sudden calmness of mind come upon him. He found himself calculating distances and arcs of fire and searching for a route that would get him nearer to the action without being seen by the Africans. Somewhere that he would be able to open fire on the black bastards and save the day.

He had slithered down off the rocky ridge running along the edge of the wadi on his belly, making sure that he kept his AK47 up in the air so that it didn't bang on to the rocks and give his position away. Then using the abandoned smuggler's pickup truck as cover he ran forward in a crouch. Frank was just about to move around the truck to where he would have a clear arc of fire at the Africans when the first BMG round hit. He stopped dead in his tracks as the sound of that shot smacked him like a punch in the guts, then ducked down as the other shots followed, not knowing who was shooting at who with that gun that sounded like a fucking canon.

When it was all over he continued to move around the pickup into a good position, only to be almost shot by the American ex-SEAL who was making sure that all of the Africans were dead. The yank looked at Frank, taking in the fact that he was holding his AK47 at the ready. Then he glanced back along the route that Frank had taken to get where he was from where he had been up on the ridge at the beginning of the contact. O'Brian's normally deadpan face eased itself into a slow smile and he nodded in acknowledgement to Frank that he knew that he had been on his way to help.

Frank nodded back. Even though he had been a little late to save the day, at least O'Brian knew that he hadn't run away when the shit had hit the fan. He hadn't abandoned his fellow team mates and had been prepared to put his own life on the line to help save theirs.

He smiled back at the American and stood a little straighter, a significant amount of his pride returned to him at last.

THIRTY-NINE

2nd July
Somewhere in the Eastern Desert, Egypt

"What?...Who?...the fuck was that?" Along with all of the members of the rescue team Dwayne Huntsbringer is in shock at the sheer brutality and speed of the violence that has played out in front of him. His face is slack as he stands and looks around at the absolute chaos. He half expects the sound of a shot to come from somewhere out in the desert, taking his own life as it had taken the lives of the African smugglers. Fearfully, he peers out into the surrounding expanse of rock, sand and sun, searching for a hint of their saviour, perhaps a reflection off a scope's lens or a distant figure waving at him, but he sees nothing.

Mike Oldport bends over and spews his guts up. He's never seen anything like the butchery that litters the ground in front of him and his face and clothes are speckled with blood, bits of bone and God knows what else. He retches and retches until there's nothing left to throw up except bile, then he retches some more. Ibrahim hands him a water bottle with a hand that is faintly shaking:

"Make sure you drink plenty of water, Mister Mike. You must not become dehydrated."

Of all of them, it's perhaps the small Egyptian who is least affected by the slaughter of the smugglers. His religious fatalism is coming to his aid. He is still alive when he believed just a few minutes ago that he was going to die. He is now absolutely convinced that he will survive this mission and rescue the tourists from the kidnappers. Inshallah, God willing.

227

O'Brian removes the magazine from the AK47 that he picked up from one of the dead smugglers, and cocks it to eject the round that's in the chamber, sending it tumbling on to the sand.

"Jeez. Who the fuck cares." He kicks out at the blood-stained mass of a smuggler's torso, his boot connecting with an audible 'thwack' that sends Oldport into paroxysms of retching again. "I guess that we've got a guardian angel out there somewhere." He shades his eyes and stares out into the desert, then gives up, swapping the position of the assault rifle around until he's holding it by the barrel and smashing it against a boulder. The wooden stock splits with a crack. He smashes it down again violently this time bending the rifle a little and making it useless. He tosses it away. "I say that we get the fuck out of here before whoever it is changes his mind and starts firing that fucking gun of his at us."

Frank Robinson walks up behind him.

"What about these bodies? We should bury them."

Frank has seen his share of bloodshed before, especially in Bosnia, but he still has to fight the urge to throw his guts up. He tries hard not to focus on any of the individual body pieces littering the ground around them. Dwayne looks up at him, noticing the slight change in his demeanour, his sudden confidence.

"Like fuck!" Dwayne says sharply. "Do you think that these guys would have buried us? Shit no! Leave them for the buzzards!"

Oldport nods his head in agreement, still feeling very nauseous. He doesn't want to touch anything. He just wants to get away from here. Subconsciously he can feel an itching between his shoulder blades as though whoever it was that killed the smugglers now has his sights set on his back.

"What the fuck happened?" Robinson looks around. "Who was it that saved you guys?"

"Let's discuss it later. I just want us to get as far away from this place as possible." Neither O'Brian's face nor his tone of voice give anything away. "Mike, you and Dwayne see if you can drive the vehicles through this mess. Frank, Ibrahim, help me to break up these guy's weapons. We don't want them to be used by any more bad guys." He looks around the faces of his team mates and can see the strain and disbelief written on all of them. He knows that they're all in deep shock at the moment and not able to really take

228

anything in, but soon enough their questions about the shooter that saved their lives will become more and more insistent. He wants to get them up and moving and out of here before the shock really sets in and they find it too hard to shift their asses. "These guy's trucks will have fucked up the kidnapper's trail, I reckon. Let's hope that they joined this wadi not too far away, so that we can find the kidnapper's spoor again." He claps his hands together to break the others from the lethargy that's already threatening to overwhelm them. "Come on fellas! Let's get a move on and get the hell away from here!"

They all begin to move.

Ibrahim comes close to him and speaks softly:

"*Dust devils*, eh?" He smiles knowingly at O'Brian and moves on.

ENGLAND

FORTY

9th July
Tesco Merseyside Superstore, St. Oswalds Street, Liverpool

The Asian man in his early thirties is clean-shaven and smartly dressed in a pair of light-coloured trousers and an open dark green jacket over a blue shirt. He is wandering along the aisle. It is still fairly early in the morning and a bit nippy outside after a heavy overnight rain storm, so no one thinks it strange that the man is wearing a jacket in the middle of July. The superstore is not that busy and the few staff on duty, including the handful of security personnel, are walking around with that early-morning look on their faces. All that each one really wants to do is go back home and climb into a nice warm, comfortable bed and pull the duvet back over their head.

The man, shopping basket in his left hand, stops to gaze along the shelves full of a bewildering variety of breakfast cereals. He pulls out box after box of Kellogg's All-Bran, Alpen, Honey Nut Cheerios, Cornflakes, Weetabix and Frosted Flakes, looks at the packets and puts them back as though finding it hard to come to a decision about which one to buy.

No one notices when he slips a packet of Rice Krispies from a large inside pocket of his jacket and puts it on to one of the middle shelves, sliding it back behind the first row of dozens of similar boxes of Rice Krispies and well out of sight of anyone wishing to buy a packet of the cereal, at least for a while. No one notices the slight shaking of his hand as he does so either, nor the sheen of sweat that has appeared on his face. Even if someone was watching him like a hawk, which of course they aren't, it is doubtful that they would notice the strain in his wrist as he lifts the heavy box, much heavier than it should be. He is just an ordinary man looking

233

to buy a breakfast cereal, one of thousands of similar people who will be using the Superstore today. No reason to suspect him of anything at all.

The man moves along the aisle a few metres, finally selects a packet of Special-K Protein Plus, places it into his basket, and then wanders off towards the milk section.

A few minutes later he's paid for his groceries and is heading towards his hire car in the Superstore's huge car park. He's relieved beyond measure to have got rid of his package. Its heavy weight had been burning a hole in his pocket and his imagination ever since he had taken it from Achmed late last night. All of the long drive northwards afterwards he had been filled with fear. Now he begins to feel the pride of doing a job well, knowing that the drive south to Coventry will be a lot more pleasant than the journey here was.

All over the north of England other young Asian men are carrying out the same task. In the Asda Supermarket on Chandler Way in Carlisle, in the Lidl Discount Supermarket along Chesterfield Road in Sheffield, in the Tesco Extra in Kingston Park in Newcastle, in Morrisons Supermarket in Westgate in Bradford, in Waitrose on Meanwood Road in Leeds, and in Sainsbury's along Regents Road in Salford, Manchester. Each of the other six men is sliding a too-heavy packet of Rice Krispies on to the rear of the breakfast cereal shelves before leaving the stores, getting into their hire cars and beginning the journey southwards.

Seven young men in total and seven packages safely delivered.

Before leaving Liverpool the first young man pulls over into a residential street and makes a call on his pay-as-you-go mobile phone:

"Hello? Liverpool Echo. News desk."

"I am a soldier of Allah. You will want to record this message."

"Excuse me?"

"Fool! Record this message. I am a soldier of ad-Dawlah al-Islāmiyah fīl-'Irāq wash-Shām, the Islamic State of Iraq and ash-Sham. The yawm al-qiyamah, the Day of Judgement, is nearly upon you and the Mahdi, the redeemer of Islam, will soon be

234

amongst us. He will rid the world of all unbelievers and your evil! The troops of the Khilafah; Amir al-Mu'minin have arrived on your shores and your evil, Godless state will soon become one with Islam! Long live the Mujahedeen! Allāhu Akbar!"

He ends the call, opens the back of the mobile and removes the battery. Then, with a smile on his lips, he restarts his journey.

Two hours later and a young woman by the name of Merissa Phillips is shopping along the breakfast cereals shelf in the Tesco Merseyside Superstore in Liverpool. She reaches up and pulls forward a box of Rice Krispies, but then stops. It feels a lot heavier than it should. She picks it up and feels the extra weight, then shakes her head, puts it down and picks up another next to it. This one is much more normal. She leans forward past the smiling form of her nine-month old daughter Yasmin who's sitting in the baby seat of the trolley, and puts the packet on top of a huge pile of other items she's collected so far in her fortnightly 'big' shop. As she straightens up, she gently strokes Yasmin's face, believing that she is the most beautiful little girl in the whole world, and is rewarded with another smile and a giggle that melts her heart. She begins to push the trolley further along the aisle.

Thankfully neither Merissa nor Yasmin feel any pain as they are abruptly taken from the land of the living. They don't even hear the bomb going off, nor do they feel the red hot wind that whips past them or the razor-sharp six-inch steel nails that penetrate their flesh and smash their bones. They are close enough to be killed instantly by the huge blast wave, which pulverises their internal organs and pops their ear-drums and implodes their eye-balls in less than a micro-second.

The people who are further away from the epicentre of the explosion are not quite so lucky, and there are a lot of them because this time on a Saturday morning is one of the busiest periods for the supermarket and it is packed with shoppers. There is only half a kilogramme of Semtex plastic explosive embedded in the heart of the packet of Rice Krispies, but packed around it in the box are literally hundreds of nails and screws. These nails and screws are driven out at almost supersonic speed in an ever-increasing circle by the terrific force of the Semtex exploding. It is three times more powerful than the same weight of ordinary plastic explosive. The lethal projectiles shred through everything that they come in contact with, whether it be the packets of biscuits and cream crackers on the opposite shelf, the tins of baked beans and plum tomatoes on the shelf beyond that, or the flesh and bone of the people who are anywhere within a forty metre range of the bomb.

Those that are not killed instantly by the blast of the explosion, like Merissa and the sweet little Yasmin are left with horrific wounds. They have six-inch long nails and screws driven into their limbs, heads and bodies. Many of the people who survive the next few critical days will require traumatic amputation. Some will be left permanently brain-injured or blinded by the steel shafts that have penetrated their skulls. Others, over the coming weeks and months will wish that they had been killed, as they try desperately to come to terms with the loss of wives, husbands, sons and daughters who were killed by the bomb. The injured lie there amongst the already dead, too shocked to feel the pain yet, but knowing even now that life will never, ever be the same again, as the cloud of stinking smoke and choking dust begins to settle in the shop and the screams of hundreds of terrified people assails their ears.

All over the north of England; in Carlisle, Sheffield, Newcastle, Bradford, Leeds and Manchester similar scenes are being enacted at exactly the same moment as the blast in Liverpool.

In a large bungalow on the north-eastern edge of Coventry in the English Midlands, Massoud Hassan watches as the first reports of the bombs going off begin to filter through on the BBC. They have interrupted one of their usual programmes on valuing antiques to break the news. Hassan smiles at his companion Achmed, the Iranian-trained bomb-maker who is sitting next to him with a shocked look on his paler-than-normal face, suddenly aware of the enormity of what he has done. Hassan recognises the look and reaches for the remote control to switch off the television, but Achmed sees what he is doing and reaches out his own hand to stop him.

"No, Colonel. I want to see the effect my bombs have had on the infidels." His voice is low, but strong.

236

Hassan smiles fiercely at him, pleased:

"Good! See how weak they are, Achmed, and how strong we are! Allāhu Akbar!"

"Allāhu Akbar!"

FORTY-ONE

9th July
Downing Street, London

The people sitting around the table in the emergency meeting in the Cabinet Office Briefing Room (COBR) are in a state of shock as they lower their heads for two minutes silence in memory of the dead. When they raise their heads again, more than one of them has unshed tears in their eyes.

The Prime Minister clears his throat with a low cough:

"Do we have an update on the number of casualties?" His question is aimed at Sir Andrew Lowe, the Director General of the Security Service, MI5. Sir Andrew turns to one of his aids who hands over a single sheet of paper.

"Yes, Prime Minister. As of five minutes ago there have been sixty-three fatalities recorded by the emergency services in the seven affected cities. The number of non-fatal casualties is estimated at two hundred and five, but these numbers are not definite as there is still some confusion at the scenes of the bombings. And, of course, many of those who are injured are in a critical state and a large percentage of them may succumb to their injuries in the next few hours and days." His voice is low and conveys the absolute shock that he feels.

"Thank you, Sir Andrew." The Prime Minister turns now to the Commander of S015, the Counter Terrorism Command. "What of the perpetrators? Do you have any news?"

Commander Vaughn looks angry rather than shocked at the sheer scale of the terrorist outrage:

"Apart from the partially recorded telephone message that we have received from the news desk of the Liverpool Echo, we have nothing else at the moment, Sir. My officers are attempting to

238

secure CCTV footage from all of the supermarkets where the devices were placed, but as you can imagine there is utter and complete chaos at the scenes. It will take some time before they can all be retrieved and trawled through."

"Play the tape again."

There are a few moments of hushed talking amongst the people around the table before the voice of a man comes out loud and clear on the room's loudspeakers:

"…soldier of ad-Dawlah al-Islāmiyah fīl-Irāq wash-Shām, the Islamic State of Iraq and ash-Sham. The yawm al-qiyamah, the Day of Judgement, is nearly upon you and the Mahdi, the redeemer of Islam, will soon be amongst us. He will rid the world of all unbelievers and your evil! The troops of the Khilafah; Amir al-Mu'minin, have arrived on your shores and your evil, Godless state will soon become one with Islam! Long live the Mujahedeen! Allāhu Akbar!"

"What do you mean? Please say that again?"

The Commander indicates to the technician who is manning the sound system to turn it off.

"The last voice you heard is the voice of the receptionist at the Echo. The call was ended and there was no reply."

The Prime Minster turns to Sir Hugh Metcalfe, the Director General of the Secret Intelligence Service, MI6:

"I'm jolly glad that this mess didn't happen *before* the elections!" His badly-chosen attempt at humour falls on deaf ears and harsh stares, but he quickly recovers from the gaffe, as only a true politician can: "What do you make of it, Sir Hugh? Is it authentic? Can the Islamic State really be responsible for this?" His voice is half pleading.

"I'm afraid so, Prime Minister. The terminology used during the call checks out with previous messages that have been received from ISIS. In particular the mention of the 'Khilafah; Amir al-Mu'minin' rings very true. This is one of the names that ISIS supporters use when referring to Abu Bakr al-Baghdadi, or Abu Bakr al-Baghdadi al-Husseini al-Qurashi as he is sometimes known. He is the self-styled leader of ISIS in Syria and Iraq; their so-called Caliph."

"Dear God. I'd hoped that we would never have to face these bastards on our own shores! It's bad enough what they have done

239

to the British hostages that they've taken in the Middle East, but this, this *outrage* beggars all belief! How have they managed to do this?"

His question is rhetorical and no one around the table appears to have an answer. Eventually Brigadier Clarkeson, the Director of UK Special Forces is the one to speak up and break the uncomfortable silence:

"I take it that the arrival of the former Iranian colonel. What's his name? Hassan? Is not a coincidence, especially as his former masters now say that he is involved with ISIS?"

Sir Andrew and Sir Hugh exchange a quick guilty look but no one else around the table seems to notice.

"That would seem to be true, Brigadier." This comes from Commander Vaughn. "It can't be just a coincidence that this Hassan has also caused an explosion so recently?"

"Are we any nearer to catching this bastard?" asks the Home Secretary in her typically sarcastic way. "After all it's been weeks since he set off the bomb in Luton! Surely we must be nearer to catching him?"

Her question is aimed at the Commander who looks distinctly unhappy.

"I'm afraid not, Madame Secretary. As you know I've had my best officers on the case, but since the murders in Small Heath the trail has gone stone cold again. All that I can add at this moment is *if* this latest attack has anything to do with Hassan, then he must now have a number of accomplices. It's extremely unlikely that one man, no matter how well he has been trained could have placed all of the explosive devices across the north of England. The distances involved are just too great."

"So you're now telling me that there must be a *group* of bloody ISIS terrorists on the loose in Britain? Not just *one* man?" The Prime Ministers voice is getting angry.

"Yes, Sir. I'm afraid I am."

"And we're no closer to apprehending him now than we were at our last meeting?"

"No, Sir."

The Prime Minister suddenly stands and leans forward, his hands placed flat on the table in front of him and his eyes roving around

240

all of the senior people sitting around him. His voice is cold and harsh:

"Then it's about bloody time that you all got your fingers out! I want every policeman, every officer of the intelligence agencies and every bloody soldier in this country on full alert and working their asses off until we find this bloody madman and his bloody accomplices! I want the north of England swamped with men so that this cannot happen again. Everything else must now go on hold, do you hear me? It must be our overriding priority to find these savages! Do I make myself clear?"

"Yes, Prime Minister." Comes the rather subdued answer in unison.

"Then why are you still sitting here? Get out there and find this bastard!"

EGYPT

FORTY-TWO

11th July
Hurghada, Egypt

Detective Inspector Helen Wright holds the mobile phone to her ear and listens to the faint dialling tone. It's her third go at calling having failed to get through on the two previous attempts. Now she holds her breath as the tone continues to ring. For God's sake Daljit, answer the bloody phone! She's standing by the large window of her plush hotel room in the 'Sol Y Mar Ivory Suites' located in the El Kawsar District of Hurghada, having found that this is the only spot in the building where she can get a decent signal. Despite the air conditioner blasting away on its maximum setting she finds that her thin silk top is still sticking to her back with her sweat. At last she hears a click, and a low indistinct voice on the other end of the line.

"Daljit? Is that you? Daljit?"
She can hear the voice again, but still can't make it out. She starts to move around the room to try and get a better signal.

"Hello? Helen?" Suddenly the big Sikhs voice booms loud and clear.

"Daljit! Thank heaven I've got hold of you!"

"Hi, Helen. Where are you? This is an awful line."
Helen turns, giving her friend a big thumbs up. Linda, who's sitting on the edge of the bed, smiles back, relieved.

"You wouldn't believe me if I told you, Daljit." And I'm not going to!

"Well, I'm glad you've called, Helen. I've been trying to get hold of John. Do you have any idea where he is?"

"He's overseas, Daljit and I'm afraid that I won't be able to talk to him for a while."

245

"Oh…well, anyway, what can I do for you, Helen?" She pauses now and tries to get her thoughts into order. With all of the hassle over the last hour trying to get hold of Daljit she hasn't really thought through what she is going to say to him, or how to put her request. Luckily, the Sikh is well ahead of her: "I'm guessing that this has something to do with the supermarket bombings up north?"

"Yes…that's right. My superiors are requesting the help of The Brotherhood. John told me that I should talk to you as their representative if he's not available…"

"Yes, he said the same thing to me a few months ago. What is it that we can do to help your…er…superiors?"

"They are hoping that you can help them locate their prime suspect, Daljit? He's a former Iranian colonel."

"Iranian? I thought that ISIS had claimed responsibility for the bombings?"

"That's right, they have. The man that the security forces believe is the leader of the bombers used to be in the Iranian Armed Forces, but now he's apparently gone rogue and joined ISIS."

"That sounds kind of implausible, Helen. You know that the majority of Iranians are Shi'a Muslims? ISIS is made up of Sunni Muslims, and they don't exactly get on with the Shiites. In fact they probably hate them worse than they hate us infidels."

"I know, Daljit. I know. But they have good intelligence that this is our man."

"Ah, that's another contradiction in terms, Helen. The intelligence services don't really have that much *intelligence*." He chuckles quietly at his own joke. "Okay, Helen. Do you have a description and a name for this guy?" She spends the next few minutes filling him in with the details. "Okay. I'll see what we can do, Helen. If this is the bastard that caused those bombings, I can't promise that we'll find him, or that we'll hand him over to the security services even if we do. You and your bosses do understand that?"

"Yes we do. I've been told that even his body will do."

"Roger that, Helen. Dead *or* alive, eh? I can live with that. Okay, we're already doing everything that we can to find the bastards of course, but this info will help us a lot. Let's hope we get him!"

"Yes."

"Thanks for your help, Helen. Make sure you tell John to get back in contact with me whenever you see him again?"

"I will, Daljit and…thanks."

"Always a pleasure to do business with you, Helen. Take care."

"Thanks. You too, Daljit. Bye."

Helen is relieved to have got that job out of the way. It's been a hard few weeks for both her and Linda since Smith and O'Brian disappeared into the desert, especially as they haven't had any news. It was good to get the call from Sir Andrew Lowe this morning so at least they feel a part of it all again.

Linda stands up and puts her arm around Helen's shoulders, giving her a gentle hug.

"He'll be okay you know?"

"I know, Linda. It's just…" She shrugs, unable to carry on. Linda gives her another squeeze.

"At least we've got each other for company, Helen. It would have driven me mad to be sitting in Norfolk and waiting on my own, and it's always going to be the same with John I'm afraid. He'll never be able to settle down to a nine to five job, or even to retire. He just won't be able to."

"I know."

"Come on then, Helen. There's nothing else we can do. We might as well try and relax a bit, especially as the government's paying the bill!" At least that brings a hint of a smile to Helen's lips. "Fancy a swim in the pool?"

"I'd rather have a chocolate ice-cream!"

"Now you're talking! Let's get down to the restaurant and order the biggest chocolate ice-cream sundaes they've got!"

FORTY-THREE

11th July
Somewhere in northern Sudan

Nine days have passed since the rescue team ran into the Sudanese smugglers, nine long, hard days of tracking and driving another one hundred and eighty kilometres. They've crossed the Egyptian border and are heading south, deep into the empty vastness of northern Sudan. Ibrahim had eventually picked up the trail of the kidnappers again seven days ago after losing it briefly because part of it had been obscured by the fresher trail made by the smuggler's vehicles, and now they know they are close. Each wad of qaad that he is finding spat out on to the side of the trail is wetter than the one before, so they know that their goal is not far away. They have slowed down now and everyone is alert with two men out on point instead of one, cautiously checking each blind turn ahead.

John Smith is continuing to follow them at a distance. Due to the hard physical exercise he is undertaking in the hot, dry climate of the desert he has become fully acclimatised to the environment. His darkly tanned face is testament to the unyielding sun and being out in the elements on his ATV. His days are spent incessantly cruising along behind the rescue team and he spends his nights in a one man bivvie pitched next to his ATV, AK47 cradled in his arms as he shivers away in the cold hours of darkness. His mind is thankfully blank at night-time now but he knows that as soon as the mission is over he will not be able to sleep properly for months and that the recollections of the faces of the smugglers he shot with the M82 will haunt him. He also knows that eventually they will fade and join the rest of his memories - of men he has killed. He's grateful for the need to be so vigilant as it tires him out and helps him sleep at night. And now at least he's got company as well.

248

A week ago he was woken in the night by a shuffling sound around his camp and he sneaked out of his bivvie to find a scrawny white and tan dog nosing around his kit. It was a bag of skin and bones and looked as though it hadn't had a decent meal in months. His first thought had been to throw a stone at the mangy mutt and send it on its way, but then he realised that it was harmless. Just hungry. He had reached into his backpack and pulled out a half-eaten candy bar from one of his MRE ration packs. He tentatively held it out to the dog but it was too scared to come closer than a couple of metres, so he left it on the ground and walked away to sit quietly on a rock.

The dog kept on sidling closer and closer to the bar, building up its nerve before scurrying away again. Smith smiled at its temerity and with his eyes drooping from tiredness he'd finally given up his vigil and had climbed back into his bivvie. In the morning both the dog and the candy bar had disappeared. He didn't see the dog again for the rest of that day but sure enough, once the darkness of the desert night descended the dog had reappeared at his next campsite. Smith had half-guessed that he'd see it again and had prepared a mixture of milk powder, margarine and minced meat which he had rolled into balls. He left the mixture with its tantalising smells on a flat rock a few metres from his camp and went back to lay on his back in the sand, looking up at the fantastic vista of millions of stars painted on the night sky. With no light pollution from towns or cities to spoil the view, it had always amazed him how clear the stars were in every desert that he'd worked in. The dog must have sensed how relaxed and at peace the man was because it had tucked into the meal with gusto as only a half-starved dog could do. It had gulped down the half a kilo of food in seconds.

Since that night Smith had made a point of sharing his rations with the dog, and slowly and surely the animal had gotten used to him and built up a confidence around him. The last couple of nights the dog had lain next to Smith's bivvie and last night he had slowly stretched out a hand and stroked it gently around its fly-nibbled ears.

God knows where the dog had appeared from and what it was doing out here on its own in the wilderness, but Smith was glad that it had turned up as it eased his growing sense of loneliness to have another soul around him. He felt a strange affinity with this half-wild animal that had found him in the middle of nowhere.

Half way through the next morning, as Smith lay on the vantage point of a high rock watching the rescue team working its way along the bottom of a ridge through his binoculars, he noticed the two men out on point, Dwayne Huntsbringer and Robert O'Brian, stop in their tracks with an unaccustomed suddenness and crouch down. He immediately swept the binos over the landscape in front of them searching for the reason that they had stopped. At first he sighted nothing but then he saw what they must have smelt on the breeze:

Smoke, trailing listlessly into the air about a kilometre and half in front of them.

FORTY-FOUR

12th July
Somewhere in northern Sudan

The man who Margot knows as Don Black coughs and then
proceeds to retch, bringing up most of the bowl of rice that she has
been painstakingly spooning into his mouth. The ex-soldier, who
one of the Somalis had badly beaten about the head with the butt of
his rifle when they were kidnapped, has been slowly deteriorating
and is now in a very bad way. Fortunately one of the members of
their group, Wim Bakker the Dutch veterinary surgeon has had lots
of experience working with the injured (even if most of his patients
up until now have had four legs). He has been a Godsend, but even
with his help Don has been slowly getting worse. Wim thinks that
he's probably got depressed fractures of the skull and is worried
that he may also have a brain injury. There are a few places around
his head which are swollen, red and warm and tender to the touch.
In addition his face is still heavily bruised even though over a
month has passed since the incident, and he continues to
sporadically bleed from his nose, eyes and ears. Black drifts in and
out of consciousness and when he is fully awake and alert (which
hasn't been often), he's complained of a crippling headache,
blurred vision and a stiff neck. At other times he has barely been
able to keep food down, vomiting it back up. Wim has also noticed
that his pupils are not reacting to light. There's no doubt about it,
he's very ill.

One of the seven Somali kidnappers has a rudimentary grasp
of English, and Wim, Margot and Sheila have used every available
opportunity to plead with him to slow down their seemingly never-
ending journey and to take more frequent stops. At first their
kidnappers were unwilling, but after Margot laid it on thick that the

sick man is an extremely well-known author of popular fiction and probably worth a couple of million to them in ransom money, they became more interested in his welfare. Thankfully their trek has now slowed down so that they are only covering five to ten kilometres a day.

The Somalis are a rum bunch. A few of them, like the guy that can just about understand English seem fairly decent and have even, on rare occasions shown some kindness towards their captives. The rest have been totally unmoved and uncaring about their well-being, being much more interested in themselves and their own comfort. The worst of the bunch are definitely the small and skinny one with the very black ashy-coloured skin and the huge yellow buck teeth that jut out from his mouth and his taller mate with the crazy eyes. They are the ones who shot and killed the Egyptian minibus driver and had then beaten Don Black after he'd opened the rear emergency door and pushed his girlfriend out. Margot has become convinced that they're both insane. They've certainly got a sadistic side to their natures and have done everything in their power to frighten and intimidate the Europeans whenever they've had the chance. They are mean ugly bastards.

The last month has been an absolute nightmare for the prisoners. It has been a tough, exacting journey travelling in extreme heat with very little rest. They've had insufficient food and drink and what has been fed to them has been disgusting; a mixture of half-cooked rice and unidentifiable bits of grey gristle that tastes foul and which is always covered in flies. It is little wonder that they've all suffered from diarrhoea at some stage. Added to this the captives have been packed into the open back of an old and battered pickup truck while they have been travelling, leaving them exposed to the direct heat of the sun and the clouds of choking dust and sand sent up by the wheels. The kidnappers on the other hand have either occupied the back of another pickup that at least has a ragged open canopy to keep the worst of the sun off their heads, or have jammed themselves into the two cabs. In order to drown out the sound of the engine and the air conditioning there they have listened to a local radio station at very high volume. Not surprisingly the prisoners have learned to loathe the sound of the North African music and singing. Margot thinks it sounds like the howling of a demented cat that's in labour.

252

Despite the hardships and barring Don Black, of course, the group has fared remarkably well so far. Margot and Sheila in particular have done a good job of keeping up everyone's morale, perhaps because they have such a strong and lasting friendship themselves which has begun to rub off on the others. They all care for each other, especially when one of them comes down with a bout of sickness and diarrhoea from the awful food, which is, of course, not helped by their constant state of semi-dehydration. When they're on their own in the back of the pickup, they have talked to each other about their respective pasts, their jobs, their families and their hopes for the future. It's all been in an effort to keep their current predicament off their minds, but it has also drawn them closer to each other. Whenever they are within earshot of their captors, especially during their frequent stops in the daytime or during their nocturnal halts, they have learned to communicate with each other using obscure hand signs and facial expressions. They have even developed nick names for each one of the Somalis. For example the buck-toothed bastard has become known to them as 'Bugs Bunny', the insane looking one as 'Crazy Eyes' while the Somali who has a rudimentary understanding of English has been christened 'Twobob'.

Three days ago Don Black's conditioned worsened to the point that they thought they were going to lose him completely. He had suffered a particularly bad attack of vomiting and lapsed into an extended period of unconsciousness. During this time Margot and Wim constantly hassled and berated Twobob, warning him that the man was in such a bad state that he would surely die if they didn't stop and rest while at the same time reminding him of the huge ransom that they would lose if he did die. At that point the Somali had opened up a little and revealed to them that most of the kidnappers did not want to hold them captive but that they had been forced into travelling into Egypt by their warlord back in their own country. He described how they had been part of a gang of pirates up until eighteen months ago which regularly boarded western ships in the Gulf of Aden and the Arabian Sea and captured their cargos and crews for millions of American dollars, (which all went to their warlord of course). He then related how the work had begun to dry up as the crews of the ships became savvier and the warships of western navies had upped the number

253

of their patrols. He told them that all of the kidnappers were from a poor fishing village on the Somali coast near a town called Bereeda, located right on the Horn of Africa, and they had no choice but to obey their warlord. If they didn't do his bidding and earn him lots of money then they and their families would be murdered.

He told them that Bereeda was where they were headed now, a distance of at least another twelve hundred kilometres. He was apologetic to them, but even so he was more worried about losing such a valuable source of income if the white man died. He took their case to the others and after lots of arguing amongst themselves they had decided to build a semi-permanent camp and to rest for a few days in the hope that the ex-soldier's condition would improve. But the Somali had also made it clear to them that they could not stop for longer than four days as their food would begin to run out. He explained that they needed to get to a place called Atbara in north-eastern Sudan, near the River Nile where they were due to replenish their stores and their fuel.

As they had journeyed south through southern Egypt and deep into northern Sudan, the bare desert had slowly begun to get slightly greener with more clumps of bushes dotting the dry desert landscape. The heat from the sun had also become more intense with each passing day as they got closer and closer to the equator. They had even begun to pass the odd oasis. It was at one of these, a dusty sand bowl surrounded by low rocky hills and ridges with a small but life-saving freshwater spring, half a dozen tall palm trees and a scant collection of thick thorny bushes that the Somalis had agreed to stop and rest.

Once they had finally decided on the place to take a break the captives were made to collect fallen palm leaves and some of the dead wood lying on the ground in order to construct two rickety lean-to shelters, one for their kidnappers and one for themselves. They weren't much but at least during the hottest part of the afternoons the thinly thatched roof of palm leaves afforded them some shelter from the incessantly blazing sun.

Here they had had the first real rest of their journey so far, even if they did have to continue to listen to the constant caterwauling from the pickup's radio. The only thing that spoiled it completely was the behaviour of Crazy Eyes, who seemed to become even more ghastly and unpleasant towards the Europeans. He constantly watched them, leering as the women were forced to relieve themselves using a rusty bucket placed behind their shelter in the bushes while at the same time cupping his genitals in his hand through his trousers, making obviously rude and suggestive remarks in his own jabbering language. Remarks that would be met with guffaws of laughter by some of the other, less affable kidnappers.

Don Black's condition has finally stabilised for a while, but they are all dreading returning to the journey which they know will happen the next day.

FORTY-FIVE

12th July
Somewhere in northern Sudan

The sun is setting as O'Brian and Dwayne make their way back to
the vehicles where the others are waiting for them, eager for news.
As the sun sinks beneath the horizon it brings with it a transient
pinky-red glow which colours the entire landscape including the
sky, rocks, sand and sparse vegetation. In another time and place it
would be something to take time out to admire and enjoy; it is so
incredibly beautiful. However the two men have other things on
their mind. By the time they reach the group dusk is starting to
settle in. The colour of the desert is gone and the dense blackness
of night is beginning to rapidly descend on their makeshift camp
about one kilometre from the Somalis. The air around them
remains intensely hot though, and they know the temperature
won't start to drop for another hour or so.
     The two men are hot and dusty when they arrive back, but
they're not given even a single moment to rest before the others
crowd around.
     "Well?" asks Mike Oldport, a quaver in his voice. "Is it
definitely them? Did you see Sheila and Margot? Are they
alright?"
Dwayne grins as he claps a hand to his friend's shoulder:
     "It's them, Mike! And yes, we saw both of them and the
others. They're looking tired and worn out but they're okay!"
Mike nearly collapses in relief. His hopes of ever finding his wife
and Margot had been pounded and worn pretty thin during their
long journey and the last few hours, as he waited for O'Brian and
his best friend to come back from their reconnaissance, seemed to

him to have been the slowest of his entire life. His mind had been awash with dire predictions and imaginings.

"Thank God! Thank God!" He grabs Dwayne in a huge bear hug. "At last!" Dwayne hugs him back, feeling a huge surge of relief himself after the most recent incredibly tense few hours.

"Let's go and get them." Frank Robinson interrupts the friends. "What are we waiting for?"

"Not so fast," replies O'Brian in a low voice. "It won't be so easy. We counted seven Somalis and they're all armed to the teeth."

"So what?" replies Robinson, still full of his new found confidence after their close call nine days ago when he had proved to himself that he wasn't a coward, slapping the stock of his AK47. "So are we! We can take the fuckers on. No problem!"

"I agree. Let's go and get them now." Mike lets go of Huntsbringer and reaches down on the ground for where he had left his own assault rifle. "It's getting dark. They won't see us coming if we hit them now!"

O'Brian steps forward and pushes the barrel of Mike's rifle down a touch.

"Just wait a minute! If we go blundering in there in the dark there's a good chance that some of the fuckers will start shooting. What if one of them hits your wife? Or Dwayne's? Or one of the other captives? Then all of this…" He waves his hand around to take them all in "…will have been for nothing!"

Mike steps back looking at him and in the very last of the day's light O'Brian can see that his point has hit home.

"But…what are we going to do then? Sit on our arses while Sheila and Margot…" His voice breaks at this point. He is tantalisingly close his wife and can't bring himself to finish his sentence.

Suddenly the low sound of sand being scuffed just behind the group causes them to turn around as one towards it. In the poor light they can just about see a man in desert combats standing roughly ten metres away. Instantly rifles are raised and fingers slip on to triggers.

"Stop!" The command from O'Brian is sharp. "Don't fire! He's with us."

"What…?" Mike squints at the figure. "Who the fuck is this?"

257

He moves threateningly forward.

"I said stop!"

There's the grating sound of O'Brian's cocking handle being pulled back and then released, followed immediately by the click of his safety catch moving from 'safe' to 'single shot'. Even Oldport has become used to the sounds after practising incessantly with his AK47 over the past weeks. He quickly turns to face O'Brian.

"What the fuck's going on Rob? Who is this bloke?"

In response to his questions the stranger steps closer:

"My name's John." His voice is dry and sounds like he hasn't used it for quite a while. They get the impression that he's tall and lean and from their brief glimpse they can see that his face is burnt as dark as their own faces from the desert sun. Then the last rays of the sun disappear over the distant line of mountains to the west and it's too dark to make out his features anymore. There's a sudden deep-throated growl from an indistinct pale shape at the man's feet. "And this is Mutt. Be careful, I think he'd like to bite you."

The group of would-be rescuers are silent for a few moments as the stranger singles out the form of O'Brian in the dusky gloom and approaches him.

"Jeez, John. Where'd you get the dog?"

"He kind of adopted me," Smith chuckles. "I think he likes your MRE rations."

"He's the only one that does then."

"Hey, compared to Brit rations they're bloody good stuff, mate."

"Mmmmm…I'll take your word on that one."

"Have you contacted the team yet?"

"Just about to. I'll get the SatCom."

O'Brian heads off towards the nearest Land Rover as the first stars start to twinkle in the night sky. John remains an indistinct shape to the rest of the group with the dog still growling every now and again at his feet.

"Just who the fuck are you?" asks Dwayne, stepping forward to try and see Smith better in the growing starlight.

"A friend."

"What the fuck does that mean?" snarls Oldport. He is completely at a loss with this latest turn of events.

"Have you been following us? Or did Rob contact you somehow?"

"Who are you?"

The questions come thick and fast from the men but Smith keeps quiet. When they start to crowd in and get too close to him the dog growls again, louder.

"Watch it! I meant what I said about the dog. He's not at all friendly."

They fall back slightly and a silence descends on the group. Their wariness and distrust remains tangible however in the atmosphere that hangs in the air.

"Are you the one that killed those smugglers?" Ibrahim asks, breaking the uncomfortable hush.

Smith doesn't answer and the silence begins to stretch again until it's broken by O'Brian re-joining the group, carrying his personal rucksack.

"I'll just climb to the top of that ridge and set up the SatCom."

"Have you got the GPS co-ordinates for the Somalis's camp?" asks Smith.

O'Brian stops and tuts.

"Jeez, John. What do you take me for?" He sounds aggrieved.

"Just checking. That's all, mate." Smith chuckles dryly again, enjoying winding O'Brian up. "I know you counted seven of the bastards, but did you clock the RPG7 in the cab of their pickup?"

There's a slight pause before the embarrassed American answers:

"No, I didn't. Thanks for the info." A shoulder-launched rocket-propelled grenade can cause havoc amongst attacking troops, so it's good that they'll be warned about it.

"A pleasure, mate. I'd hate for your blokes to be surprised by that."

O'Brian goes off into the darkness without another word. A full minute of silence goes by as the men stand around, shuffling their feet. Then Robinson can't help himself. He has to ask the question they've all been thinking:

"How do you know they've got a bloody RPG in their cab?"

They can just about see the whiteness of Smith's teeth as he smiles.

"I went and had a look, mate."

"Fuck me…"

"No thanks. I think the dog's a bit lonely though…."

O'Brian re-joins them after about fifteen minutes.

"That's it. They've got the info. The Van Amstel is still positioned off the Egyptian coast, so that makes them about five hundred kilometres away. The guys should be here within three to four hours."

Just as he finishes talking the distinct crack of a gunshot rents the night air, coming from the direction of the Somalis's camp.

FORTY-SIX

"Here, take the dog." Smith shoves a piece of rope into
Robinson's hands. "I've made a makeshift harness for him but if I
were you I'd tie him up to the Land Rover, and I wouldn't try to
pet him, mate."
He heads off leaving a bemused Robinson holding a snarling dog
on the end of a rope and disappears for less than a minute. Then he
reappears with his backpack. He rummages around inside and pulls
out three sets of night vision goggles, one of which he hands to
O'Brian. He hesitates just a few seconds then hands the second set
to Huntsbringer.
"Do you know how to use these?"
"Sure."
"Good. Come on both of you, let's take a look at the camp and
see what's happening. The rest of you stay here!"
Mike Oldport begins to complain but Dwayne grabs his upper arm
and quiets his friend.
"I don't know who the fuck this guy is, Mike, but he's right.
We shouldn't all go blundering over there. Let us have a look to
see what's going on first and then we can all decide what to do.
Okay?"
"I guess so."
Mike doesn't sound that convinced and being so near to Sheila at
long last he finds it hard to back down, but he trusts Dwayne. He
nods his head in agreement, a movement that can be seen plainly
now as the stars have brightened considerably since dusk.
O'Brian goes to his own backpack first and pulls out a small
box which Smith recognises instantly. It contains another Heckler

and Koch Mk 23 semi-automatic handgun. He loads a magazine and cocks it, before he slips it into a holster which he straps to his thigh. Smith grins at him and slaps his own thigh holster containing his Mk 23.

The three men then head out in the direction of the kidnapper's camp, O'Brian acting as point, Smith behind him and Huntsbringer bringing up the rear.

It's another twenty minutes before the trio halt their advance, when they reach the place that O'Brian and Huntsbringer had been watching the camp from that evening. It's a natural dip between two low ridges of rock on a forward slope. O'Brian had hung a small camouflage net in the gap between the two ridges, a simple but effective way of hiding them while they had watched the kidnappers about a hundred and fifty metres away. He indicates a shallow slope that leads away foreward from the position, then whispers to the other two:

"This slope carries on down to the level of the oasis about eighty metres further on. There's plenty of cover from big loose rocks along the way but once we hit level ground there's a patch of sand about forty metres wide with no cover at all. Once we get across that we'll start to hit the bushes growing around the waterhole. That's where their camp is."

Smith nods as the picture of the ground ahead begins to form in his mind.

"That fits with what I saw earlier too. I snuck in from the other side of the camp. There are two pickups parked off to the left just inside the cover of the bushes and two of their guys are always hanging around the trucks. I think that they're probably the drivers. It doesn't look like it's a regular sentry system or anything like that. They just seem to like to stay close to their trucks, I guess. Beyond them is the kidnapper's lean-to made of bits of wood with a palm-leaf thatch on top and down the sides. They look like they regularly have a small camp-fire going in front of it at night as I could see the pile of cold ashes. Beyond that is another lean-to similar to the kidnapper's but this one holds the civilians. Okay so far? Does this fit in with what you've seen?"

O'Brian nods in the affirmative and Huntsbringer whispers:

"Yeah."

"Okay. There are seven targets, all black and all young males. They appear to be armed with AK47s, most of them pretty old and battered and probably of Chinese manufacture, with wooden stocks and folding metal butts, a lot like the shit ones that we've got." Here he indicates the assault rifle being carried by Huntsbringer. "At least two of them are also armed with handguns but I couldn't figure out the type, although my impression was that they were semi-autos of some kind rather than revolvers. Each of the targets is also carrying a nasty looking machete at their belt. I haven't seen any larger weapons apart from the RPG and a box of spare warheads. I managed to get a quick peek at the box and read the stencils on it. If it still contains the original warheads then they're of the OG-7V type, which are anti-personnel high-explosive fragmentation. The Somalis look like they can handle themselves in a scrap but I wouldn't think that they're great shots."

O'Brian chips in here:

"From what we saw earlier the civilians are confined to their lean-to and there's always at least two armed guards posted there during the day. We don't, of course know what they do at night-time. The only time we saw the civilians leave their shelter was on a handful of occasions when they went to the toilet – they have the use of a bucket in the bushes behind their shelter. They were always accompanied by a guard on those occasions, leaving just a single guard to watch the rest of them. We identified all of the civilians during the day as they went to the toilet except for the British writer. We haven't seen him at all. How about you?"

"Afraid not."

"He might still be okay," adds Huntsbringer. "He might not have wanted to relieve himself, that's all. Most of the others seemed to go fairly regularly so I'd say that they've all got a case of the squits."

Smith grimaces in sympathy:

"Okay. Here's how it's going to happen: We will all move forward down the slope. At the bottom, Huntsbringer, you will stay put and cover the two of us with your AK in case we have to withdraw in a hurry. We two will then move across the open stretch of sand one at a time, me first and then you, Rob. Then we'll crawl through the bushes until we're level with the two trucks but on the right, so that we're about twenty metres from them. From that position we should be able to see all of the elements of the camp, though we won't be able to see inside the civilians's lean-to, and we'll be able to make out what's going down and what the shooting was all about. I envisage that we'll withdraw agai....." Suddenly he's interrupted by another loud burst of gunfire that shatters the quiet of the night, followed by the unmistakable sounds of women screaming and men shouting, in anger or fear they can't tell. "....or not, as the case may be!"

"Okay. Let's move out!" and with that Smith slides forward through the netting on his belly. O'Brian follows, content to let the older man lead for the moment, especially as his plan seems to be a sound one.

The L-3 AN/PVS-31 Generation Three Binocular Night Vision Device is a compact dual-tube head-mounted binocular that works off just four AA batteries contained in a remote battery pack. The device weighs less than half a kilogramme and the power pack is located at the back of the head so that it counterbalances the binocular itself. Not all operators like forward-looking infra-red devices such as this one. Some prefer image intensifiers which intensify any low ambient light source such as stars. But not Smith, The sometimes fatal drawback of image intensifiers is that they will 'flare' if faced with a sudden bright light source (such as the flash of a weapon discharging) and the operator will temporarily lose sight of his target. With infra-red, the device works off its own light source that's invisible to the human eye, so you don't have that problem. The target is always lit, though with some systems the range of the infra-red light source is limited to only thirty or forty metres.

With the benefit of their night vision goggles Smith, O'Brian and Huntsbringer easily work their way down the slope without making any noise. In front of them they hear a lot of shouting coming from the kidnapper's camp but thankfully no more shooting. When they hit the bottom of the slope Smith waves Huntsbringer into the cover of a big rock and indicates that he is to stay there and cover them. The big American ex-Ranger does as he's told even though it's clear that he would like nothing better than to charge straight into the camp and shoot the bastards that have kidnapped his wife and the others. Once he's in position and facing forward the other two men quickly scoot across the forty metres of open sand in a low crouch, Mk 23 pistols in their hands and night vision goggles swinging from side to side as they scan for hidden enemies. It's only a matter of seconds before they reach the cover of a few straggly bushes growing at the edge of the oasis and feel relatively safe again.

From here they crawl forward slowly another fifteen metres through the bushes, trying not to get their clothes snagged on the vicious thorns, until Smith raises his hand to indicate that they've gone far enough. O'Brian then crawls forward to lie next to the Englishman.

In front of them lies the kidnapper's camp. To their left about twenty metres away are the two pickup trucks. Fifteen metres to their fore is the Somalis's lean-to, and off to the right at an angle of about thirty degrees and a distance of forty metres is the civilians's lean-to. Of the latter they can only see one side and just a slim portion of the open front. The Somalis are everywhere around them. There are two of them standing by the nearest pickup shouting questions at the others. They look like they're trying to find out for themselves what's going on. There are another two men squatting in front of their lean-to and tending a big pot of something, probably food of some kind that's bubbling away over the flames of the small camp-fire. They have their backs towards Smith and O'Brian and are also shouting out questions, though they don't appear to be too worried by the shooting. The remaining three Somalis are standing in front of the civilians's lean-to. They're obviously angry and are arguing with their captives and ignoring the shouted demands from their comrades. One of them in particular is leaning forward and shouting loudly, almost screaming in anger and waving the barrel of his AK47 threateningly at the people inside the shelter. Even as the two ex-Special Forces soldiers watch, this man fires another round into the shelter and a small cloud of dust spurts from the ground. More screams erupt from inside.

"Shit, mate! It's going to be too late by the time your lot get here," hisses Smith into O'Brian's ear. "We've got to do something now. That nutter looks like he's going to kill one or more of the civilians, *if* he hasn't shot any already."
O'Brian looks pensive, then he nods curtly:

"Okay, I agree. How are we going to do this?"

"Follow me."

Smith glides off back along the way that they came, crawling on his belly like some huge snake, and O'Brian obediently follows.

FORTY-SEVEN

12th July
Somewhere in northern Sudan

The Somali kidnapper known to the captives as Crazy Eyes is almost frothing at the mouth in anger. Sheila is sure that he's been drinking alcohol or smoking dope or something similar. His eyes are red-rimmed and wide-open with staring pupils and he looks absolutely insane. His mouth is slack and there is drool dribbling from one corner of his lips. He raises the barrel of his gun and fires another bullet into the ground, just missing Don Black's feet. The shock of the very loud noise, the sickening stink of expended gunpowder and the cloud of dust created by the bullet striking the ground all add to the growing sense of terror amongst the captives. Both the lorry driver's wife and the female BBC producer react by screaming loudly and their voices are filled with unadulterated fear. Sheila manages to stay quiet but only just. She can feel her heart hammering inside her chest and the blood pulsing through her veins. It's still fairly hot and the back of her dirty shirt is sticking to her back with the sweat that's trickling down between her shoulder-blades. She reaches out and grabs Margot's hand for comfort but even this small movement seems to send the tall ugly Somali into another paroxysm of hate-filled shouting. Margot winces as the man's spittle coats her face and hair but she still finds the courage to squeeze Sheila's hand back in reassurance.

One of the other two Somalis, the one that the captives have christened Bugs Bunny laughs harshly and kicks the unconscious form of Don Black in the top of his thigh. The third Somali laughs as well and spits a gobbet of phlegm on to Black's trousers. Crazy Eyes just looks madder by the second.

Sheila prays that Twobob will appear soon and help to calm the mad man, like he has before, but he doesn't materialise. She can hear questions being shouted from some of the other kidnappers out in the darkness of the camp but Crazy Eyes and his two cronies are not bothering to answer them. Although she doesn't have a clue about what they've done to set off his insanity, she can see that he's obviously close to breaking point and his two mates are egging him on, seemingly amused by it all. They've had to face his angry outbursts before during the last month but she senses that there's something different about this one. She gets the feeling that this is going to end in some sort of irrational extreme violence against the captives. She feels totally helpless to avert the coming tragedy though. What can she or any of the others do?

It's the lorry driver that inadvertently sparks it all off. One of Crazy Eye's gang makes an obscene gesture at the lorry driver's wife and the large man snaps. He rises up, his face contorted in anger and his fists clenched. The Somali that had made the gesture backs up quickly, fear written all over his face, and the lorry driver subsides again, but this just seems to madden Crazy Eyes even more. He launches into the British man, kicking him repeatedly in the chest and face with his heavy boots, screaming invective and spraying foaming spittle all over the place. The lorry driver curls up into a ball, trying to absorb the attack and his wife tries to come to his aid, adding to the racket by screaming herself hoarse. Wim the Dutch vet grabs her and holds her back. The other Somalis grin and start to pitch in themselves, kicking the man who now has blood all over his face and the front of his shirt from a shattered nose and a deep cut on his cheek.

Sheila closes her eyes, knowing in her heart of hearts that this is the beginning of the end. Crazy Eyes is totally out of control now. How long will it be before one of them, perhaps all of them, are killed? She feels her body starting to shake uncontrollably.

Meanwhile Smith and O'Brian have held a short conversation using hand signals and split up. They have silently crawled to a short distance behind each of the two Somali drivers who are now squatting by the side of one of the pickups, having given up trying to get an answer from their comrades at the captive's lean-to. The westerners can tell that the two men are not happy about what's happening as they are muttering to each other in dejected tones, but it's also obvious that neither of the men is prepared to stick their necks out and help the foreigners. Both of them have their AKs lying on the ground by their sides. They've got to be taken out.

Smith and O'Brian have been counting in their heads as they crawled forward. As the agreed count of one hundred is reached, O'Brian, who's counted fractionally faster than Smith rises out of the darkness behind his target, quickly followed by the English man behind his own mark. They have different methods of attack but both are equally effective. O'Brian clamps a hard calloused hand over his man's mouth then stabs up into his back with his SEAL knife, the seven-inch blade slicing through the Somali's thin shirt and the muscles of his back as it seeks out his heart. Smith prefers to throw his left arm around his target's head so that the Somali's mouth is muffled in the crook of Smith's elbow as he pulls his arm back towards his own chest. Then he swiftly stabs upward with the black partly-serrated blade of his borrowed SEAL knife in his right hand, stabbing into the front of the man's chest below his ribs. Once he feels the blade cut through the muscle and enter the heart he starts to twist it in a corkscrew motion, severing the veins and arteries that are clustered around the organ. Both of the kidnappers jerk violently and attempt to fight back as the blades are stabbed into their bodies but the pain is intense and debilitating and they quickly succumb to the immense loss of blood as their hearts are sliced and diced. Within two minutes they are so weak that they can't even control their bowels or bladders and they empty in a gush, the night air suddenly filled with the stench of their contents. Within three minutes they're both dead and Smith and O'Brian are already on their way towards the camp fire and their next two targets.

Crazy Eyes' chest is heaving with the exertion of laying into the British lorry driver. He draws back from the attack to try and regain his breath, sweat streaming down his face and dripping into the dust. But his eyes are crazier than ever. He starts to mutter to himself and staggers slightly as he swings the barrel of his AK47 around the ring of frightened faces looking up at him. Each of them flinches involuntarily as the barrel points at them during its erratic wanderings and he laughs, the sound like dry leaves being blown in the wind. Finally, he settles his barrel so that it's aiming directly at the Dutch veterinary surgeon Wim, who stares back aghast. The Somali grins and pulls the trigger and the inside of the lean-to is lit up briefly by the flash of the weapon firing. Everyone inside is deafened by the crash of the shot.

The ground around the two Somalis crouching in front of their lean-to is exposed and too well-lit from the camp-fire's flames for Smith and O'Brian to attempt a close approach as they did with their first two targets. Instead they crawl to a position just outside the ring of light about fifteen metres away. They exchange glances in the semi-dark and withdraw their Heckler and Koch Mk 23 semi-automatic pistols from their thigh holsters. Both weapons are fitted with long suppressors, or 'silencers' as many people know them, almost as long as the rest of the pistol body. They don't need to use their infra-red goggles for this shot as the light from the fire is enough to aim by.

The men hold the heavy 2.29 kilogramme pistols in two-handed grips in front of them, their butts resting firmly on the ground. They aim the pistols at the centre of their target's backs using the fitted Laser Aiming Modules, small red dots from the lasers showing exactly where the rounds are going to strike. Breathing deeply to steady themselves they fire two rounds apiece within micro-seconds of each other. No silencer in the world can suppress all of the sound produced by an exploding cartridge in the confines of the weapon's chamber, but they can reduce the noise sufficiently so that all that is heard is a loud 'click' and that's quiet enough.

The two Somalis are thrown forward by the impacts of the .45 US Army rounds, each one with a diameter of 11.5mm and a weight of 15 grams, travelling through the air at eight hundred and thirty feet per second. Both men are quite dead before their bodies fall forward on to the camp fire, sending a shower of sparks into the night sky and upsetting the cooking bowl, which spills its contents on to the bone-dry ground where it disappears as it is absorbed immediately.

Smith and O'Brian glance to their right to see if any of the Somalis at the civilians's lean-to has noticed their colleagues being killed, but they're too involved in whatevers going on to have noticed.

Four down; three to go.

Crazy Eyes fires his AK47 twice. The first round hits Wim high in his left shoulder. Luckily it goes straight through the meat of his body and into the ground rather than hitting anyone behind him. The second round hits him in the upper left arm, smashing his humerus bone. The AK47 fires a high velocity round, which means it has a hell of a kick and does a hell of a lot of damage when it hits something relatively solid like a body. Wim is thrown backwards in a shower of blood and his left arm is more-or-less left attached to his shattered shoulder by only a few strands of gristle and sinew. He groans out loudly with the shock but it'll be a few minutes before the full pain of the wound will hit him.

In response Wim's wife throws herself across her husband's body to try and protect him from further shots but Crazy Eyes is already lowering his rifle. His head is thrown back and he is cackling away like some old hag in a movie. Everybody else in the lean-to, including his two Somali buddies, is motionless, bought to a standstill by the shock of what's just happened. Then the insane Somali suddenly stops laughing. He lowers his eyes and again begins to move the barrel of his rifle around the group of Europeans, seeking out another random target. His barrel stops moving and points directly at Sheila's face. She keeps absolutely still but she can't help but look up into his eyes, and what she sees there is deep insanity. His finger begins to tighten on his trigger.

O'Brian fires first. His round takes Crazy Eyes high in his left temple and leaves a small entry hole where it hits. The other side of his head blows out in a shower of bone fragments, brains, snot and gore, temporarily blinding the kidnapper on the far side of him who gets a face full of his friend. Not that it matters much because O'Brian's second round hits the other man through his open mouth and exits through the back of his neck, taking a substantial part of his upper spine with it. The third Somali is shot by Smith. Two rounds in the back of his head placed about one centimetre apart blow his heard apart like an overripe melon.

All three are dead before their bodies hit the ground.

271

Five minutes later Smith and O'Brian are crouching beside the Dutchman, giving him emergency first aid. Smith has his fingers digging deep and hard into the pressure point in the veterinary surgeon's armpit, doing a good job of staunching the arterial bleed caused by the Somali's gunshot into his upper arm. O'Brian is wrapping a third First Field Dressing around the shoulder wound as the first two that he applied are already soaked with blood. Wim is calmly telling them what to do, even though he's in shock and wincing from the enormous pain, not realising that the ex-soldiers have previously treated many such wounds between them during their respective years of combat. Smith and O'Brian let him chatter on; it's not doing any harm, though they can't stop grinning at each other every now and then.

Dwayne Huntsbringer had come running into the camp as soon as he heard their shouts that it was all over. He is still hugging his wife Margot as though he never wants to let her go. In the near distance they can hear the shouts of Mike Oldport and the others as they too run towards the camp, unable to resist the temptation of joining them any longer even though they don't yet know that the captives are safe.

Smith eases away his fingers from the pressure point as the American ties off the dressing. The flow of blood from the wound has partly congealed and almost stopped. He wriggles his cramped fingers to get some life back into them and grins at O'Brian:

"Your lot are going to be well pissed off that we took the Somalis out before they got here. They've been waiting for weeks for this action!"

"Jeez, John. What is it you limey soldiers say: 'Tango Sierra', Tough Shit!"

"You're right there, mate. Better give them a call on the SatCom and give them a SitRep (Situation Report) though. We don't want them to come in hot."

"Roger that. They'll be doubly pissed off because they'll have to wait around here while their helo ferries the civilians and us back to the Dutch ship. Then they'll have to clean this place up, look for any intel they can find and pick-up your ATV and kit as well. It'll be a long night and day for them!"

"Well, as long as it's not you and me, mate. All I want right now is an Ice Cold in Alex."

"A what?"

"You must remember that old Second World War movie; Ice Cold in Alex?"

"Jeez, John. Remember that we're not all as old as you are, fella."

"Mmmmm…"

"What was it about?"

"What?"

"The movie."

"Oh, that. It was a great film starring John Mills, Silvia Syms and Anthony Quayle if I remember correctly. It's about a bunch of British squaddies making a journey across the North African desert with a couple of nurses during the evacuation from Tobruk. They have all sorts of adventures, of course, but the film ends with a really memorable scene where they drink an ice-cold glass of beer in a bar in Alexandria."

O'Brian stretches his tired body and smiles.

"Well, I can dig that, John. I could sink one or two cold beers myself right about now. I'll have to look up this movie when I get Stateside again. Do you think they'll have a bar on board the Van Amstel?"

"Of course, mate. It's a Dutch ship!"

"Cool."

"God knows what they'll make of my dog."

"You're going to bring that flea-bitten hound with you?"

"Of course, mate."

"Jeez, John. I'll enjoy seeing the look on their faces when you step off the helo!"

"Like you said, mate. Cool!"

ENGLAND

FORTY-EIGHT

12th July
Maidenhair Drive, Rugby, England

"I just don't understand it, Nina."

"Understand what, Michael?"

Nina Robbins looks across the breakfast table towards the field supervisor of the team assigned to watch John Smith's eldest son. He pauses to consider how to put his thoughts into words, then decides 'to hell with it' and just blurts it out:

"Look, Nina. Ever since the supermarket bombs went off, every field agent in both the Firm and the Box have been reassigned to find the bastards that set them! Not to mention that all of the bloody coppers and squaddies have had their leaves cancelled as well. What I don't understand is why two full teams of experienced operatives like this one and the other that's watching Smith's youngest son are still stuck doing this dead-end duty. It's been eleven months since the surveillance was set up and in all of that time there's been absolutely no sign of Smith. Which isn't that surprising considering that the bugger has been reported dead! This is a crazy waste of resources." He's slightly breathless after his rant.

Nina considers her answer before speaking. Privately she totally agrees with the field agent. That this is a huge waste of resources that could be used elsewhere, but there's no way that she's going to say that to him. Especially as the other three agents assigned to this surveillance job are all in the same room, along with her second in command Rebecca Harris. They may be doing their best to look as though they're not eavesdropping, but of course they are.

"What you are doing is far too important, Michael. The Brotherhood is still very active and we're making no headway at all with our other enquiries. I can't tell you everything of course, but both of the Director Generals of the security services are pretty convinced that Smith may still be alive and that he is the leader of the vigilantes. Besides which, the police and the boys from SO15 have identified all of the supermarket bombers. They got their IDs from the CCTV coverage at both the supermarkets and the companies where they hired their cars. Their names, faces and descriptions have been splashed all over the TV, newspapers and social media. It's only a matter of time before they're arrested, so we're not needed."

The supervisor sighs, and Nina can almost hear the others sighing too. She smiles gently at him:

"I know that this job is a real bummer, Michael. But it's still our best chance of getting to grips with The Brotherhood, so we'll just have to stick with it. I also know that you and the rest of the team…," she waves a hand around the room, "…are pretty fed up with being stuck here, and I know that you want to help with catching the bombers. It's only natural; you're all highly trained and effective field agents. But this is the way it's got to be, at least for the foreseeable future. We need to be in a position for when Smith eventually feels the need to contact one or both of his sons so that we can nab him. You know this guy's history and you've heard about his capabilities. Getting hold of him when he finally breaks cover should be exciting enough for any of you!"

Even Michael has to grin in anticipation of this:

"There's four of us and we're all armed. Even Smith shouldn't be too much trouble!"

Rebecca Harris chooses to chip in here:

"I wouldn't bank on it, Michael, or become too complacent. Smith's a real hard bastard. It'll need all four of you to take him down I reckon, and that's if he's on his own and he hasn't got a load of ex-squaddies from The Brotherhood to back him up!"

Michael just shrugs his shoulders:

"Well, that's why you're here today, isn't it? Too make sure that we're not falling asleep on the job!"

Nina squirms a bit at his directness.

"Not at all! We just wanted to let you know that you're not on your own, that's all! We know how isolated you guys can begin to feel when you're carrying out a long term surveillance like this!"

"Plus we need to talk about the rota as well, guys," adds Rebecca.

"Yes, that's right." Nina looks at her colleague thankfully, a look that's not missed by the field supervisor. "We'd like you to let us know when you want leave etc., so that we can work out the arrangements."

"Mmmmm."

The uncomfortable silence continues for a few moments until the female agent monitoring the listening devices placed in the target's house speaks:

"There's movement." The rather frumpy-looking woman is concentrating on the sounds coming through the headphones she's wearing draped over one ear. "He's getting ready to leave for work and it sounds like she's off down to the shops as well."
The supervisor looks at his watch, then jots down a note in the logbook lying on the table and consults a hand-written rota pinned to the wall:

"Here we go again, ladies and gentlemen. Gina, it's your turn on the bike. I'll take the Audi. Jim and Barry, you'll both be on foot behind his wife." He looks across at his bosses. "In an ideal situation I'd have a larger team and I'd be able to leave at least a pair of agents here to watch the empty house, but we have to make do with what we've got. I refuse to split my team up into less than pairs for any job, for safety's sake." He smiles to make it sound less like a lecture and quickly changes the subject: "I don't know what your plans are? Are you staying here or coming with us? It's only a half hour drive to the factory that Smith's son works in. We've got a comfortable observation post set up in an office overlooking it across the street. Perhaps we could talk more about the rota there?"

"That sounds good." Despite the fact that Nina's only been in the house used by the surveillance team for the past forty minutes, she's already feeling a touch claustrophobic. No wonder the team is getting a bit stir crazy! This particular team has been here for the past thirteen weeks. She also knows that it's going to be hard to give them much time off from now on since Sir Andrew has reduced the overall number of agents working on her 'desk'. It's with a faint touch of guilt that she feels the impending relief of getting out of the house. "We'll follow you in our car, if that's okay with you? I want to go straight over and talk to the other team this afternoon once I leave you."

"That's fine, boss. Gina will be about a hundred to a hundred and fifty metres behind the target's vehicle on the bike but I'll be hanging back out of sight about four or five hundred metres behind them, so there's no chance that you'll blow our cover. We've fitted his mate's Land Rover - the guy who gives Smith's son a lift to work every morning - with a tracking device, so I don't have to be too close," he explains. "There's a mobile tracking screen in the Audi and another here in the back room."

"Great."
The female agent hands over her headset to Barry, one of the other two field agents on the team.

"I'll slip into my leathers. His lift will be here in a few minutes."
Barry grins at her. After more than three months stuck together in close proximity on this job, even Gina is beginning to look attractive to him, especially in her biker's outfit, which somehow shows up her substantial curves a lot better than the dowdy skirts and cardigans that she normally wears on the job. His imagination has been starting to take hold of him recently, almost to the point that he's seriously considering making a pass at her. Gina smiles back at him as she leaves the room, her eyes friendly.

Mmmmm, he thinks. Perhaps I will. My missus would never find out!

A few minutes later Nina watches an old battered Series 1 Land Rover pulling up in the street outside and jumps a little as the driver honks his horn loudly. I bet the neighbours love him! A man emerges from the target's house. He's in his early thirties and has a mop of bright ginger hair on his head and a moustache and goatee beard. He's tall, quite stocky in build and wearing a black T-shirt and jeans. A woman also emerges from the front door and the man helps her to lift a heavy-looking three-wheeled Mountain Buggy over the doorstep. She's a very attractive woman of about the same age. The ginger-haired man grins at her and gives her a quick kiss before half-jogging around to the passenger side of the Land Rover and climbing in. The driver honks his horn again as he pulls away and his passenger waves his hand through the open window over the top of the cab so that the woman can see it. She waves back and then starts to push the buggy up the footpath running alongside the road.

Inside the house occupied by the surveillance team there's suddenly a lot activity. Barry and Jim throw on a pair of lightweight jackets. It's only seven-thirty in the morning but already it looks like the day is going to be a scorcher. Unfortunately for the two field agents they need to wear something to conceal their shoulder holsters and pistols. They wait a few moments to give the target's wife a fifty metre start then Barry slips out of the front door and strolls along after her. Jim waits another minute before tagging along behind. Gina had left almost as soon as the target had pulled away from the curb in the Land Rover, sitting astride the powerful Honda CBR900RR Fireblade motorbike. Michael climbs into the Audi Q7 SUV, but waits a couple of minutes before pulling out of the garage sited beside the house and turning to follow Gina. He uses a remote control to close the garage doors behind him. Nina and Rebecca follow quickly from the front door. Their BMW pool car is parked on the roadside in front of the house, just like a regular visitor. They climb in and Nina guns the souped-up engine to accelerate away and pull in behind the Audi as it sprints away.

FORTY-NINE

12th July
Campion Way, Rugby, England

About three hundred metres from his house along a residential street called Campion Way, Robert Smith's best mate John Scott slows down as he follows a white Ford Transit van decked out in the white, blue and yellow of Warwickshire Police towards the T-junction with the busier Newton Manor Lane. John's a bit of a maverick when it comes to driving, preferring to drive a lot faster than the speed limit, but on this occasion, stuck behind a police van, he does the sensible thing and slows down to the thirty miles an hour speed limit. He swears under his breath.

"Bastard coppers!"
Robert laughs at his friend's dilemma:
"You could always overtake."
"Nah. Knowing my luck they'd be stuck on my arse all the way to work. At least if I'm behind them I don't have to watch my speedo. I'll just tag along at the same speed they're doing."
"Wimp."
"Wanker." The two men have been best friends for the past ten years and this is the usual way they start their working days, with a bit of friendly banter. "How's Gemma doing? She looks like she's got over her cold?"
"Yeah, she's fine thanks, mate. This is the first time she's been out of the house since Friday."
"Crikey, I bet that was fun. Being stuck in the house all weekend together with your missus with a stinking cold!"
Robert grimaced.
"You can say that again!"
"Crikey, I bet that was fun, being...."

282

"Okay. Shut the fuck up, smartarse."

"Jesus! What's this arsehole doing?"

The police van had suddenly accelerated, but instead of keeping to the left hand side of the road it swerves sideways into the middle of the road and then stops abruptly.

"Fuck!"

John has to slam his own brakes on to avoid crashing into the side of the van.

The side door slides open and two men dressed completely in black, including black ski masks leap out in front of the Land Rover. But it's not their clothes that grab the two friend's attention. It's the small sub-machine guns that each of the men is carrying in their hands. John, having long been a fan of war and action movies can't help himself as he thinks: Uzis! They've got fucking Uzis! The two men in black open fire with their Uzi sub-machine guns as they move to cover both sides of the Land Rover, each of them spraying the car's tyres with short controlled bursts of 9mm rounds. The four-by-four instantly sags as the tyres deflate almost explosively, sinking down to settle on the wheel rims. Robert and John both huddle in their seats making themselves as small as they possibly can as the loud staccato bangs of gunfire fill the air. The ambushers jerk open both of the front doors of the Land Rover and grab the two men inside by the scruff of their necks.

"Out! Get fucking out!" the men shout in broad Birmingham accents. The two friends tumble out and are roughly shoved towards the open door of the police van. "Get inside, Kuffir!" shouts one of the men, while the other turns and faces back towards the road as he hears the roar of an approaching motorbike.

Gina sees the action unfold in front of her as she rides along about a hundred metres behind the Land Rover. She slams down on her brake pedal but a big heavy motorbike like the Honda Fireblade, even when it's only travelling at thirty miles per hour, takes a little while to come to a full stop. Unfortunately, she brakes so hard that the rear wheel locks and starts to swerve and she loses control. The bike falls to one side, trapping her right leg beneath it as it slides along the tarmac. She eventually comes to a stop, still caught beneath the bike about thirty metres away from the two masked men ushering their captives into the police van.

One of the men turns towards her, but he doesn't shoot at her immediately. He just aims his Uzi at her and waits. Gina struggles to free herself, very aware of the black hole in the muzzle of the sub-machine gun pointing at her. She kicks at the bike with her free leg to get loose.

After a few seconds that seem to last a lifetime for Gina she liberates her leg and crawls backwards. She tries to stand but her right leg won't take her weight as she's broken her tibia. Sweating now inside her bike leathers and fearful of the man with the Uzi, she begins to crawl further away, desperately trying to unzip her jacket and reach inside for the familiar butt of her handgun in its shoulder holster. Unnervingly the man still doesn't fire, he just stands there watching her while his partner pushes the two men inside the van and climbs in after them.

When Michael hears the first unmistakeable shots being fired he still hasn't left the street where Smith's son lives. It takes a second or two for the impact of the shooting to sink into his brain but then he slams his foot down on the accelerator pedal and the Audi powers forward to the junction with Larkspur which he takes in a long shuddering skid, hardly slowing down at all. The big car's souped-up engine screams as he forces even more speed from it and after another seventy metres he hauls the steering wheel hard over to the left, screeching around the next junction with Campion Way narrowly missing the car of another commuter, which has to brake hard and consequently skids off the road and into a garden wall.

He continues along a long right-hand bend at an ever-increasing speed and then as he swings around the end of the curve he gets his first view of the scene of the shooting about a hundred and sixty metres in front of him. He realises immediately that Smith's son and his friend are being kidnapped at gunpoint but that's not his major concern at this particular moment in time; the fate of Gina, a long-term colleague, a valued member of his team and a personal friend, is. Very much so. He can see that Gina's come off her bike and is struggling to crawl away from a masked man pointing a gun of some type at her, and all that he can think of is to drive forward as fast as possible and put the bulk of his car between her and the gunman. How he deals with the situation after

284

that doesn't even enter his mind at that moment. As far as he's concerned that's a problem for later. Right now he has to protect Gina.

Even though it looks quite normal from the outside the Audi Q7 SUV is more than just a pool car. It's armoured like a tank with Kevlar body inserts, a titanium roof and underbody armour. The fuel tank is self-sealing, the Pirelli tyres have the Road Guard run-flat system (which allows the car to be driven even if the tyres are riddled with bullet holes) and the whole car has a sturdier suspension to handle the added weight of the protective measures. It also has a tamper-proof exhaust, alarm sirens and an independent oxygen supply to both the front and rear compartments. The B7 ballistic protection on all of the Audi's windows is strong enough to stop an armour-piercing round from a high-powered rifle and to provide full protection from the blast of a hand grenade. Michael is secure in the knowledge that no matter what the masked gunman fires at him, it won't be able to pierce this car, no way.

He swerves slightly to overtake a parked car and it's then, in the last half second of his life that he realises the enormity of the mistake that he's just made. He can see that the masked man is no longer aiming his weapon at Gina. Now he's holding something that looks like a switch of some kind by the way that it's held in his fist with a raised a thumb above it.

Michael's mind goes into overdrive. He sees the thumb pressing down on the switch, he sees the parked car that he's overtaking from the corner of his eye and he sees Gina crawling backwards and helpless in front of the masked man. He now knows why the man hasn't yet fired at Gina. He has used her abject helplessness to draw Michael into driving thoughtlessly to her aid in the heat of the moment, knowing that any agent would do anything to protect a comrade from enemy fire. By doing so he has forced Michael to swing out past the parked car and just as he does so the gunman hits the remote switch in his hand with his thumb, igniting a ten kilogram shaped charge of Semtex plastic explosive packed with a thousand six-inch nails and bolts which is sited in the boot of the car.

The directed blast hits the side of the Audi spot on target and despite the heavy armour and ballistic protection the nails and bolts pierce the passenger window, door and side panels with massive force, shredding everything inside the car including Michael's body into small pieces, at the same time tossing the big heavy vehicle into the air and across the street.

Massoud Hassan instinctively crouches down in anticipation of the explosion, even though he knows that the force of the blast is directed away from where he stands. He's very glad and relieved that he has when he feels the powerful shock and heat wave wash over him, nearly knocking him from his feet.

At the same time he feels a small thrill of pleasure that his plan to take out the troublesome SUV has worked so well. Then he notices the female agent who had been crawling away has stopped and finally managed to draw her weapon. With almost contemptuous ease he raises the barrel of his Uzi and sends a stream of 9mm rounds scything into her upper body, the multiple impacts causing a line of closely-spaced ragged red holes to appear across her leather jacket as she is thrown backwards to the surface of the road, instantly dead.

Hassan allows himself a tight smile of satisfaction, then turns back to the police van's open side door.

It's then that he hears a car accelerating towards him.

Of course, there's no way on Earth that Massoud Hassan could have anticipated a flying visit to the team's location by the surveillance team's bosses. Nor that they would be driving a BMW saloon car only a short distance behind the Audi SUV when it was destroyed by the car bomb. Nor that, in spite of the massive shock of watching one of their agents blown apart and killed right in front of their eyes, that they would still have the courage and the presence of mind to accelerate their own vehicle and attempt an attack on the kidnappers.

But none of this really matters. Hassan is one of the most highly-trained and experienced operatives in the world. This type of overt operation is the bread and butter of his life; the reason why he exists. He doesn't have to think when he hears the car accelerating towards him, he just acts. He dives to one side, rolling a few metres to get clear, then he comes up into a crouch, his Uzi sub-machine gun already in the firing position, its telescopic butt pressed tight into his shoulder. He zeros in on the startled and terrified, but still determined female face behind the driving wheel of the car and sends a short controlled burst straight at her. Her face disappears in a splash of gore behind the shattered windscreen and the car slews out of control, narrowly missing the police van and smashing into the opposite curb. It bounces up into the air before slamming down on to its roof on the opposite footpath.

Hassan is by its side in seconds. He peers into the battered front and sees that there is another woman in the passenger seat, still alive, though barely aware of what's happening around her. He grabs her by her long auburn hair and drags her screaming from the door, which has been flung open by the impact of the crash. He slaps her hard across the face repeatedly until she stops screaming. Then he quickly runs a hand over her upper body and waist, searching for a hidden gun. She's not armed, so, not knowing who the hell she is or what she's doing there, but knowing that somehow she might turn out to be important, he drags her across the road and literally throws her into the van.

He then climbs in behind her, screaming in Arabic for the driver to get them the fuck out of there.

The scream of the van's tyres spinning on the tarmac as the van roars away hides the distant sound of yet more gunfire a few hundred metres away.

FIFTY

12th July
Maidenhair Drive, Rugby, England

Barry and Jim, the two field agents who are on foot following the young mother of Smith's grandson as she walks along the street to the shops, react quickly when they initially hear the distant gunfire and then watch their supervisor accelerate away to the end of the residential street and skid around the corner. Barry's the closest one to the woman. He sprints up behind her, pulling out both his ID card and his SIG Sauer P226 semi-automatic pistol as he goes. She's already stopped dead in her tracks at the sound of the shots breaking the early morning hush, and almost screams in panic as she glances behind her and sees this big lumbering man who she recognises as one of her neighbours, coming charging towards her with a big chunky gun in his hand.

Barry doesn't worry about the niceties or introducing himself. He just grabs her and the Mountain Buggy containing her son and bundles both of them off the street and into the driveway of a house so that they are partially hidden from view by a large laurel hedge. Only then does he flash his ID card right into her face and tells her calmly and quietly that he is from the security services. The woman is speechless with shock. The nearest that she's ever come to anything like this is when she watched a TV programme about her father-in-law's exploits. A father-in-law that she's never met and about whom her husband Robert never speaks.

Jim, who is about sixty metres behind Barry and the woman takes cover behind a low wall surrounding a front garden. He too has his P226 pistol out of its holster but is holding it out of sight while he searches the street for any sign of attack. It doesn't take long to materialise.

A white Mercedes Sprinter van pulls into the street just after the bosses Audi disappears around the corner. The van stops about ten metres from the house that the surveillance team has been occupying. The side door on the opposite side of the van from the house slides quietly open and four men, dressed completely in black and with ski masks hiding their faces, pile out using the van's body to cover them from view.

From their separate locations further up the street the two field agents have a clear view of the masked men as they hoist their weapons up ready to move. Each of the men is armed with an Uzi sub-machine gun which is instantly recognisable to the agents. Jim keeps his head down low but risks a quick look back up the street towards Barry and the woman. He sees Barry's face, as pale as a sheet, peeking out from the side of the hedge. Quietly he speaks into his short-wave radio mike hidden beneath the collar of his shirt:

"Barry. I reckon they're gonna split up, mate. Some will attack our OP and some will go for the son's house!"

"Fuck, mate. I agree with you. Who the fuck are they?"

"God knows, mate, but they don't look friendly. Listen, I'll stay here and give covering fire if it's needed. You should try and get the girl and the kid into the back garden of that house where you are. With any luck they won't know where you are. They probably think that we're all still inside!"

"Okay Jim, willdo. Be careful, mate. They outnumber and outgun us."

"Yeah. Roger that, Barry." A few seconds pass and nothing happens. The masked men are still hiding behind the van. "What the fuck are they waiting for?"

"I don't know, Barry."
Just then there's the sound of a terrific explosion. Even the agents can feel its massive shockwave hit the street as one or two windows in the houses shatter.

"This is it, Barry!" Jim shouts down his radio. "Get them the fuck out of here!"

EGYPT

FIFTY-ONE

15th July
Hurghada, Egypt

Doctor Linda Webb lies back on her bed. The last few weeks have
been a nightmare of worry for her, especially as she hasn't heard
from John at all since he disappeared into the Eastern Desert.
She'd really meant what she'd said to her new-found friend Helen
Wright a few days ago; she'd have gone mad if they hadn't had
each other for company, or if she had been stuck back on her own
in Norfolk not knowing anything about what was happening in
Egypt. What on Earth ever possessed me to fall in love with a man
like John Smith? A man who would never be happy with living a
mundane life instead of gallivanting all over the world in search of
adventure. And that's what drives him, she is sure. Oh, he might
talk passionately about doing the right thing or risking his life to
help others who can't help themselves, but Linda knows what
really pushes his buttons. It's the need for excitement and the
adrenaline rush that goes with combat. Still, love doesn't abide by
any rules, and she knows deep down that she wouldn't have him
any other way. She'll just have to put up with his occasional
absences and hope against hope that he survives his skirmishes
with death. After all, he has survived a lifetime of wars and
conflicts and if anybody can pull through, it will be John. He
seems to have an uncanny knack of surviving just about anything.
    She groans slightly as she shifts her body weight on to her side
in an effort to get comfortable. And now this. Her body is
beginning to fail her. Over the last few months she hasn't been
able to eat properly and has steadily been losing weight. She also
has a slight swelling in the left side of her abdomen which causes
occasional bouts of pain. It must be the worry, but I really must go

and see my GP when I get home. Suddenly she laughs at herself; Doctors! We make the worst patients! I probably won't get around to it for months!

Her musings are interrupted by a sharp knock on the door of her hotel room which startles her. She sits up.

"Hello. Who is it?" she calls.

"Room service!"

Linda sighs.

"Room service? I haven't ordered anything?"

"Special delivery from the kitchens, Madame. Courtesy of Miss Wright."

She smiles to herself. It's just like Helen to order me something tasty, knowing that I'm not eating too well. She's such a sweet person. She slides off the bed, feeling just one sharp twinge of pain from her abdomen, and walks to the door.

"I'm not sure I want anything right n...."

She starts as she opens the door.

Outside she sees a grinning John Smith with another man - a short, stocky man with very close-cut hair who is wearing a pair of wraparound sun-glasses and chewing gum. Both of them are burnt very brown by the desert sun.

"John!" She throws herself into his arms. "You're back!"

"Yep!"

He hugs her back with a fierce intensity.

It takes a discreet cough from Smith's companion some moments later to eventually get the two to break apart.

"Ah sorry, Rob. Linda, this is my new buddy, Robert O'Brian. Rob, this is the love of my life, Doctor Linda Webb. She's beautiful and a surgeon! God knows what she sees in me!"

O'Brian smiles while extending his right hand to shake hers and removing his shades with his left hand, revealing his startlingly pale blue eyes.

"Pleased to meet you, Ma'm".

"Bloody hell! You're honoured, Linda. He *never* takes his bloody sunglasses off! Ever!"

O'Brian smiles at her, doing his best to ignore Smith.

"All the better to see your beauty, Ma'm!"

Linda blushes.

"Why thank you, Mister O'Brian. You're very kind."

"Just being truthful, Ma'm. Please call me Robert."

"Okay, Robert, but only if you drop the Ma'm and call me Linda?"

"That's a deal....Linda."

Smith sighs.

"Alright, that's enough, Yank. Linda's the love of *my* life, remember?"

"Jeez, John. I was only saying hello, buddy." O'Brian laughs. "You'd better watch out though. I'm looking for Mrs O'Brian number three and Linda here sure is a stunner!"

Smith rolls his eyes.

"Just ignore him, Linda. He's only looking for number three because the first two couldn't stand his snoring and farting at night, and I should know, I've just spent a few nights banged up in the same cabin with him on a frigate!"

It's Linda's turn to laugh as she looks back to Smith.

"I'm so glad you're *both* safe!"

She stands there looking up into his eyes.

"The job wasn't that dangerous, Linda. A piece of cake." He grabs her again. "Are you gonna invite us in then, or what? I've got someone else to introduce to you."

'The someone else' turns out to be a rather large but skinny dog that Smith and O'Brian have smuggled into the hotel inside a large holdall. As soon as Linda and the dog set eyes on each other they fall instantly in love. The dog stands up on his back legs and places his front feet on Linda's shoulders. Then he begins to lick her face while she dissolves into fits of giggling.

It takes at least half an hour for Linda's heart to finally stop fluttering. She feels more relaxed now than she has for God knows how long; now that she knows that the mission is over and John is safe back with her. The sense of relief is so intense that she almost feels faint. Smith gives her a very brief run down on the successful operation to rescue the kidnapped holidaymakers. Very brief, and he obviously misses out the bad bits, not that she wants to hear about the bad bits anyway as she listens to him, the dog lying by her side, enjoying being stroked around the ears:

"Anyway, we flew back in the chopper with them, landed on the Dutch frigate and that was the last that we saw of them."

"Didn't they want to say thank you when the shock had worn off?"

"Sure they did, but you know how it is, Linda. We're the 'grey men'. We live in the shadows. It's enough for us to know that we've rescued them and that they're gonna be alright. We've done our job."

"Are they going to be alright? How about the Dutch vet, what was his name; Wim? And what about the man who was beaten up?"

"Don Black? Oh, he's fine now, thanks to a very good surgeon on the frigate. He and his team operated on them both as soon as we got on board. You'd love his sickbay, Linda, It's like something out of Star Trek."

"Well, that's really good news. I'm glad they're all okay. What about the kidnappers; the Somalis? What will happen to them?" Smith and O'Brian exchange a quick look which Linda can't fail to miss. There's a moments embarassed silence. "Oh, I see…none of them made it then?"

It's O'Brian who finally answers in a low voice:

"Like John says, Linda. We did our job and the victims are okay. That's all that matters really."

Linda smiles gently and lays a hand on each of their arms. The dog doesn't seem to mind that he's not the centre of attention for a moment.

"It's okay, I understand, really."

Smith decides to change the subject:

"Where's Helen? I thought she'd be with you?"

"Oh, she had an urgent message from London come in. She had to go to Cairo to see the chief spy there so that she could download it or something. She said that she'd be back by this evening. With any luck it'll only be an hour or two."

"Super."

Linda smiles a little mischievously as she reaches out for an official-looking envelope on the table:

"Helen had to disappear back to England last week to pick this up. It's for you, John. I think you'll like what's inside." Smith looks at her quizzically, but she just smiles again and hands the envelope to him: "Go on, read it. I'll keep Robert entertained." Smith takes the envelope and stands up, retiring across the room to sit on the edge of the bed. The envelope has already been opened so he just slips in two fingers and pulls out the sheet of paper that's inside. It's headed: 'Her Majesty's Court of Appeal in England' and is from the Lord Chief Justice himself, Lord Thomas of Cwngiedd. Smith skims down the paper, his eyes settling briefly on phrases such as 'Access to Justice Act, 1999' and 'Civil Procedures Rules, 1998' which he doesn't understand, before finally landing on the key line towards the end: 'In the Case of Smith, John, versus the Crown, heard at Peterborough Crown Court on 15th October 2013, Her Majesty's Court of Appeal in England finds that the case made against the appellant has no basis in truth and therefore the Appeal is upheld.'

Smith looks across to Linda, who's sitting watching him with tears rolling down her face beside a bemused but smiling O'Brian.

"Does this mean what I think it means?"

His voice is choked.

"Yes, John. It does."

It's close to ten o'clock at night when Helen Wright turns up at Linda's door. She's looking weary and the palest that Smith has ever seen her (despite the sun-bathing of the last few weeks). Smith answers her knock and the look she gives him when she sees him is enough to make the hairs on the back of his neck stand up. He'd been planning to grab her into the biggest bear hug ever and thank her profusely for putting into motion the appeal that had found him not guilty of abducting, raping and murdering thirteen year old Mary Knightly. But the look that he sees in her eyes makes him hold back.

"What's up?" he asks, knowing in his heart that it's got to be something serious. "Are you okay?" She doesn't answer immediately and just walks into the room. Silently she puts her computer bag on to Linda's table and takes out her laptop, taking her time about plugging it in and switching it on, all the time avoiding everyone's eyes. Linda looks across at Smith with a querying look on her face. Smith just shrugs his shoulders. They wait in tense silence while Helen taps a few buttons.

Finally, Helen takes a deep breath and looks up into Smith's eyes, her own finally brimming over as tears begin to roll down her face.

"It's Robert, your son. He's been taken, John."

Smith looks back at her, uncomprehending.

"What do you mean? *Taken*?"

"London sent me a high-priority message. There's been a video released on the internet. It's Islamic State extremists, John."

As the two women look at John Smith's face they see the emotions wash over him. First of all there's the questioning look in his coal black eyes. Why? Why Robert? Why Islamic State? What the fuck have I ever done to them? Then the rage takes over as the enormity of what Helen has said sinks in; the uncontrollable hate-filled rage that tightens the muscles of his face and makes his eyes blaze. Everyone in the room suffers from a brief and irrational surge of gut-wrenching fear as they feel the strength of the white-hot rage pouring out of him. Then slowly the rage subsides and is replaced by…nothing.

Smith's eyes become blank and there's no emotion in them at all. They look like the eyes of a dead shark and somehow this is the most frightening thing of all.

His voice is like a cold water stream flowing over sharp gravel:

"Get me booked on a plane home, Helen. Then I want to see this video."

Author's note

The scene involving the Muslim protesters at the beginning of this book was particularly hard to write, as I wanted to try and express the opinions of both sides; the small minority of Muslims who feel that their religion is oppressed in Britain and the vast majority who are glad that they're British and proud of it. I hope that I got this across okay. I chose to do it in this fashion, involving a protest made during a military parade, because of the protests that have actually taken place in the recent past and in similar circumstances. The slogans on the placards carried by the protesters in this story are ones that have been used in real life.

Egypt was a lot easier to depict because I could rely on my own memory to a large extent. Linda and I once took a diving safari along the coast of the Red Sea in Egypt, though it was thankfully in more peaceful times. The strange and scary habit of Egyptian drivers switching off their headlights while driving at night is true!

Bringing back the character of Massoud Hassan was also an easy progression, as I'd always felt his future had been very uncertain at the end of Heart of Stone. Obviously, we shall be seeing quite a lot more of him in the next book!

I try to base all of the sub-plots and stories within my works on real-life people and happenings. In the case of the massacre that took place in Tehran's Jaleh Square, this really did happen pretty much as depicted, in September 1978, and was one of the reasons that the Shah of Iran was deposed soon after. Also the Colombian city of Bogotá was really as bad as I've said it was in the 1980s. Tens of thousands of street kids, themselves orphaned by the tides of drug-related murders that constantly swept through the city, were killed by death squads paid for by local businesses, and many of their bodies really did end up feeding pigs in local pig farms. I can only hope that the city has changed for the better in the intervening years, though you can still hear about similar death squads that have operated or are still operating in even large well-known South American cities such as Buenos Aries, so perhaps not.

The ex-SEAL CIA agent Robert O'Brian in this novel is based upon another real-life character; Robert O'Neil, one of the men who claims to have shot Osama bin Laden in Pakistan in 2011 (another ex-SEAL, Matt Bissonnette, also claims to have shot the Al-Qaeda leader). One of the recurring criticisms that the character of John Smith receives from certain reviewers is the great amount of combat that he's seen during his service career. Let me just set the record straight here; although someone serving in so many operations is unusual, it's by no means unheard of. For example Robert O'Neal served for sixteen years in SEAL Team Six. During that period it is on record that he took part in over four hundred separate combat missions, and was decorated *fifty-two* times, including two Silver Stars and four Bronze Stars with Valour! Believe me when I say that there are real John Smiths out there.

John Smith will be back of course, but what will happen to him and his kidnapped son is undetermined and unknown, even by me! I look forward to discovering the story even as I begin to pen it....

Craig William Emms
April 2015

Become a friend of John Smith, 22 SAS on Facebook, or 'Like' the 'John Smith Series' page on Facebook (there are occasional competitions and freebies on this page). Published by Cold Fish Books, please visit their website at www.coldfishbooks.com for more information or contact the author: craig@coldfishbooks.com.

OTHER BOOKS IN THE JOHN SMITH SERIES

One Heartbeat
A Minute

Craig William Emms

ONE HEARTBEAT A MINUTE

'Quite simply one of the best books I've ever read, and I read a lot. Difficult to imagine that this is the author's first book. It's much too good. Makes Chris Ryan et al read like comics. Outstanding, well done to the author'
Sean 0801

Meet John Smith. He's as cold as ice and as tough as they come. Whatever you do, don't make him angry, because he's a killer who's about to go off the rails. Annoy him and there's a very good chance that you'll end up dead. Smith, ex-Special Forces soldier, spy and assassin, is framed for a brutal murder that he did not commit by a government that he almost gave his life for. He knows too many of their dark secrets and they want to keep him quiet for ever.

But Smith has the skills and the determination to blast his way through anyone or anything that stands in his way and he does so in a bloody orgy of violence and revenge!

'Not for the squeamish, this tale about a Special Forces squaddie is at times graphic enough to make you cringe. Some of the scenes actually cause you to question whether people could survive such treatment. Merging fact and fiction wonderfully, the story leaves you pondering what is true or imagined and what really goes on behind the scenes. How many clandestine missions are carried out and then denied by governments or shadowy organisations? Read it if you like hard-hitting action, not if you prefer your books pink and fluffy.'
Rick Wilson, Soldier, the official magazine of the British Army

'A good book is one that you just can't put away once you've got into it and which leaves you with a sense of emptiness and sadness (like losing a good friend) as soon as you've finished it. You just don't want it to end, you want to know what's going to happen

next. One Heartbeat a Minute is just one of these books. You follow John Smith into the abyss of a broken mind, through the twists and turns of intelligence services, military operations, secrets and lies and sometimes you just don't know if you should weep for him or slap him in the face! A brilliant, fast-paced book that makes you wonder how much of it is actually true...'
Sandra "sanried"

'A superb thriller, excellently written, well woven in with real-life events, riveting, satisfying and totally unputdownable! Can't wait for the next one!'
J. A. Hobby

PUBLIC ENEMY

CRAIG WILLIAM EMMS

PUBLIC ENEMY

'Just finished Public Enemy. What a fantastic read. As an ex para and prison officer everything seemed so real. Craig is quickly becoming my favourite author.
Now to read book three.'
Michael Bradshaw

John Smith is wanted for waging a war against his former masters that left a swathe of destruction and dead bodies behind him in One Heartbeat a Minute.

Now the Secret Intelligence Service has been ordered to bring Smith to justice, but they don't want him to go on trial. They want him dead.
But they're not the only ones.

Smith must fight for his life against a group of fanatical terrorists, survive a face to face encounter with an ex-IRA hit man who wants bloody vengeance for the murder of his brother, face a life sentence for a crime that he did not commit and rescue two members of the Royal Family kidnapped by a gang of vicious thugs.
Will his luck finally run out?

'Hard as nails, tough as army boots, and a stone-cold-killer, former spy and government assassin John Smith makes the action heroes of Andy McNab and Chris Ryan look like sensitive souls by comparison. No wonder lovers of blood-and-guts action-man thrillers have taken to the books by former soldier Emms in droves. The latest is raw and edgy as smith wages war against his former masters and old enemies alike.'
Alex Gordon, Peterborough Telegraph

'Great second book in the series, again another excellent page turner. Couldn't put it down. Just when you think nothing else could possibly happen - it does! Highly recommended.'
Doe

'If you want a book that is believable, exciting, full of humour and incredible action sequences then for God's sake get this and the first book in the series!!!! Couldn't put it down and can't wait for more.'
Mike Thompson

'Another belting book which I could not put down. I am so sorry that I finished it. I just loved all the different aspects of this John Smith and the different directions the reader was taken throughout the entire book including the superb ending. Keep them coming please, Craig.'
Spanners

HEART OF STONE

A JOHN SMITH SHORT STORY

CRAIG WILLIAM EMMS

HEART OF STONE

'These books get better and better, you can't put them down, looking forward to the next one. Keep up the good work Emms.'
Johhny 2 bad

Having escaped from a life sentence in prison, John Smith is now living an idyllic life with his soul mate Doctor Linda Webb in Norway. But with a half a million pound reward on his head, his nemesis Detective Chief Inspector Alan Davies and the Iranian Secret Service are out to get him. They will stop at nothing to take down their target in the Norwegian wilderness.

But have they taken on more than they can cope with? Will the hunters become the hunted?

'Just so good, working my way through John Smith and his life, cannot put the story down, would stay up all night, these books grab you by the throat, fantastic.'
Rodders

'A short story but fast paced. The research that goes into Craig's books is first class. Another excellent read. If you haven't read any of his books then please do so.'
Michael Bradshaw

'This short story has cemented John Smith among the heroes we need in life, like Bond, Biggles, Reacher, Hope and a handful of others we read and love throughout our lives. Craig William Emms is carrying on writing about Smith and he has somehow made the character more real and exciting. The storyline has made the reader keep on reading in case he misses out on the action. I can hardly wait for the next book.
Congratulations Mr Emms, keep them coming.'
Steve1

'I literally can't get enough of John Smith. Brilliant! Even after a hard day's work I still look forward to this ruthless hero!'
Martin

'Can't wait for the next book!! A film to follow hopefully. Can't stress enough how good these are. Emms, yet again, well done!'
Fraser Wiseman

MEET JOHN SMITH

PUBLIC ENEMY
CRAIG WILLIAM EMMS

HEART OF STONE
A JOHN SMITH SHORT STORY
CRAIG WILLIAM EMMS

One Heartbeat A Minute
Craig William Emms

HIS FIRST THREE ADVENTURES IN ONE BOX SET

THE JOHN SMITH COLLECTION VOLUME ONE

The first three novels in the John Smith series One Heartbeat a Minute, Public Enemy and Heart of Stone are also available in a single volume:
"The John Smith Collection Volume One" **on kindle only** at a 15% discount.

Please see Amazon for details.

THE SMILING COAST

COAST

CRAIG WILLIAM EMMS

THE SMILING COAST

'My goodness, these stories just get better. I've read all four and the intricate plots have me glued. I've always given 5 stars and same again for this. Mr Emms, you are such a clever author. John Smith fans won't be disappointed. Read this - it's great!'
Paula Potier

Smith's ex-army pals form themselves into a vigilante group they call 'The Brotherhood' and declare war on organised criminals in the UK. They soon find themselves doing the job that our police force and the courts should be doing - fighting the drug dealers and human traffickers on the streets, and at the same time also meting out violent judgment and punishment on the thugs and rapists who have escaped justice.

Meanwhile, Smith is in West Africa again. In the company of a Dutch wildlife expert he finds himself up against a bunch of vicious Nigerian gangsters who are trafficking wild animals and young sex-slaves for profit. What can the two of them accomplish against dozens of armed thugs who will not stop at any form of depravity to get what they want? And why have the Russian Mafia turned up? It's time to call in the troops.

'Another great chapter in the John Smith series, superbly written and pretty realistic. I felt like I was back in the Forces reading it! Well done again Mr Emms, keep them coming!'
Amazon customer

'More John Smith please!'
Topfox

'Never been disappointed by a John Smith story. They take twists and turns and are always full of action. The Smiling Coast was

brilliant and I can't wait for the next one. The suspense is crippling!!'
Graham L

'All the John Smith books to date have been gripping stuff but The Smiling Coast is the best yet. Fast paced and packed so full of action it's difficult to put down. The John Smith character is without doubt the baddest ass in the "Special Forces" genre and I'm really looking forward to the next instalment. I urge you to get them on Amazon quickly because they are reasonably well priced at the moment but when the word gets out you'll be paying full whack for these little gems. Move over Chris Ryan and Andy McNab it's time to set a new place at the table because Craig William Emms has arrived.'
Kevin Scanlan

THE BROTHERHOOD
CRAIG WILLIAM EMMS

THE BROTHERHOOD

'I think this is his best one so far - love the pace, twists and story. We need more good books like this one. Read the set!'
J.V.Tully

Sergeant John Smith is back, and this time with a vengeance!

Ex-Special Forces soldier, spy and assassin, Smith is a hard and brutal man whose character and attitude have been forged in the blood and gore of a dozen wars around the globe. A man without pity for those who oppose him. In The Brotherhood Smith joins forces with a group of hardened veterans who are fighting organised crime on their own terms.

Corrupt politicians, paedophile gangs or the Albanian Mafia. They're all the same to him.

'Yet another fantastic adrenaline filled adventure for John Smith fans, superb read and yet again attention to detail in every aspect of the themes of the story. I have to admit I am as much of a Craig Emms fan as I am a John Smith fan. If you like a good action-filled read then forget the rest, get some John Smith in your life. Keep up the good work Craig. Looking forward to John Smith 6.
Mark Murray

'At last, Sgt John Smith is back. Once more Craig William Emms brings the shadowy world of the grey man to life. Emms evidently has an intimate understanding of his subject and combines this with a world class ability to conjure up a gripping story. What I love about this the most, however, is that Sgt Smith is a creature of contradictions. Yes, he is a killer, a man who ends lives without pity or remorse. Yet, for all of that, he is driven by a rigid code of what is right. As you read The Brotherhood, Sgt John Smith will take you off on a roller coaster ride as he tackles some of our

society's most pressing and current concerns in his own, unique way. For now though all I can say is hold on, it's going to get very bumpy!'
John Waite

'Cannot wait for the next adventure, absolutely brilliant, gripping and very clever writing. I've really enjoyed being lost in all these books. Love your work, Mr Emms.'
Matt Bush

'Definitely one for the barrack room shelf.'
Andy Kay, Soldier, the official magazine of the British Army

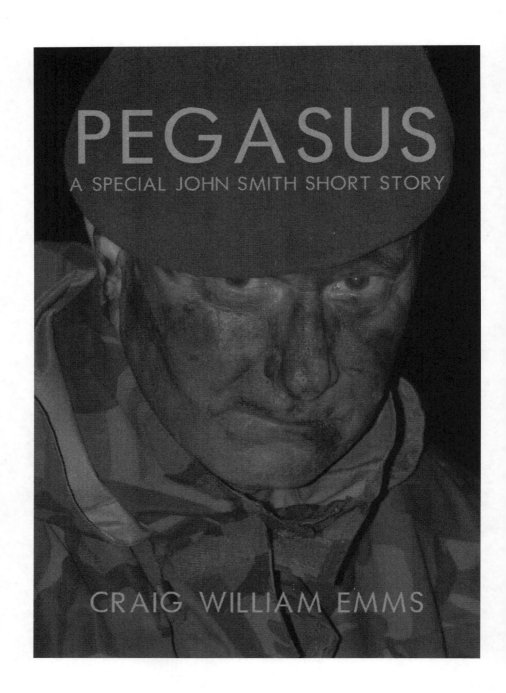

PEGASUS

A SPECIAL JOHN SMITH SHORT STORY

CRAIG WILLIAM EMMS

PEGASUS

'This story is like a really good starter in a restaurant. It leaves you with a hunger for more and a little sad that it's over already. This author is peerless in his description of combat. History and fiction is interwoven in a way that hasn't gripped me since Wilbur Smith's rage. A truly outstanding novella.'
Sean0801

In this special short story, John Smith is recuperating from the wounds he received in The Brotherhood, when he has a chance meeting in the local pub with a hero of the airborne landings on D-Day. Smith is totally gripped by the old man's tale and learns how the Oxfordshire and Buckinghamshire Light Infantry took the bridges over the River Orne and the Caen Canal, and held them against overwhelming odds until they were relieved by Lord Lovat's Commandos.

The two old warriors discover that they have a lot in common, and over numerous pints of beer their conversation makes it easier for Smith to begin to put his own ghosts to rest.

'John Smith gets better and better. Being ex-Forces I can feel everything that Craig writes about. Roll on book 7.'
Michael Bradshaw

'Just finished this one, such a good writer. All the John Smith books to date have been so good I wait with great anticipation for the next. Would recommend as the best reads for years.'
Rodders

'Craig William Emms never lets us down. This short story is up to his usual high standard and makes us the readers feel that the characters are someone we all know, someone we lesser mortals wish to emulate. War is always with us in some fashion or another

and Craig brings our heroes to life in his own special way. The next time you see an old soldier, buy him a pint. You may owe him your freedom. Lest we forget.'
Steve

'What can I say, another excellent trip into the world of John Smith. Craig Emms continues to produce excellent books with such an eye for detail and drama. Carry on the good work, Craig. One word says it all. Super!!!!!!'
Mark Murray